A Romance with Chaos

A Romance with Chaos

Nishant Kaushik

Rupa & Co

Copyright © Nishant Kaushik 2009

First Published 2009
Sixth Impression 2010

Published by
Rupa Publications India Pvt. Ltd.
7/16, Ansari Road, Daryaganj,
New Delhi 110 002

Sales Centres:

Allahabad Bengaluru Chandigarh Chennai
Hyderabad Jaipur Kathmandu
Kolkata Mumbai

All rights reserved.
No part of this publication may be reproduced, stored in a
retrieval system, or transmitted, in any form or by any means,
electronic, mechanical, photocopying, recording or otherwise,
without the prior permission of the publishers.

The author asserts the moral right to be identified
as the author of this work.

Typeset by
Mindways Design
1410 Chiranjiv Tower
43 Nehru Place
New Delhi 110 019

Printed in India by
Nutech Photolithographers
B-240, Okhla Industrial Area, Phase-I,
New Delhi 110 020, India

In loving memory of my late grandfather, who always encouraged me with the art of storytelling as he patiently listened to and admired all the fairy tales I narrated to him as a toddler.

Contents

Acknowledgements — ix

1. We, the Bytes — 1
2. Small Talk with a PYT — 13
3. Who's Eric? — 20
4. I'm Not SRK — 32
5. Of Sushi and *Vada Pav* — 45
6. Jogging *Kachori* — 57
7. be-compassionate.com — 68
8. Symbiosis — 79
9. Eagles in the Air — 91
10. Two Strawberry Shakes, Cutting — 101
11. Erratica Erotica — 115
12. Happy Hours — 122
13. To Each His Own — 133
14. Smart Ass — 146
15. A World of Jackals — 162
16. Payback Time — 169
17. Kisses have Variety — 179
18. The 'X' Element — 195
19. The 6 a.m. Romance — 211
20. The Redemption — 222
21. The World isn't a Supermarket — 231

Acknowledgements

I'd like to first thank my parents and other family members for supporting and guiding me throughout my endeavour. They've been my severest critics as well as my kindest guides – I love you all.

Kamini, Abhijit: My round-the-clock friends, who patiently went through endless reviews and recommendations on my work, and for being there always.

Abhay: For sharing with me some important (and some dark!) insights into the corporate world, that helped me shape my story.

Mirat: For always inspiring me with his sense of humour and for introducing me to the funny nothings of life.

Last, but certainly not the least: My sincerest gratitude to Shri R.K. Mehra, Shri Kapish Mehra, Gunjana and the entire editorial team at Rupa Publications for showing faith in my work and for helping it see the light of the day.

We, the Bytes

I got a resounding thwack on the back. I turned around to see Cheapo Chaudhary towering over me like the shadow of the devil himself.

'I didn't know you were that good,' he grinned, 'you've proven me wrong this time.'

'That's OK, Chirayu.' I winked with due vanity. 'We all make mistakes.'

'Ha ha,' he roared, his expansive belly juggling like a mound of jelly as he laughed. 'But remember – a tough cookie I am and a tough cookie I'll remain. More work to follow.'

'Sure!' I smiled cheerfully before I faced the stage again.

Short-Skirt Shirley got onto the stage with her usual élan, following her staunch principle of minimal clothing.

'We are proud to have with us tonight three employees, who together share the award for the Young Achiever of the Year,' Shirley spoke into the mike. 'Can we please have Nakul Kapoor on stage first to share his experiences with us?'

If the deafening sound of the applause was music to my ears, the icing on the cake soon followed. As I reached the podium, Shirley strode up to me, leaned forward, and planted a kiss on my cheek – in front of some few thousand people! I felt faint. I somehow held my own and walked up to the mike.

'Thanks folks,' I began, when a ring went off in the audience.

Rinnnggg! I woke up, looking up at an email pop-up alert on my computer screen. I hate Vishal's habit of tinkering with the settings of my machine. His latest discovery was this obnoxiously loud ringtone that goes off in my mailbox every time I get a new mail alert.

From: Anand Pai
To: Resources_BuyMe
Subject: Note of thanks from BuyMe

[Yawn!]

> Dear All,
>
> *Great news! At the closure of our project, BuyMe has expressed extreme satisfaction with the work we put in. In the words of their chief programme lead, Friedrich, 'the dedication, discipline and agility exhibited by your team is an example that other vendors might want to follow, and is a reason for us to believe that our relations shall only go higher in the future.'*

[Prolonged yawn. . . .]

> *In my experience of over seven years in the industry, I have worked with and led several teams, but believe me when I say it, this duration together with all of you has been special. . . .*

'Chuck it,' I heard a grunt. That was Vishal. 'Usual *gyan*, you can give it a miss,' he advised.

'Save me the trouble then,' I said, 'and tell me the important part.'

'We have a week off – compensatory holidays starting tomorrow.'

'That's it?' I asked in disbelief.

'What did you expect to read?' he asked bitterly. 'Anand plans to put your name in the Bytesphere hall of fame?'

I stared at him disbelievingly. 'But Cheapo had promised he would be recommending my name to Anand for the annual award. . . .'

'We haven't named him Cheapo for nothing, dude,' Vishal interrupted me. 'When he reports to Anand, all he remembers are his ass-licking techniques.'

'Big deal!' I laughed it off. 'I'm anyway planning to shift to a new project now. I've had enough of Cheapo Chaudhary.'

Sulking in Vishal's presence was a bad idea. For one, I could never beat him at the game. Instead, my sulking would only serve as a catalyst for his eternally long period of glumness. Saying that Vishal Tiwari was an unhappy, dissatisfied employee, would be an understatement. That Vishal Tiwari would be the perfect model for the 'before' part of an anti-depressant's ad would be more like it. With a coveted IIT degree, he often complained that he deserved better. He had declined an attractive campus offer for a job in the United States so that he could visit his ailing mother in Allahabad more frequently. Thus, shelving the dream of a career in Boston, he settled for Bytesphere in Mumbai. But he always regretted his decision. One, he obviously lost out on the dollar multiplier factor. Two, the frequency of his visits to Allahabad from here was no better than what it would have been from Boston.

In his first year at Bytesphere, he had somehow managed to thump off all forms of politics and competition within his peer group, and had succeeded in displaying his sheer brilliance at work. By the end of the year, he had been promoted from the rank of a software engineer to a senior software engineer, which, by any standard, was a commendable speed in rise. In the following three years, his personal life had come a full circle. He had got married to his college sweetheart after a long courtship, had a baby boy, and was now also on the brink of a divorce. But sadly, his professional life was not even half as dynamic. His wheel of fortune had come unstuck after his first raise, and thereon, his position and responsibilities in office had stagnated at a rather mediocre level. The frustration that resulted had brought him to appear a decade older than his actual age. He was losing hair and gaining pounds at a rate much faster than the rate at which his super-genius countenance once coded Java programs. The last time I had seen him smile was when he had laughed his guts out on reading a terribly hackneyed joke forwarded by someone about six months ago.

To be honest, I had my share of worries, too. I was anything but what I had visualised myself as about two years ago. I needed a more exciting career, more status in the mélange of people I stood with, and a lot more money. To top it all, the ongoing recession ensured that I was to get none of these in some time to come. Only, I avoided discussing these issues with Vishal, in the lame hope that he could stop spreading his contagious depression. So what I could do was either to bring him out of his perennial despair or nod in silent acquiescence each time he complained that 'life is such a bitch'. The first option I had dismissed long ago; it had exceeded my capacity.

'Life is such a bitch, I tell you,' Vishal bemoaned as we wound our way down the shiny spiral staircase across four levels. 'I really need a reprieve now.'

'Hmm, true.' I nodded absently, looking around and marvelling for the millionth time at the architectural delight that Bytesphere was.

'I don't think you are listening to me right now.' Vishal shook me by the shoulder. 'Preoccupied?'

'No, I am listening. You said that life is a bitch.'

'I said I need a reprieve! It's been the same routine for the last three years: I drag my bum here everyday and offer it to a bunch of idiots who possibly have less expertise than I do, but who have the impudence to demean me every now and then.'

'Self-esteem issues?'

'Yes, and everything like that. Even Shirley has stopped asking for me now.'

Short-Skirt Shirley was the single biggest contributor to the smile quotient of all men in the office. Seated at the reception desk, she greeted us daily with her ultra-seductive smile and stare, and a cross-legged posture that provided a fulsome view to a few hundred lusty eyes. A number of female HR executives had strongly objected to her sense of dressing and had urged the dress code committee of the company to issue her warnings. But nothing of the sort happened. The members of the dress code committee were all guys. Obviously, they were all as happy to see Short-Skirt Shirley in her usual attire as the rest of us were. Rumour had it, in fact, that when Shirley had walked into Bytesphere for an interview six years back, the then lecherous personnel manager, Kamal Kothari, had taken an hour-long interview with her, but had hardly asked her any questions. The interview was of a special kind. How do we know? Ask Jassi – the living repository of all the gossip needed to keep the post-lunch coffee sessions in the cafeteria alive. Nobody ever figured out how, but Jassi always knew exactly who was next in line to get a promotion, who was being henpecked by his wife at home and whom had Shirley been keeping happy of late.

Interesting stories he had in his kitty. I liked spending time with him whenever I was bored with work, or worse, had no work. Having said that, he was also known to be the kind of person who could not ever be trusted.

'What do you think about the stories he narrates about Shirley?' I asked Vishal as we walked out of the building into the sweltering heat.

'I don't know,' Vishal replied indifferently, 'but this Jassi is a telltale rascal. He spices up stories about people only to make his gossip more thrilling to listen to.'

'Looks like you are a victim too, eh?'

'Nah.' He shook his head. 'Boring people don't make for spicy stories, buddy.'

'You must not keep saying that, man,' I pleaded. 'You will run into depression one day.'

'You're right,' he said. 'I am not too far from it. OK, no more sulking. Come, let's hit the *ghosla*, I need a fag.'

The ghosla, or nest, was the name coined for a semicircular cemented area in one corner of the Bytesphere lawns, shaded with straw. It had earned its name, courtesy the several lovebirds in office who often stole a few precious moments from work to cosy up there in the afternoons. Later, when the frequency and the intensity of the romance increased, the senior management got concerned. It issued a notice that no couple should be spotted performing PDA, or public displays of affection, on office premises as it was detrimental to the reputation of the company. A board was put up with a symbol of a cross over two lips, and below it read: NO INDECENT BEHAVIOUR ALLOWED. ACTION WILL BE TAKEN AGAINST OFFENDERS.

And so, the ghosla ceased to become a romantic spot and turned into a smoking zone for the company employees. But the name stuck.

Bytesphere is housed in a corporate park in one of the plushest real estate locations in downtown Mumbai. Dayanand Lalwani, the founder of the company, had invested huge sums of money, saved from his father's erstwhile textile business, to ensure that his office looked the snazziest, not only in the corporate park, but in the entire city of Mumbai. Nobody knew why and how Lalwani made this awkward migration from textile to information technology. But apparently, around the dotcom boom, someone told the affluent merchant that information technology was the next big thing in the market and that he would make much more money in this field. Lalwani smelled the green, followed his nose and built Bytesphere. The company is currently one of the top players in the Indian stock market and we are its proud employees, called Bytes (don't ask me whether I like being called that, I don't have a choice anyway).

'So, what plans?' Vishal asked, as he lit his cigarette and emitted smoke rings into the air.

'I'm going home tomorrow,' I said. 'Folks have shifted back from Chandigarh to good old Baroda.'

'Is Baroda where you did your schooling?'

'Yes, which explains my fondness for the city. I have got some awesome memories of those times.'

'You bet,' Vishal said. 'That was the only time I used to smile tax-free.'

'I feel you over-think your job woes,' I said cautiously. 'Is it really such a big deal?'

'It probably wouldn't have been so by itself,' he replied. 'But it's like a cascade – one thing leads to the other. My job woes render me feeling low even at home. My wife, on the other hand, is doing extremely well at her job. And I might sound cheap saying this, but this adds to my problems. It makes me feel like an incompetent mutt. And I feel somewhere things moved too fast. We needed more time to settle in. We now have a son and I am afraid I am not making a fine example in front of him.'

'There's nothing like that,' I said rather softly, not sure how convincing I sounded. 'I am sure you make a nice father. And I don't think our condition is that bad here. . . .'

'Talk for yourself, smarty,' he cut in. 'You are an MBA, *na*? Try living on the salary that we get as engineers and you'll know.'

'How come you never thought of doing an MBA?' I asked.

'Nah, MBA is not my thing. All gas and gyan,' he scoffed, stubbing his cigarette butt under his shoe.

I fumed. 'Bullshit! What makes you comment on a course you have not taken?'

'Let's see,' he said. 'For starters, can you tell me where you can fit the BCG matrix in our BuyMe project?'

'Very funny,' I protested. 'Every theory won't fit everywhere.'

'OK, leave that,' he continued. 'You tell me a theory that fits into the context of our project.'

'Shut up now.' I put my hands up. 'Enough of your MBA bashing. I give up.'

There we go again, with the famous duel between the two groups. The world of IT can be classified broadly into two categories: the MBA and the non-MBA, or as the latter would like to hear it – the MBA and the intellectuals. The scene is not too different in Bytesphere. The intellectuals like to believe that an MBA is meant to be pursued by nitwits who could not tell a programmable logic converter from a P-N junction diode back in engineering days. Such morons, they claim, take this two-year-long, good-for-nothing course in order to learn to make flowery statements without substance and impress other fools like them. And when their gassy theories don't sail them through if an application encounters a bug, they have to revert to the non-MBAs, or the real intellectuals, for help.

I walked back to the cubicle after hearing some more bickering from Vishal about his wife and her tantrums. I began to pack my stuff, preparing to leave. The prospect of taking a week off to visit home was a delightful one, especially coming after a tough project schedule. There was only one thing that could kill this moment of joy.

'Nakul,' I heard Cheapo Chaudhary croak as he stepped out of his cabin. 'Come here.'

'Yeah, coming,' I shouted, swearing under my breath. It was amazing how instinctively I could swear on hearing the mention of Cheapo's name, leave alone taking orders from him. His buffoonery at work, combined with his insatiable hunger for undue attention and respect, made a perfect reason for me to despise him.

'Yes, Chirayu?' I walked in.

He was slouched in his armchair, looking like the fattest teapot there ever was. 'There is a presentation I need to submit to Anand,' he said. 'You can call it a project summary report. I need you to help me with some points.'

By the way, 'help me with some points' should best be understood as 'I am bored, please make the whole goddamn presentation', or

'I am a good-for-nothing dodo, how about you do the work and I take the credit?'

'Well, I was planning to leave in the next ten minutes,' I replied. 'I've some packing to do before I travel home.'

'Leaving already?' he asked, twitching his eyebrows with displeasure. 'It's only four.'

'Some compensation, after all,' I said, faking a big smile, 'for all the times you've made me work till midnight!'

He looked at me dryly, without the remotest of acknowledgement.

'Hmm, OK,' he grunted. 'Go ahead and enjoy your holidays. I'll see you next week. Let's hope we work together again on the next project.'

'Yeah, it will be a pleasure,' I said. 'See you.'

I am superstitious and feared what he said might turn out to be true. I muttered a quiet prayer and scampered away to safety before he could stop me again.

'So you escaped, huh?' Vishal said without looking up from his computer screen. 'For all you know, that measly presentation work will now be handed over to me.'

'Sorry *yaar*,' I said, 'but I really need to leave.'

'I know.' Vishal nodded. 'Was just kidding. In any case, I am not going home early. So I'd rather help him with that presentation.'

'Why, don't you have plans with Anita?' I asked.

'Plans with Anita, did you say?' Vishal smirked. 'My rich and famous wife doesn't have time for me, Sir! And if by chance she is free and at home early today, my gut feeling tells me there will be an argument over something. So weighing my options, I vote to sit here longer!'

I almost began advising him on something, but then stopped short. 'Alright.' I sighed. 'Bye then.'

He raised his hand in bye, still not looking up from his screen.

It is not often that I get a chance to leave office while the sun is still at work. I began an arduous walk towards Haji-Ali under the ruthless April sun, but I was not complaining, for a week off was as exciting today as a three-month long summer break was fifteen years back as a school kid. I permitted myself the luxury of fifteen minutes by the Haji-Ali seaside. Once a favourite hangout zone in college days, it now looked destitute and forlorn. As I walked across it, I could faintly feel the presence of my friends around me. I saw the bench where we used to sit and talk crap, letting time pass by, like we didn't care. I saw myself with them, dressed in a tee and three-fourths, and I suddenly wanted to go back there. . . .

I looked at myself. Suddenly I felt my formal attire and that loathsome necktie shackle me. I loosened the tie, rolled up my sleeves and ambled over to the bench. Instinctively, I bent low and checked the inscriptions on one corner of the bench. Yes, it was still there.

A tramp I am, and a tramp I shall be, wild and free, till death be unto me, Amen. – Aryan Nair, AD 2006, Nakul Kapoor, AD 2006.

I smiled, took out my phone, and dialled Aryan.

'Nakul . . .' Aryan spoke hurriedly, as he picked my call.

'Hi . . .' I began.

'Will call you back,' he said. 'Boss on ass-kicking spree.'

'No prob. . . .'

The tramp had hung up already. This is the first time in one year that we connected, but he did not have the time to sound thrilled, let alone talk. I could not complain though. I had myself felt quarantined from my social circle for the past six months. Someone's boss was kicking ass, someone's was licking ass. But we were all screwed any way.

Who am I anyway? Permit me to describe myself in the lingo of an IT consultant that I am so used to:

Product	Nakul Kapoor (In case you are wondering, I feel as lifeless as a product at times).
As-is Environment	Beginning to sense an identity crisis. Too few know the first name, nobody knows the second. Boss, in fact, refers to him as 'the resource'.
To-be Environment	Be everything that he is currently not: Make n times more money, have women swooning over him, own a sexy car and be the cover story of the business magazines in the country.
Project Objective	Product upgrade from as-is to to-be. Needs to be effected soon before product crosses the maturity stage of its lifecycle.
Challenges	Huge gap between as-is and to-be. Needs either a lifetime or the miracle of a Tooth Fairy to be executed within desired timelines.

That's me – a byte among a thousand bytes, a struggler among a million strugglers, who has learnt to live on eternal hope and to die a thousand deaths of fear and failure. I have submitted to the will of my own greed. I am beginning to forget how to enjoy my life and I can hardly narrate my dilemma to anyone, for everyone around me has the same lament.

I soaked in the ambience around me for a while and vowed to see the lovely sunset from Haji Ali every evening after office hours. But I knew that wouldn't happen. The sun always beats me in the race back home.

I read the inscription on the bench once again:

A tramp I am, and a tramp I shall be, wild and free, till death be unto me, Amen. – Aryan Nair, AD 2006, Nakul Kapoor, AD 2006.

'Rubbish,' I muttered to myself, and scratched out the *Amen* I had once written. I picked up a stone, and with a heavy heart, inscribed on the bench:

The tramp is held captive, and so am I,
This shitty life leaves us high and dry,
We can't find a freeway now, much that we try.

Small Talk with a PYT

'Hi, Tisya!' I shouted into the phone. 'Are you in office?'

'Oh, you know I exist?' a staid voice shot back from the other end.

'You are being sarcastic. . . .'

'No, of course not!' Sarcasm was now replaced by mock-sweetness, though both really meant the same here. 'You've been such a caring brother, you did come and meet me six months back, didn't you? You cut my call a thousand times and then don't call back, and you've almost forgotten that we stay in the same city. . . .'

Tisya Kapoor is the epitome of the Indian super-sister. She is married, well-settled with a newborn kid, has a gruelling job, and worst of all – she plies daily between home and work on the roads of Mumbai. Yet, she never fails to find time to exercise her right of teaching her brother a thing or two about the good ways of life. My reduced frequency of visiting her had deprived her of this right for long now. And she was not impressed.

'OK, stop,' I said. 'I'll come and meet you once I return.'

'Return? Where are you off to?' she asked.

'Home. I am already at the airport, in fact.'

'Hmm, that explains that noise in the background. So now you don't even tell me your plans.'

'Nothing like that,' I said. 'It was planned just yesterday. Nobody knows about my travel yet.'

'Except your designer girlfriend?' she asked.

I sighed. 'Her name's Kavya, Tisya. And she's not my girlfriend yet. We are just good friends. . . .'

'OK, whatever. For how many days are you off?'

'A week,' I said. 'Will be back next Monday.'

'A week off? Have you lost it?' she snapped. 'You should be saving up, Nakul. You'll need to collect a good number of leaves for your wedding.'

When will they ever stop? From the time my voice cracked, my marriage issue has been steadily assuming the importance of global-warming. My mother chairs a panel (comprising my sister, a couple of close aunts, and dozens of not-so-close aunts who know no more about me than my being *shaadi ke layak*) that debates regularly on how to convince me into falling prey to the nuptial trap. And when the panel is not in progress, there is a one-on-one 'chat' that would read something like:

Mom: How is Kavya?
Me: Beautiful, mom.
Mom: I am serious, Nakul. What's happening between you two?
Me: What do you think? I think we hit it off pretty well.
Mom: So when do you plan to marry?
Me: Not thought about it yet. We need some time.
Mom: Still, is there a ballpark estimate?
Me: Umm, I don't know . . . how about tomorrow?
Mom: Forget it, Nakul. I've given up on you. This is the last time I am asking you. . . .

And in a span of twenty-four hours, the discussion is repeated . . . Occasionally, Daddy Dearest comes to the rescue and assures me there is no need to rush things. But then Mom rebuffs the idea and kind of wins the battle.

Wow, that rings an ominous bell. I am going to be home for one whole week. If I am not alert, I might find myself a married man at the end of next week, and the rest shall be history. . . .

'Do you ever have anything else to talk about other than my marriage?' I asked Tisya.

'It's not just the wedding factor, Nakul,' she said sternly. 'These are not good times. You know about the job cuts, don't you? Why do you want to give your company a reason to forget about your existence? One week's leave is a little too much.'

'I've not taken leave,' I replied. 'These are compensatory offs. In any case, our company is not laying off resources.'

'They won't warn anyone before they start the layoffs,' Tisya declared, giving me the go-ahead. 'Everyone around is falling prey. Anyway, I don't want to freak you out right now. Go, enjoy your comp-offs.'

She couldn't freak me out any more than I already was. The ghost of recession used to poke its ghastly face at me every night in my dreams. And it used to linger on the next morning too, until I reached my office and checked my mails to ensure that all was well. If that were not enough, the balance time was for people to fill me up on how many acquaintances had been axed of late. The latest question added to the list of pleasantries at social gatherings was, 'Are you still with Bytesphere?' asked with a mixed tone of near disbelief and pre-empted sympathy. But for the sake of a relaxed week ahead, I decided to stash away my worries for some other time.

I got into the plane, shoving my ample self through the narrow aisle. I performed a stampede over a few dozen hapless passengers who looked at me petulantly as I knocked their heads around with my heavy luggage. I finally reached seat 18C, which was an emergency aisle seat. Thank God for small mercies, for I usually have to recoil like the Anaconda on the regular seats to accommodate my XL frame. I settled down in anticipation of a nice nap through the journey. I was beginning to drift into a light sleep when I heard a girl's voice.

'Excuse me,' she spoke in a clear, intelligible voice. 'Could you please help me with this?'

I looked at her irritably. She had a bonsai frame and looked sort of emaciated. She stood next to me with a huge Samsonite trolley in tow, almost her own size, and a Reebok bag flung on her frail shoulders.

I seized her trolley rather indifferently and shoved it in the overhead locker with all my might. The girl had got to have some solid power to carry that giant of a bag all by herself, I decided. As she settled down, I felt a compulsive urge to size her up. *Not happening.* I shook my head in dismay. I mean, c'mon, whatever happened to the all-pervasive feminine mania for grooming details? This one seemed least bothered about her loosely packed hair bun, thick-rimmed glasses and her pale skin. Her oversized chequered kurta and baggy-white pajamas looked like a sack of rice thrown over a couple of bones stapled together.

'Bytesphere!' She chuckled loudly, like she had spied an alien in a flight reserved for humans. Or maybe it was sheer admiration – I could not tell from her tone.

I looked around and saw the piece of glaring evidence: the Bytesphere logo embossed on my T-shirt, which had been gifted to all the Bytes at the time of their induction.

'Yeah.' I smiled lightly.

'That's some name to be associated with!' she said.

So it was admiration after all. I felt better. I smiled again, not sure if I wanted to extend this conversation. I was sleepy and tired, and didn't have much incentive for a chat. I was just beginning to lie down, when she threw in the real punch.

'You guys are all over the place, aren't you?' She giggled.

Now, this was getting a bit too gutsy. 'Sorry?' I said indignantly.

'Don't get me wrong,' she added. 'All I meant is there has been a deluge of your clan. . . .'

'Clan?'

'The IT clan. I mean, I am quite impressed. Most students from my engineering college are also headed there, so I guess the clan's going to multiply further!'

'We are not chicken in a poultry farm, ma'am,' I said, offended. 'You do seem to know a lot about the IT industry, don't you?' I gauged somehow that she didn't.

'No, in fact, I hardly know anything,' she said, still smiling affably, as though trying to erode my vexation. 'I'm sorry if I offended you. I was only trying to make small talk.'

Small talk! This was the first time a girl was proactively trying to make small talk with me. I was pleased with the prospect, but not with the subject. It made me uneasy.

'Alright,' I said. 'I agree there has been a deluge in the Indian IT sector. But what the hell, we are driving the economy, aren't we?'

'Of course, you are,' she said, 'but I wonder if it drives anything other than the sensex. I mean, what happens to the real value addition to the country?'

'And what is the *real* value addition?' I asked, now a little amused. 'Are you alluding to philanthropy, by any chance?'

'Why, does that sound absurd?' She knitted her eyebrows into two little cones. 'How hard is it to consider the shocking gap in our society? The revolution you are referring to is hardly even understood by the rural people.'

'Are you a social worker?' I asked, just about half in earnest.

'I wouldn't mind being labelled one,' she said, 'though I know there is much I need to do before I can claim to be one. But I do believe we owe something to the society in which we prosper by the day.'

'Appreciable,' I remarked. 'But I prefer keeping quiet on subject matters I am not equipped to deal with. I have a lot in my head I think one must do, but the head is where it all remains. I need to eat, and I can only find so much time as to earn my own square meal, rather than fending for someone else's. I might sound insensitive, but am just plain practical.'

'If we all think thus,' she mused, 'nothing will happen anyway. You are right.'

I smiled wider this time. 'Ah, am pleased to see that someone can think like a true revolutionary. But then, if social work is what you are inclined towards, why did you choose an engineering degree?'

'You don't expect I would walk off with a *jhola*, telling my parents I wanted to pursue a career in social service, do you? They would ask me some really tough questions. They are very orthodox when it comes to viewing a career as in or out of vogue.'

'There you are,' I said triumphantly, 'you just seconded my opinion.'

'No, I didn't,' she cut in. 'I still believe in what I say. Pursuing this alongside one's career cannot be all that tough.'

'Right,' I said softly, more in an attempt to call off the debate. I was getting increasingly sleepy, and if her incessant talk was any indication, I was not going to be able to weasel out easily. Man, she had some energy! I wondered if she had darted right into a truck of Red Bull just before boarding the flight.

I decided to be abrupt. I knocked off my floaters, sighed loudly and lay back on my reclined seat.

'Sleeping?' she persisted.

'Yes,' I said, gritting my teeth. 'I'm beat.'

'Okie,' she said in the same effervescent tone, and began to flip a magazine.

I awoke after about forty minutes, when the pilot's jarring voice pierced through my ears, informing us that we had commenced descent over Baroda. It was sunny outside, and the beautiful landscape of the city was now vaguely visible through the fast disappearing sheets of clouds. It was a familiar scene, one that I gladly viewed every time we were returning from a family vacation. Oddly, I always looked forward to my return home more than I looked forward to the vacation. For, in the township where I stayed, I had my own set of adventures. I ran on the empty roads in the morning to take in the scented air. I played self-created games with friends in the evening. At night, I talked to the stars from the sprawling terrace of that paradise I called home.

Eight years ago, my family had shifted to Chandigarh, and had returned to this place only a year back. And this was going to be my first trip back here, after the exile. I sensed an insane excitement surge within me. I felt I could recognise each element of those streets from twenty thousand feet high. I took off on a parallel journey of nostalgia, making the fifteen minutes to landing unbearable.

Who's Eric?

The township that we stayed in was arguably the best gift mom and dad gave their two kids. It was a bold decision for them to take a sabbatical from their civil service profiles and join OCIL, a giant chemical manufacturing company, on deputation. The overwhelmed company executives gave them a neat little house ensconced between dense foliage, some interesting neighbours and some chronicles that comprised an unforgettable childhood.

Less working hours now meant they could give more attention to the children, who were not the self-motivated kinds to practise discipline without supervision. Tisya is just two years elder to me. And two kids home alone on a post-school afternoon aren't really angels for the neighbouring housewives trying to catch up on their siestas.

'Mrs Kapoor, please control your children.' A hassled Rao Aunty would storm into our house every other evening. 'They make such a racket, I tell you. I can't sleep. Look, I am getting dark circles under my eyes.' She would thrust her face upwards for dramatic effect.

Per force, Mom had to opt for a profile that had a shorter shift. She began coming home early in the afternoons, and ensured that we did our lessons like good, civilised children. When we failed to do so, we would be greeted with the usual embargos on TV, dessert, and everything else we were likely to beg for. Tisya often got away with her lachrymose stunts (all moms give in to histrionics), while

I would be a silent victim. Anyway, Tisya was always an edge more academically responsive than I was and managed to scamper out with her eight noisy friends in the evening, while I struggled with percentages and equations.

These nine girls played a wacky 'Story-Story' game every evening, where they would cook up some imaginary fable set in a dreamland and then enact it. I can't poke fun at their madness, for in early days, I belonged to their group, too. While other boys in the township would busy themselves with GI-Joes and cricket, I found comfort in the company of nine girls. Initially, it was my reticence that made me stick around with my sister. But soon after, that reason changed to Zoya. Friendly, suave and beautifully easy on the eyes, she was the first to make me realise the concept of puppy love. I often tried to be her husband in 'Story-Story'. I never got even close to succeeding, but I still savoured every moment of those evenings when she would tug at my cheek and go, 'You are *cchho chweeeeet*. . . .'

Often, some boys jeered at me while cycling off to the playground. But I didn't care, for Zoya pulling my cheeks was always a bigger motivation than clubbing a few sixes on the ground. Anyone could play cricket, but being loved at six was not everyone's forte. I did play cricket later, however, when dad intercepted and warned me that he would dress me in a frock if I played with the girls again. There again, I was lucky enough to find that Zoya's younger brother played cricket at the lawns and that she would often come to pick him up on her Atlas cycle. As she waited on the park bench for her brother's game to end, I would rise to the occasion and display some fabulous batting or pull off an excellent diving catch where it was not necessary to dive. I would then hear her cheer for me. Cricket had begun to pay off, too.

As I grew from knickers to denim, though, I began to realise that I was but a kid brother to Zoya (ouch). I began to mingle more with the cricket freaks, most of who were a little older than me. But I hit it off pretty well with them, especially with the undisputed leader of the pack, whom we fondly called Shomu *da*. Our friendship began by accident, well, quite literally. During my first week at the cricket ground, he had aimed the ball in my direction to run me out, but the ball had found its place right on my temple. In a fit of panic, he had rushed me to the township hospital and had got the treatment done out of his pocket money.

'Who did it?' Mom had asked. 'I fell while running,' had been my prompt reply. I got a chiding for my carelessness, but Shomu da was relieved. In return, he began calling me every evening after the game to his house, where his mother would serve *sondesh* – her claim to fame in the whole township.

Under his guidance, I learnt not only to play good cricket, but also some important lessons like: to never smoke, to never lie to my parents and to not always blabber the truth in front of his parents. For example, he poked me in the chest and said, 'Don't *ever* tell my parents that I am going with my friends for this!' He pointed at a steamy poster of *Basic Instinct* outside the open-air theatre. Sharon Stone clung to Michael Douglas and pouted her lips lecherously. On top was the invite, an English message written in Gujarati font: 'Don't miss sexy kitten Sharon Stone: *Basic Instinct*, screening tonight at 9 p.m.'

An intrigued ten-year-old, I had gone home and asked dad: 'What does sexy mean?'

He was scandalised to say the least. 'Who taught you that word?'

'The theatre says Sharon Stone is a sexy kitten.'

Dad sighed. 'Don't bother about them, the theatre guys are nuts. You just remember, you won't use that word.'

'OK, but how can a girl be a kitten?'

'Ah, forget it!' dad said, exasperated, and began to walk off. Then he turned to me and said, 'By the way, that movie is not for you. So don't watch it!'

Dad had made a big mistake. By denying a child the possibility to explore the unknown, he had only strengthened his resolve all the more. I had then approached Shomu da and his friends, and they somehow managed to sneak me in under the lazy security guy's nose. I loved the movie, and oh yes, the story was OK, too.

Over the Sunday noon cycling adventures, and over the lazy conversations by the lakeside, Shomu da and I had fostered a unique friendship, which we believed would stand the test of time. And then came adulthood. . . .

The plane screeched to an exaggerated halt at the Vadodara airport at around 10.15 in the morning. I saw dad wait eagerly at the arrivals terminal, craning his neck every now and then to spot me. I ran to him, waving excitedly, and hugged him.

'A year seems like a lifetime, son,' he said. 'How have you been?'

'Absolutely great,' I replied.

'Looks like it,' dad said. 'You've put on weight. A lot of it, in fact.'

I twitched uncomfortably. 'Every parent who sees his child after a long time feels he has lost weight. . . .'

'I can't lie,' he interrupted me.

'Alright, I'll pull down.' I patted him. 'First, let's get home. I can't wait to meet mom and be home.'

As we proceeded towards the parking, my philanthropic co-passenger tapped me on the shoulder as she darted past me.

'Hey,' she called, hurling a card at me. 'That's my contact. Let's keep in touch!'

I missed the catch and the card fell on the ground. I was too lazy to pick it up. I looked up and saw her; clumsy yet queerly confident, with luggage in tow, slowly wafting out of sight.

'Mom has a surprise for you when we get home,' dad said, smiling widely. That smile was a sign that portended matrimonial discussions were in the offing.

'What's the surprise?' I asked hesitantly. 'Don't tell me it's about a girl. . . .'

'It won't be a surprise if I told you, Nakul,' dad said, roaring with laughter in sync with the car's engine as it sped towards home.

As the car wound its way into the alley, I caught the first glimpse of the house. It brought back all the associated memories and I swear I would have killed to get those days back. Only the kitchen garden at the rear was in a mess. 'It wasn't taken care of while we were away,' dad explained woefully.

'Nakul *beta*!' Mom exclaimed before I actually stepped in. Of all the therapies the world may have to offer, nothing can possibly match a mother's hand brushing through your hair. 'You've become so weak!' she said, examining me thoughtfully from head to toe. There, she scores a brownie point over Dad already. Moms always feel their child needs to be fed, even the ones who look like overgrown potatoes.

'How have you been?' I asked.

'I am good only when you come home, son,' she said ruefully, 'otherwise all is dull.'

If you are among the kind of people who visit home occasionally, you need to make your mother promise she won't get schmaltzy. It just gets too difficult when you need to go back in a few days.

'Oh, by the way,' she said cheerfully, wiping her tears, 'I have a surprise for you!'

'Yeah, dad told me,' I replied nervously, walking towards the bathroom. Evasion was the only solution, if at all. 'What is it?'

'A new uncle called Saxena Uncle has moved into our block. They have called us for dinner.'

'OK . . . and?'

'Their daughter, Payal, is the prettiest girl I've seen. She is in her final year of dentistry. . . .'

'I don't think I will come, Ma,' I said. 'I am too tired from the trip.'

'I am not asking you,' she said sternly. 'I'm telling you. You will come. I am not asking you to marry her, but you can at least socialise.'

Socialise! That's the most misleading term in such discussions. You never know when the noose falls around your neck. When I had howled once in a dentist's clinic as he extracted a milk tooth, mom had promised me she would never take me to a dentist again. And now she was marrying me off to one. Someone should tell her she was breaking her promise.

'I am not ready for marriage,' I said as boldly as I could.

'Why?' she asked earnestly. 'See, even your beard has begun to grow.' She pinched at my stubble.

'It's been growing for the last nine years,' I said.

'Whatever – you'd better shave before we leave tonight. And please, for God's sake, don't wear pink!'

'But I don't. . . .'

'Shh,' she admonished. 'What's your apprehension? Kavya?'

'Oh God. . . .' I moaned.

'OK then.' She clapped her hands. 'It's done. You're coming. Now freshen up, I am making *double ka meetha* for your breakfast.'

Double ka meetha was my favourite dish, and today, the sweetest bait for me to give in to her plea. I gorged on a bowl full of the dessert, after which mom asked a drowsy me. 'So are you better now? You'll come in the evening, na?'

'Uh-huh, yeah,' I mumbled, and plopped into bed.

I was woken up at five: three hours before the dinner. 'Get ready!' Mom said excitedly.

'Huh? There's three hours!' I protested.

'You'll need time. Try out these new clothes. If they don't fit, we'll have to go buy.'

I turned to see a navy blue kurta pyjama kept at my bedside. 'What? Are you serious? I am not wearing that bridegroom outfit!'

Thankfully, dad intervened. 'Wear what you are comfortable in,' he said. He then turned to mom and whispered, 'Don't make him conscious, or he will run away.'

Fine, so he was part of the conspiracy. I got up grumpily and began to get ready. At sharp eight, we rang the doorbell at the Saxenas.

'Hello, hello,' Mr Saxena folded his hands in greeting. 'So nice of you to make it.'

I bowed and folded my hands in return. 'Hello, Nakul,' he said, shaking my hand. Somehow I felt the handshake to be a few seconds longer than necessary. He kept grinning. I smiled back in return and retrieved my sweaty hand from his clasp. Mrs Saxena followed suit, coming out from the kitchen, leading a delicious aroma of lentils. The same pleasantries were exchanged with my parents once again. Once again, I did the customary bow.

'Nice!' She looked at me. I could feel it in my bones that I was being scanned. She beckoned me to sit by her side on the sofa. Embarrassed, I kept gazing at the carpet and she kept asking me questions about my work, my hobbies, my favourite cuisine, etc. Within ten minutes, I was hoping that this Payal came in soon!

'He is very shy,' uncle looked at dad, 'isn't it? Even Payal is like that only. Payal beta, come here.'

I stalled my breath and refused to look above the carpet. But like the ostrich can't escape trouble by burying its head in the sand, I was no exception. Payal was anything but shy. She came into the room and greeted my parents, then turned to me and said hello. I muttered a quick hello, and must have looked at her for a flash of a second before I made the carpet my object of study again.

'Payal is a fabulous painter!' Mrs Saxena beamed at me, waiting for me to acknowledge.

'That's great,' mom said. 'Nakul is fond of art, too.'

Now that I was being marketed so aggressively, mom wouldn't be unjustified in even claiming that I was Da Vinci reincarnated.

'I've taken to fabric painting,' Payal said to me. 'Would you like to take a look? It's in my room.'

I looked up at my parents for their response. A girl was inviting me to her room – this was no joke. *Please say 'no'! Let's storm out of the house saying, 'our culture doesn't allow this . . .' or something like that!*

'Go, Nakul!' Dad said.

I followed her reluctantly. Her room was adorned with her own works of art. I must admit they were indeed some fabulous pieces. For a person like me with sedate interests in plaster and enamel, the colourful strokes on her walls, on her cupboards, and on every inanimate object, were strikingly impressive. I can be very sure I don't remember what Payal looks like, but I distinctly remember one of her pencil sketches on her window shades: A young man on the road, surrounded by whirls of a dangerous tornado, stared at a signpost from which arrows jutted out in four different directions.

'I call this one "Eric in Chaos",' she explained.

'Who's Eric?' I asked.

'A little bit of him is in all of us, you can say,' she said. 'It's a series of sketches I'm trying to make for an art exhibition – the story of a boy called Eric, who, like millions of other people, is in a quest for the ever-elusive phenomenon called success. It's like all these people are in a race of sorts and the finishing line is this pinnacle of success. En route, he encounters obstacles of all kinds and tries to either jump over the obstacles or find alternate paths to that pinnacle. The story should end with the last sketch depicting how he does manage to hit the pinnacle eventually.'

'Wow.' I smiled for the first time. 'That's quite some thought. It pretty much summarises what we face everyday at work!'

'That's what I was telling my uncle,' she explained, 'who is incidentally also in some IT company. I told him that the unrest and chaos I see in his hectic life was my inspiration to make these sketches.'

'I'm impressed!' I said in due appreciation of her artistic abilities, though I didn't understand the concept of chaos entirely then. Art was anyway always too deep for me to analyse and so I decided to let the discussion die right there.

The dinner was an epitome of dilemmas. The food was so delicious I could have hogged on it like a pig, if it was not for the constant gaze of the foursome. The icing on the cake was when Payal's leg accidentally brushed against mine under the table. It sent shivers down my spine, but I held myself until she spoke – 'Oops, sorry!' – and brought everyone's attention to the fore. Mom looked mighty pleased.

I was finally relieved to be back home by bedtime. As I lay down to sleep, I burped and brooded over 'Eric in Chaos'. For some reason, that image did not leave my mind.

It took me two days to come out of my laziness, before I decided to explore the township and meet old friends.

'Zoya is married,' mom told me at breakfast. 'She stays in the US with her husband. So no need going around looking for her.'

'Hah, big deal!' I laughed. Somehow, I did not find it funny. I still expected Zoya to pull my cheeks and ruffle my hair. The thought of her being married off to some weirdo in the US disgusted me.

'I want to meet only Shomu da,' I said. 'Does he still stay at the same place?'

'I'm not sure, you can go and check,' mom said. 'We've not got a chance to meet too many people since the time we've returned. From what I hear, a lot of people have relocated in the past few years.'

I hurried with my breakfast and sprinted three blocks across to where Shomu da stayed. To my pleasant surprise, I saw him right outside at the porch of his house. He sported long tresses and a beard so dishevelled it looked like a cyclone had lived there. He was dressed in tattered shorts and a worn out tee, and was busy cleaning his vintage Enfield bike.

'Shomu da!' I called out.

He turned back at me quizzically. 'Yes?' After a brief pause, he cried out, 'Nakul! *Bondhu, kemon acho!*' How are you!

As he shook hands with me, I could sense a tinge of formality, a queer coldness in him. He had been sprightlier before; his face also was eroded of youth already. His eyes had rolled into deep sockets. The veins running through his thin hands were thick as tree trunks.

'I did hear about uncle and aunty shifting back to Baroda,' he began. 'Sorry, I just didn't get a chance to meet them.'

'That's OK,' I said. 'They're themselves still settling back in. It feels awesome to be back here though, after so long.'

'Yeah,' he said, a bit indifferently. 'It's been long since I heard from you.'

'I know,' I replied. 'I have so often craved for aunty's handmade sondesh. I can't wait to feast on it now!'

'Well, I'm afraid you can't,' he said curtly. 'Mom died three years back.'

I felt a vacuum descend on us. His words droned in my ears painfully as I absorbed them over and over.

'But . . . how?' I babbled stupidly, and then changed the line. 'You never told me. . . .'

'You never gave me your new numbers as they changed by the month.' He smiled this time. 'My number was the same, though. . . .'

This was the politest way to say that it was I who had stayed out of touch. I had nothing to say in defence. He was right. I jumped from Baroda to Chandigarh, from school to high school to graduation to post-graduation. And in the mad scheme of events, I forgot that there stayed a Shomu da in my neighbourhood whom I considered an elder brother. I had been preachy and wordy on maintaining relations before, and now I suddenly found myself very hollow and fake. My guilty self could look nowhere above the cobblestone road beneath us.

'I got depressed after she went,' he continued as I looked at nothing. 'And got on the turkey. I was finally sent to rehab to get off it. But I'm fine now and am trying to make a life.'

'Where do you work?' I attempted feebly.

'OCIL – in the operations and logistics team,' he said. 'Dad gave the jack. Anyway, you tell me – how have things shaped up all these years?'

'There's a lot to talk about,' I said. 'We will need to sit at length.'

'Would you like to go by the lakeside once again?' he asked. 'I haven't been there in ages.'

'Yeah, sure . . . , ' I began, when my phone beeped.

1 New Message.

Vishal Tiwari

Cheapo can't reach u . . . has called us back urgently . . . some P1 task is up. Make it by tomorrow if possible . . . Cheerio.

'Shit,' I muttered. 'I'm afraid I'll have to leave tonight. My manager wants me back.'

'Whoa, that was fast,' he laughed. 'No worries, we'll plan later. When do you come next?'

'I have no idea,' I shrugged. 'I am at the mercy of my organisation!'

'We all are.' He laughed louder this time. 'Anyway, so long.'

'Catch you later,' I called back.

I trudged back home with a heavy heart. The tears wouldn't stop. It was very embarrassing when people ogled at a burly bloke sob on the road, but I couldn't erase the lovable image of Shomu da's mother in my mind.

It was only after I boarded my train that night for Mumbai that I began wondering of Cheapo's urgent requirement. Must be offloading some work he cannot handle himself, I thought. Or could it be a new project? Could I be in for a bigger role? Was there an issue in my annual appraisal? The tears finally dried up and tension began to brew.

I'm Not SRK

'We have some interesting P1 work up our sleeve,' Cheapo leaned forward in his chair as he spoke, ready to roll off anytime. He paused, waiting in anticipation for someone to ask him what P1 meant.

Sure enough, a new member in the team asked. 'What's P1, Chirayu?'

Chirayu smiled triumphantly. 'P1 means Priority1,' he said with dramatic stress. 'Very important work. This could make or break you in the initial phase of your career.'

If you ask me, this explanation of P1 was an anticlimax of sorts. Come on, everything in this company is P1. It doesn't even strike me often, but I am handed some hundred P1s a day. What could be so important that he curtailed our leave?

'Most of you are new to this team,' he continued. 'So I'd like to tell you a little about myself and my style of working, first. I am a tough cookie. . . .' The new guys kept staring at him blankly, their heads nodding up and down involuntarily like yoyos, even as he went on singing his laurels.

A sneak peek into the 'team' till Cheapo continues his wordy gyan: Lekha Rao, Vishal Tiwari and I are the three trusted soldiers of his small team. So far, we were, simply put – body shoppers. The three of us had had to pay a price for being extra active in our days of training. We volunteered to get trained on multiple packages and applications. As a result, we became the unofficial gypsies of the batch. We were thrown as fillers from one project to the other, as and when their requirement came by. This time, Cheapo had promised us that Bytesphere was going to win a new client deal and the project would be ours. If that would be so, the three of us would be the spearheads of the team that would drive this project. So far, everything was 'in the pipeline'.

The members paying attention to Cheapo right now in the conference room are new to our team. They have no idea what they are in for. They are fresh out of college and are wearing the Bytesphere tag. That is enough to boast about in front of their friends. They are not ruffled by issues like staid growth, monotonous tasks and a pesky manager. As a result, statements like, 'This could make or break you in the initial phase of your career,' send an adrenaline rush through them. For us, such statements were wisps at best.

'So, what's the work?' a disgruntled Vishal interrupted him.

'Britcell is a new player in the European telecom market,' Cheapo said. 'And Bytesphere is pitching for testing their MIS application. Shh, it's between us, OK?'

We nodded dutifully. 'When's the bid?' I asked.

'There's speculation that it will happen in about three weeks,' he said.

'Then?'

'We need to prepare ourselves,' he spoke like an army chief. 'Ours is a small team, and this is going to be a huge project. If we don't showcase our competency, the other teams will snatch this from us. And we will be left freelancing for them again. I want my team to win it this time.'

'So what do we need to do right now?' I asked. 'Until the proposal is sent to us, we have no info.'

'Speculation is rife that they will opt for Xabre as their application,' he said. 'It's new and it's hot property in the telecom market. We need to get trained on Xabre in the meantime.'

'We don't have licences to install Xabre,' Vishal said. 'How do we get trained on it?'

Cheapo thrust his palm towards Vishal and then placed it on his own chest. 'Relax,' he assured, 'what am I here for? I've asked for these licences already. They will be installed on our machines in the next couple of days. We also have arranged for a trainer who will be in by next week.'

'Then why did you call us back so soon?' I asked agitatedly. 'We don't start until next week.'

'Read up,' he said. 'There's a lot you guys need to know about the telecom market. Look up the net and get cracking!'

'You curtailed our leave for this?' I asked, still in disbelief.

'Look, Nakul,' he growled. 'You can't imagine how intense the competition is. Do you know how many vendors fight each other for a single bid on an average?' He paused and then shouted, 'Many!'

Anticlimax, again. I ignored his comment. The guy doesn't even know his numbers right, tch tch.

'But I could have accessed the internet from home!' I complained.

Cheapo harrumph-ed. 'Work is worship, and this place is your temple. Please appreciate the spirit of the team, we need to work together!'

I'm sure he himself didn't know what he was saying, but he said it anyway and then bounced back to his seat. I seethed. 'What crap is that!'

Vishal did not respond. Lekha looked at me and grinned. 'Chill,' she said. '*Hota hai*. It happens. You should be used to it by now.'

'It's easy for you, Lekhaji,' I mocked. 'You live here. I don't get to go home often. This Cheapo doesn't understand.'

'OK, leave him.' She tugged at my arm. 'You need to cool down. Come, let's have some iced tea.'

Lekha dragged me off my chair towards the staircase. Her name is a misnomer, as it has an uncanny resemblance to the petite, fragile silver-screen damsel of the 70s. Lekha was anything but feminine. She sported short, almost spiky hair, a demon-faced tattoo on her forever exposed arm, and she rode a Pulsar to office.

'Are you coming?' I asked Vishal. He clicked his tongue in 'no', without looking up from his screen. We left him to be and headed for the cafeteria.

'A Long Island Iced Tea, please,' Lekha announced.

The attendant turned to me. 'Cappuccino,' I said dryly.

The attendant smiled and pulled a fast one. 'You always take the same thing, don't you, Sir? Whatever happened to the adage "variety is the spice of life"?'

'I'm looking forward to that,' I said, and forced back a smile.

'You want to talk variety?' I looked at Lekha when he left. 'If I had it in me, I would alternate between cognac and Chateau Margaux everyday at the Marriott!'

'What's wrong?' she asked. 'All this sulking just after the annual hike. . . .'

'Hike! Heck, yeah!' I sniggered. 'A six percent hike! Maybe now I can go buy some new underwear!'

Lekha laughed out loud, pouring a fountain of water from her mouth all over me.

'Sorry,' she blurted, 'but you are damn funny when depressed.'

'I'm not depressed,' I protested. 'Don't make me so by saying that. All I'm saying is I need more money. I live in a cramped one-room place and I'm still struggling with the rent!'

'You live in Bandra, my boy,' she said. 'And you are not SRK. So live with it. Why don't you get yourself a roomie?'

'I'm looking for one,' I said. 'But I haven't found anyone yet. My landlord introduced me to a few.'

'What happened?'

'I need someone who is non-interfering, non-pesky and fun to talk to.'

'I fulfil all three criteria,' she said mischievously, winking. 'What if I moved in?'

I winced. 'Sorry, I missed out the last one,' I said. 'I need a guy. The thought of my parents paying a surprise visit someday scares me.'

My phone rang. 'Golu!' Kavya's voice echoed through the phone. The whole cafeteria must now know what she calls me.

'Hi,' I said as laconically and softly as possible. 'What's up?'

'My class just ended, Golu,' she meowed affectionately. 'I was missing you.'

'Aha,' I said, trying to cover the earpiece with my palm. 'Nice, nice.'

'Weren't you missing me?' she asked.

'Yeah, yeah, of course,' I said as surreptitiously as possible. 'It goes without saying.'

'Then say it,' she demanded.

'Hmm, I am in office.' I dropped a hint.

'So? I called on your mobile na, dumbo? Mobile means you can move away and talk.'

'Of course,' I laughed. 'How could I forget that?'

I excused myself from the scene and spent some time with Kavya, the most refreshing voice that ever was. Only, there was one problem: I was more of a listener and she the talker. While I was pretty comfortable with this arrangement, she often mistook my silence for disinterest.

'You don't feel like talking to me?' she asked after I must have responded to her in 'hmm' a zillion times.

'No, baby, I am listening,' I clarified. 'Go on.'

'What did I say last?' she tried to test me.

'Your friend Richa broke up with her boyfriend Manas because she caught him making out with your other friend . . . now what was her name? Yeah, Gagandeep!'

'Imagine that wretch! All men are. . . .'

'Pigs. I know,' I sighed. 'You told me.'

'Except you,' she said romantically. 'You are my cutie pie. Oh, by the way, I have to give you a surprise, so hold your breath!'

'You're coming to Mumbai?' I asked.

'You're so irritating,' she moaned. 'Why do you have to spoil the fun? I wanted to say it.'

'But I guessed it . . . ' I attempted to reason.

'OK, leave it,' she said. 'Yes, I am coming in about two weeks – under the pretext of some project work.'

'Great, I'll look forward to it,' I said. 'I hope it's a weekend though?'

'Why, are you trying to say you won't meet me on a weekday?'

'Of course, I will,' I got onto damage control. 'Only that weekends would give us more time together.'

'OK, let me try for a weekend,' she said. 'I'll plan and inform you.'

She then quizzed me on a few standard questions that marked the end of every conversation.

It was like going through a compliance audit on every call.

'Are you keeping your cupboard in order now?'

'Yes.'

'Are you keeping away from other girls?'

'Yes.'

'Will you call and sing me a song tonight?'

'Yes.'

We hung up. I looked at the list of recurring reminders on my phone: 'Wake up Kavya for her morning class – 7 a.m.', 'Say "I miss you" – 1 p.m.', 'Sing her a nice goodnight song – 10 p.m.'. These were no obligations I carried out for her. Believe me, Kavya was special. But excessive working hours and pressure in office smoked out these important must-dos from my memory much too often.

Kavya was a budding fashion designer in a premier institute on the outskirts of Pune. Well into her final year, she had just finished her internship under the guidance of some big fashion maestro of Bollywood. All this on her own merit, for she had the mettle. I tested application defects, classifying them into high, critical and super-critical all day long, day after day. She could design for and dine with the Hrithik Roshans and Aishwarya Rais of the world. I would have loved to live her life, if only I could tell a sewing machine from a typewriter.

I had first met Kavya when she came to visit her brother in Mumbai when he worked with Bytesphere. I had just joined the company then, and her brother had invited me courteously to his place for dinner. I met her there and fell in love instantly – with her culinary skills. We had got talking, and we exchanged phone numbers and email addresses. I had taken the first initiative to call, but thereon there was no looking back from her end. Her brother quit Bytesphere soon after, but our calls went on. The funniest part of our relationship was, as we liked to claim, that we were not in a relationship. We were 'just very good friends'. This phrase always eluded my understanding, but Kavya had her definitions set very well.

'My social circle is split into four rings,' she once explained, drawing rings with her finger on the beach sand. 'The outermost has those people whom I consider furniture. They have no importance in my life. I either hate them or I don't care. The second one is formal acquaintances – for whom I reserve my plastic smiles. You need to be cordial with those kinds for your daily needs. The third circle is that of my best-est friends: I can be myself with them. And yeah, they are the only ones whom I would bother waking in the middle of the night to crib. The fourth circle,' she said finally, 'has my parents, my brother, and soon. . . .' She halted and looked into my eyes. She blushed gently, and her hair blew against the westerly sea winds. I am sure she never looked more beautiful than that.

'You lie somewhere here,' she then said, pointing at the third ring, hence breaking that brief spell of enchantment.

I returned to the café to find Lekha playing with the straw in her iced tea.

'You took long, Golu,' she smirked.

'Shit, you heard . . . ' I muttered. 'Look, please don't tell anyone.'

'I'll think about it,' she grinned. 'Why does she call you Golu, though? Isn't it a funny name?'

'What's funny?' I asked. 'She calls me that out of affection.'

'Or maybe because you are pudgy?' she suggested. Nobody in the world could get as blunt and obnoxiously rude as Lekha Rao.

'I'm not pudgy,' I said indignantly. 'I'm pretty fit. Just the stomach has begun to peep out a bit.'

'A lot of things are peeping out.'

'Come off it,' I said in irritation. 'Talk something else.'

'Why don't you start coming with me to the gym?'

'I don't need to.'

'You do.'

'I don't have the time either,' I said virtuously. 'Training's going to begin.'

'That will be only till 5 p.m.,' she insisted. 'You can come after that.'

'Are you stubborn or what!' I raised my hands in protest. 'Talk something else, I'll tell you when I feel the need to be Arnold Schwarr-whatever!'

'Hmm, so what do you think of this Britcell thingy?' she asked.

'Who knows,' I said. 'It's like shooting in the dark. We have no idea if we will win it.'

'If we win it, we will lead the team from Mumbai,' she said excitedly. 'Because Cheapo is sure to work from the client location.'

'Yeah,' I said. 'Leading a big team does sound exciting. For a change, we can boss over someone.'

'And there is going to be an addition to your team,' I heard Jassi call out from behind me. The joyous Surd came trotting along to our table, in eager anticipation of providing us with some BBC newsflash. 'Some new employee has joined today. I overheard Anand mention that he might join Chirayu's team.'

'Who?'

'I don't remember the name,' he said. 'But he is some guy from Pali. His name sounded like that of some medieval warrior.'

Jassi then narrated us the latest gossip doing the rounds in office. Thanks to him, we never felt the need of a leisure-oriented Bulletin Board. We all had him as a single point of reference for leisure. And luckily, he was always available at the right time, when we needed to kill time – which was most of the time. Today would have been no exception, had Cheapo not called in at the most inopportune moment.

'Your cubicle misses you, Sir,' he mocked. 'You've left it alone for too long. Now come up, we have a meeting.'

'Come on,' I told Lekha as I hung up the phone. 'We've been summoned by His Majesty.'

'You do hate Chirayu, don't you?' Jassi asked me.

'Why?'

'I can always sense that sarcasm.'

'Oh no, Chirayu is an angel,' I shot back. 'He is a sucker when it comes to understanding business nuances of the client, but who cares – he is a "team player"! He takes credit for the work that we do, but who cares – he is our boss, isn't it? He is as stingy about our leave as a merchant would be about his gold, but who cares – he is the "driving force" in our team, thanks to whom we deliver all our projects in time. Man, Jassi, you got to be kidding me! How can I hate him?'

'See, sarcasm again,' Jassi said triumphantly.

I didn't respond. We turned our backs to him and walked out of the cafeteria.

'You shouldn't have said that in front of Jassi,' Lekha pondered. 'This guy can't keep things to himself. He could create trouble.'

'Like I care,' I said disinterestedly. I did care! Shit, what if Jassi told Cheapo what I thought of him! Could he please hold on to his *Narada* instincts, at least till my appraisal for this year was cleared? A senseless fear gripped my mind, which was thankfully eased by crossing Short-Skirt Shirley in the hallway. With her kind of dressing, she was impossible to miss even if she were at the end of the corridor. Fridays were when she took that extra liberty and went off-shoulder, indulged in her lavender specials, and white hot pants that were sized no better than a handkerchief. What topped it all was her suggestive gait. I could have ogled longer, had I not spotted Lekha looking at me disparagingly.

'Shameless!' she snorted and stormed up the staircase.

'What?' I tried following her. 'What did I do?'

'You know.'

'But what pissed you off?' I asked.

She didn't reply. She just huffed and puffed her way back to the cubicle.

My phone beeped as we walked towards the meeting room.

1 New Message

Hey, dis is Vishal's wife Anita . . . sry 2 bother you like dis . . . but I nd 2 talk . . . classified discussion . . . wl it b possible 4 u 2 meet me Mon evening at 6, at the Marriott?

I was taken aback, not just because of the abrupt request, but more because of the venue she had suggested. I would have to spend no less than a few hundred bucks in order to listen to her classified information. I was just about to request a cheaper place, when another message saved me the trouble.

Btw, pl consider it my treat. And pl don't tell Vishal abt it. . . .

I felt better. Sure, I typed back.

'What?' Vishal asked.

'Nothing,' I replied. 'Let's go.'

We entered the MR. Chirayu sat on the revolving chair, and next to him stood a boy with his head bowed, hands crossed in front. He fiddled with his fingers from time to time, and every few seconds, produced a cracking sound, redolent of extreme nervousness. Small beads of sweat negotiated their path along the frame of his soda glasses. All this demureness was a perfect antithesis to his hulk-like frame.

'Team, meet Kohinoor Pratap Kesari,' Chirayu said, gesturing towards the hulk. 'He is joining us from today.'

The name rang a bell. He had got to be that guy Jassi mentioned about. His name did sound like that of some medieval warrior. I could almost hear the trumpets in the background when Chirayu spoke out his name.

Kohinoor looked at us for a split second, and then shuffled his feet uncomfortably, looking downward again.

'Why don't you give the whole team your introduction, Kohinoor?' Chirayu suggested. 'It will help you mix with all of them faster.'

Kohinoor cleared his throat. 'Hello, dear brothers and sisters,' he had just begun when Lekha burst into a giggle. She got a glare from all of us, though we all found it funny. But it wasn't funny anymore when we saw Kohinoor's eyes well up in a jiffy. His voice began to quiver.

'Lekha, maybe you need some coffee,' Chirayu growled. 'Go, get some.'

Lekha walked out, and Kohinoor was egged on to continue. 'I am from Pali,' he said. 'And I have come here to make life in this city of dreams.'

Now, is that vision or what! I have already spent three years in this city of dreams, and all I have done so far is to collect those dreams each of the million times they scattered around.

'My name means a precious diamond . . .' he continued. '. . . I have studied software and coding is my passion. . . .'

I refuse to believe that, boss!

'Above all, I am here to make all of you my friends.'

Neat: you should say that again during your appraisal.

'That's awesome,' Chirayu said, mildly amused himself. 'We are all your friends. Make yourself comfortable today. Nakul,' he turned to me. 'You will be his mentor for the next one month. Help him with all office-related issues.'

I nodded. Kohinoor looked at me with an expression of exaggerated gratitude. I helped him with opening his bank account, and showing him around the cafeteria, gymnasium and the designated smoking zone – the ghosla.

'Oh no, dear brother!' he said in alarm. 'I don't smoke. They allow smoking to happen in office?'

I looked at him with perplexity. Before I could reply, he went on, 'I hope food is veg?'

'You get both,' I said.

'Separate kitchen?'

'Yes,' I said.

He could finally smile. 'This city is so big, brother. It is scary.'

'You can call me Nakul,' I said uncomfortably. 'Dear brother' was not in, man! 'And don't worry about the city. You will take some time, but once you do, you wouldn't want to leave it.'

'But it is very much expensive,' he added.

'Ask me about it,' I smiled. 'I pay a bomb for my house.'

'Bomb?' he asked, aghast at my comment.

'I mean, I've been paying a lot of money.'

He looked relieved. 'I thought you were dealing in bombs part-time! Ha, ha. . . .'

I didn't know what to say. I roared back in courtesy after making sure there was no one around to see that I found such humour worth a laugh.

'I am looking for someone to share the house with me,' I said.

'Oh, can I come?' he asked. 'I need a house.'

I looked at him. I needed time, but I could see the plea in his eyes. More than that, I could feel the desperate urge for me to save some money. I usually worked on impulse, and that day was no exception. I looked at him for a second and then nodded. 'OK, move in.'

Of Sushi and *Vada Pav*

I had never slept so undisturbed. The sublime calm, soothing weather and a long day at work made for a very rewarding sleep. It was all so perfect until an elephant began trumpeting outside the apartment in the wee hours of the night. What did an elephant want at this time, and that too in suburban Bandra? The noise didn't cease; instead, it grew all the louder. It kept grunting continuously, and very systematically, every two seconds, in a standard melody. I was now growing increasingly irritated. I tossed and turned in bed, tried to cover my ear with my pillow, but somehow the volume kept rising, till I could feel my bed tremble under the beast's breath. It was closing in on me. . . .

I woke up with a start and looked outside. The sun was not yet out, but dawn was about to break. I looked to my left and saw the elephant, Kohinoor, sitting on the bed adjacent to mine in a mendicant posture. He inhaled air forcefully through his wide nostrils and then let it out with a loud burst, tucking his stomach inside each time. The entire movement made his bed creak. He kept repeating the same movement till I got ticked off.

'What are you doing?' I asked.

'*Pranayama*,' he replied as briefly as possible and then got back to the same exercise.

I waited for him impatiently to finish his next five-six-seven hundred grunts, before saying, 'Your pranayama thing makes some kinda noise. It's not letting me sleep.'

'Oh, don't call it noise, brother,' he exclaimed as if I had committed blasphemy. 'Say positive vibrations.'

'Yeah, it's causing quite some vibration, too,' I said disdainfully. 'Listen, if you don't mind – can you do this workout of yours in the living room? I want to sleep.'

'Oh no, you must get up now, dear,' he said, tugging at my blanket. 'Mummyji says that only if we beat the sun in the race to rise every morning, can we win the race of life.'

'I don't want to win any race, Kohinoor,' I begged, pushing his hand away from my blanket. 'Please, let me sleep!'

I flipped over to the other side and tried to go back to sleep. But within a minute, I heard some sniffling sound. I turned over and saw Kohinoor in tears.

'What happened, Kohinoor?' I sat up, startled at his sudden change in behaviour. One thing was now certain; his tear glands were hyperactive.

'I think you are very angry with me,' he spoke between sniffles. 'Sorry.'

'It's OK, buddy,' I said, now fully awake. 'Good that I got up early for a change. I'll try getting to office early.'

I got up sleepily and slowly made my way towards the bathroom. The moment I got up, Kohinoor got back to his cheery self and resumed pumping air in his humongous body with the same vigour. I got ready and began fishing for something to eat in the fridge.

'There was a carton of Nestle's milk in the fridge last night.' I turned to him. 'I can't seem to find it now. Did you use it by any chance?'

'Oh yes, I gave it to pussy,' he said.

'What?'

'There was a pussy meowing near our door in the morning. I thought it was hungry, so I gave her that milk in a bowl.' He beamed with pride at his act of kindness.

'But why did you give her Nestle?' I asked. 'I mean, cats are not brand conscious, yaar. That milk was expensive. Let's please use it only for ourselves.'

I opened the door of the house to find the bowl lying outside.

'Is this the bowl you fed the cat in?' I asked, holding a big chinaware bowl in my hand.

'Yes!' He nodded proudly.

'Boss, this is my cereal bowl,' I said in disgust. 'I eat in it!'

'Oh, sorry! Should I wash it?'

'No, leave it,' I said. 'Keep it for your pussy now. I will buy another one.'

The thought of serving myself breakfast in a bowl licked all over by an abandoned street cat was sickening. I ransacked the fridge and found a couple of loaves of bread and some Nutella spread to go with it. I must have been less than halfway through, when Kohinoor came running out of the bathroom and into the kitchen, water dripping from his hands.

'Hey brother, do you have shit soap?'

The sandwich stuck in my throat even as I cringed at the mention of the word. He had tactfully chosen the apt moment. Suddenly, the Nutella spread oozing out of the bread no longer looked tempting. I gave up on the entire breakfast-eating urge, and walked out of home, scores of questions buzzing through my mind. When would our training begin? Would I get to go onsite at all? Was the landlord likely to raise the rent? Did I make a mistake by bringing Kohinoor in? Sadly, I never had an answer to any of my own questions.

I met Vishal at the entrance near the ghosla. 'How's work, mate?' I quizzed.

'Guess.'

'Same old, huh? Any news of the training?'

'Yes. It starts tomorrow. Some Canadian dude is coming for two days to train us.'

'Two days, that's it? How can we learn it all in two days?'

'They can't afford him for more than that. So the rest, as they usually say, will be self-explanatory and for self-practice.'

'Hmm. Hey, by the way, has Lekha come to office already?'

'Yeah, she is up in the cubicle. Why?'

'She got sort of upset with me on Friday morning. I wonder what's with her.'

'What are you upto, Nakul? You naughty kid!'

'God knows.' I shrugged. 'We just crossed Shirley that day in the hallway, and she was, you know, dressed as always. Now I just glanced at her routine, like we usually do, and suddenly I find Lekha giving me a dirty look. Then she called me shameless and stormed off.'

'First of all, your glances are not routine,' Vishal interrupted me. 'They are meaningful, lecherous stares.'

'Look who's talking!' I mocked.

'Hmm,' Vishal deliberated over the matter. 'Or maybe Lekha likes you.'

'Yeah, of course,' I taunted. 'I should have expected this brilliant answer from you!'

'It's only logical, Nakul,' he argued. 'She got jealous because you were staring at another girl.'

'That's preposterous!' I shook my head and began walking in. Inwardly, of course, I was bloating with pride. If this were true, it was a first of sorts, when a girl had proactively taken an interest in me. Maybe I should put this date down in Dear Diary, I mused. Yes, I would have wished for someone more feminine than Lekha, but a record is a record.

She looked at me as I walked into the cubicle. Thankfully, she had cooled down.

'Good morning,' she said. 'You're in early today. What's the sweat?'

'No sweat,' I replied. 'Just some extraneous circumstances got me to wake up early.'

'How's Kohinoor Pratap Kesari?' she asked and winked.

We discussed and laughed over the pranayama and the pussycat and the shit soap. But I dared not ask her the reason she had got cheesed off with me that day. I decided to let it lie.

'Ah, Nakul! Pleasant surprise to see you in office so early!' Chirayu stuck his grinning face over the cubicle fence after a while. 'On this good note, let me have you come and see me in my cabin.'

I followed him in and examined his cabin. A plush leather chair faced his shiny glass desk. His Vaio laptop was a sleek beauty. His Blackberry device was securely tied to his enormous waist. His overall cunningness and incompetence notwithstanding, these gadgets always fascinated me and forced me to respect him for those brief moments. After all, even if it were pure luck, he had reached somewhere in life.

'OK, there is news for you,' he said. 'The project manager of the Japanese CME team called on Friday. They want you on board for their new project with that broadcasting company in Tokyo.'

'Wow!' I said, hardly able to contain my excitement.

'What wow? You'll be working in a team of sixty. You won't get any recognition.'

'I agree, but to be honest, Chirayu, I didn't get much recognition in my previous project either,' I said, gathering all courage. 'And I'm not sure how I'm going to attain any specific recognition in Britcell. At least in this case, I get to go onsite.'

'And do what? Watch women dressed in kimonos offer you sushi all day long?' he asked. 'Look dude, think about your career growth. Do you really want to freelance around with other teams or do you want to establish your identity in the telecom vertical? Onsite-vonsite will keep happening in other projects also. This Japanese project is already through the development, and they are calling you only in the deployment phase. Why? So that you do all the shoddy clerical work as just another resource, and then they shove you somewhere else.'

'But can I bank on the Britcell project right now?' I asked. 'The bid hasn't even happened as yet.'

He tilted his head to one side and looked at me disapprovingly. 'Don't you trust me?'

Now, now, you wouldn't want to know the truth, Sir! 'I do,' I said.

'Hold on to that trust,' he patted me. 'We will get it.'

'And will I get to go onsite? Or at least will I get some kind of promotion, or a more important role?'

'Let us get the project first,' he smiled. 'We will do the onsite-offshore allocation after that. A lot of factors like resource rotation, the client budget etc. will go into deciding that part. But I can assure you that you being one of the senior resources in the team, you will be one of the frontrunners. As for your role, I'll ensure I give you something that is in conjunction with the metrics of your professional aspirations.'

'Alright,' I submitted. 'I'll go with your judgement.'

'That's my boy!' He clapped and rubbed his hands in excitement and dialed the project manager through his speakerphone.

'Hi Sujit, this is Chirayu. . . .'

'Hi Chirayu. Give me some good news, please. Has Nakul agreed?'

'Unfortunately, no,' Chirayu said, quite satisfied with himself. 'I just spoke to him and he is keen to stay on in the telecom vertical. I'm afraid you'll have to make do.'

'I'd like to speak to him too,' Sujit fought back. 'This resource is of urgent need to us, please. It is needed with immediate effect.'

It! I am referred to as an 'it'! This is a perfect case in point of self-dignity gone to the dogs.

'It is needed here as well,' Chirayu cut in.

'It's only acting as a buffer for you, Chirayu.' Sujit raised his voice now. 'Be reasonable.'

OK that does it! Will one of you please stop using 'it'? This is thoroughly demeaning.

Two dorks were objectifying me and playing 'passing the parcel'. And funnily, this was not at all funny. I finally heard the climax of the conversation as Chirayu barked a mouthful on the phone and slammed the phone down.

'Done,' he said, breathing finally. 'You will stay with us. We have Anand's backing on this decision.'

'OK,' I spoke in a deadpan tone, not sure if I had played a smart gamble or snapped up a bait. 'I'll be off, then.'

I went back to my desk, confused like never before. At this moment, I was no longer bothered if I should have chosen Tokyo's sushi or Mumbai's *vada pav*. All that bothered me right now was the 'it'. I'm not sure how long I brooded, but the day had almost ended when I came back to my senses.

'Oh, drat!' I looked at my watch in dismay: 5 p.m. 'I'm late.'

'For what?' Vishal asked in surprise. 'It's only 5!'

'I've to meet someone,' I said without looking at him, and sped off.

∾

One look at the posh JW Marriott, Juhu, and one knows why it is off limits for people like me. My rickshaw tuk-tuked and came to a stop right in front of the gate. A Mercedes honked from behind with a blaring sound, shouting for way.

The guard came and rapped on the rickshaw. '*Aage karo, saab log ko jaane do!*' *Move aside, let the big shots through.*

My vehicle may have been a misfit, but I showed the panache I needed at the entrance to the grand hotel. I walked up the ramp that led to the coffee shop.

'A very good evening, sir!' The sentry bowed in affable greeting.

'Good evening,' I nodded back.

'Have you got your valet parking token, sir?' he asked.

'I don't need one, thanks!' I winked.

I walked straight to the coffee shop where I was supposed to meet Anita. She had not come in yet, so I decided to be entertained by the pianist playing some soulful Kenny G numbers. Nothing was as soothing as a melodious rendition on an evening after work.

'Good evening, sir, what would you like?' A stewardess came to me and disrupted the reverie.

'Ah, I'm waiting for a friend,' I said.

'Sure, would you like something in the meantime?' she asked, thrusting the menu card down my throat.

'Yeah, I could do with some iced tea,' I said slowly, hurriedly looking for the price tag on the menu. Oops, Rs 295. Well yeah, that's a lot less expensive than three hundred. 'Or on second thoughts, I'll wait for my friend.' I smiled back at her and returned the menu card.

Anita came in about fifteen minutes late. 'I'm so sorry, have you been waiting long?'

'No, that's fine.' I got up to shake hands with her.

One look at Anita Tiwari and you'd know why she preferred the Marriott to a CCD, even for a simple coffee. You'd know why it was impossible not to admire Anita for the elegance she generated so effortlessly. And you'd know why Vishal suffered from the much talked about inferiority complex because of her. She looked full of beans even after what must have been at least ten straight hours of work. Hair tied back firmly in a ponytail and a laptop slung over confident shoulders. She was dressed all in black, with her shirt neatly tucked into her trousers. The metal of her Swatch glinted every few seconds.

I hate to meow, but Anita and Vishal Tiwari weren't the coolest combo you could think of. Anita was hot – a perfect figure, and a pleasant and youthful face even after motherhood, and mannerisms that were uber-sophisticated. Vishal, on the other hand, looked like a forlorn Hercules who was forced to carry the weight of all the brutalities of the world on his shoulders. Anita and Vishal together would give you the feeling of a spicy chicken sizzler being served along with a tumbler of fizzled-out cola that had been kept in the open for too long. But love found its way through all odds, I guess. And theirs had, too. So far.

'Pleased to meet you,' I said. 'I've heard much about you from Vishal.'

'Well, I hope they are nice things!' she laughed.

'Of course!' I laughed back. I hoped I looked honest enough while saying that. 'So what brings us here?' I asked without much ado.

My question was interrupted by the now restless stewardess. 'What would you like now, sir?'

I passed the menu to Anita. 'Do you like Cheese Twisters?' she asked me.

'Sure.'

'We'll have a serving of Cheese Twisters and two café lattes,' she said to the stewardess. Then she turned to me. 'Actually, I wanted to talk to you about Vishal,' she began hesitantly when the stewardess walked away. 'He's been going through a lot lately at work.'

'Yeah, he has mentioned it to me.'

'I don't remember the last time he came home a happy person,' she lamented. 'It really upsets me.'

'I can understand.' I nodded back in agreement. His unhappiness could upset anyone in the world. And then, she was his wife. She must have to handle it everyday.

'Tell me, Nakul,' she continued. 'What do you think could be the problem? Are there issues with his performance?'

'I don't think so, Anita,' I said. 'In fact, Vishal is understood to be a highly capable resource. Our boss, Chaudhary, also holds him in good regard.'

'Then what's the matter? He projects his job as something that demeans what his qualifications stand for.'

'I think it's just a phase,' I said. 'You see, with a company the size of Bytesphere, it's only natural that one's calibre will often go unnoticed.'

'It's not just that,' she said. 'The bitter fact in this whole game is that one needs to be political at times to get one's way through. But Vishal is just not the kind who will take this advice. Call it his ethics, his ego, his self-respect or whatever.'

'Cutting through so many layers of hierarchy is not so easy in my opinion,' I said, leaning back for the stewardess to lay the order on the table. 'There are a lot of people above Vishal right now waiting for a ray of light.'

'Why is it not easy?' she demanded. 'When so many people have done that to him in the past, why is it not easy for him?'

'Done what?'

'He has been working for five long years now, Nakul!' she said. 'And he has lost himself somewhere in this miasma. People have literally trampled over him to move above him. And he has just stood watching the show. There was a time when he was so full of life . . . now all he brings home is his misery. And I fear this is going to affect our family . . . I'm losing control. . . .' She broke down.

I struggled to understand what I was doing here. Why was she telling *me* all this? I began sipping on my latte to avoid eye contact.

'You might wonder why I am discussing this with you,' she said.

I nodded affirmatively.

'Vishal told me you guys are now expecting some major breakthrough in a telecom project in the UK?'

'That's right,' I said. 'But there's no surety. The slowdown has impacted all clients, and consequently our business too. Even if this project does happen, it's a long way from now. We haven't even got the quote request from the client yet.'

'I know,' she said. 'But in the event of it happening, I am sure there will be a possibility of some ramp-up?'

'I can't say,' I said. 'That's for Chaudhary to decide, really. But yes, given that Vishal and I are among the senior members of the telecom vertical, Vishal does stand a good chance to get a promotion or at least travel onsite. But then again, the scene in our company is just too dynamic – people keep shuffling across verticals. And if these new guys are senior to us, we are again stuck.'

'Nakul, this is where you can help me,' she said, placing her hand on mine.

I was taken aback by the urgent desperation. 'I can?' I asked, bewildered.

'See, if this project comes through, you and Vishal can surely talk to this Chaudhary guy and play an important role in the resource allocation. From what Vishal tells me, I understand that you can pull some strings with Chaudhary.'

'Really?' I asked in surprise. 'Is that what Vishal told you?'

'Yes,' she nodded. 'I know Chaudhary trusts you in a lot of decisions. What's more, I know that Vishal will not pull these strings even if he wants. And I really feel this is his chance to move ahead. Even an onsite opportunity could be a welcome change for him.'

'Well, I am not exactly what you would call street-smart either,' I said defensively. 'So if you are suggesting I put in a reference to Chaudhary for Vishal. . . .'

'Why just Vishal?' she cut in. 'I'm talking about both of you. Don't you think it is only fair that you ask for your dues from the management?'

'Yes, that's true. But why are you telling me all this?' I finally asked her.

'Because if I tell Vishal, he thinks I am being preachy, and I'm trying to put him down or something. You can't imagine how thoughtful I've to be while talking to him. . . .' Her voice began to quiver again.

'Alright, alright,' I said, trying to pacify her. 'I'll do the best in my capacity. But the rest is up to our fate.'

She nodded and smiled. 'Thanks! It's difficult to put into words, but even talking about it to you has made a world of difference.

And though it goes without saying, please don't mention about our meeting to Vishal.'

'Sure,' I smiled back. 'Don't worry, my mouth's zipped.'

She slid a five-hundred-rupee note into the cheque booklet for a bill of four hundred. We got up and left without waiting for the change.

I stopped on my way back at Bandra's sea-facing Bandstand. I opened my laptop and logged on to my blog to read the scores of responses to my posts on my fears at work. I got empathy from people who echoed my concerns, I got reprimanded by people who were happy with their jobs and thought I was making a big deal out of my problems, and I got suggestions from some Good Samaritans who felt it was time I looked for a new job – something that gave me that 'ever-evasive happiness'. *But what finally will define that happiness?* Yet another patron questioned me.

I looked behind me at the high-rise apartments facing the Arabian Sea. I had seen them first when I had come to Mumbai more than three years ago to pursue my MBA. I had associated my happiness with the flat on the top floor of the apartment. *It's out of bounds, boy,* Aryan had warned. *We'll reach for it,* I had replied positively.

Why had my positivity come to decline over time? Was I beginning to reconcile to what my life offered me? Strangely, the apartment now looked a little taller than what it had looked three years back. I wondered if they had built another floor or two on top, or if I had simply shrunk. The tower loomed over me in the dim moonlight. *I can still dream of getting you, can't I?* I looked up at it questioningly, and the sea waves came crashing to the rocks in cackling laughter.

Jogging *Kachori*

Lekha: Good morning, fellas!
Nakul: Good morning. What's up?
Lekha: Nothing ya . . . a black cat crossed my path this morning.
Nakul: Oh really? Do you believe in superstitions?
Lekha: Vishal . . . ? Buzzzzzzz . . . you there?
Lekha: Superstitions? Naah . . . what's the worst that could happen anyway?
Nakul: Maybe you'll spend the entire day with Kohinoor Pratap Kesari!
Nakul: Maybe he asks you for a date! Match that!
Lekha: Eeks! What's *your* problem with him by the way?
Nakul: Try staying with him for a few days and you'll know. That guy's got some strange antics up his sleeve all the time. . . .
Lekha: Why, what happened?
Nakul: He is crazy, man. . . . He borrowed Paulo Coelho's *The Alchemist* from me yesterday. When I returned from my walk last evening, I saw him jotting down notes alongside reading the book!
Lekha: Ha ha! You got to be kidding.
Nakul: *Arre,* he is a psycho, seriously. When I peeped in, I saw him scribbling some crap on a page which he had titled: My moral value lessons from *The Alchemist*!

Lekha: Whoa! That's some psycho! :D By the way, Vishal, why are you not responding?
Nakul: Knock, knock!
Lekha: Who's there?
Nakul: Vishal.
Lekha: Vishal who?
Nakul: Vi-shal-respond to friends who ping! ☺
Lekha: LOL! Vi-shal-not sulk!
Nakul: Vi-shal-laugh at Kohinoor jokes!

Vishal finally turned to us with an irritated look. 'What's your problem, guys?'

'We said good morning,' Lekha scoffed. 'You can at least respond.'

'What is so good about this morning, if I may ask?' he asked, frowning intensely.

I looked at Lekha. None of us had an answer. I shrugged and sank into my chair.

'And what's this novel way of wasting time?' Vishal continued. 'We are all in this two-by-two goddamn cramped cubicle, so why the messenger chat?'

'Just like that, yaar,' Lekha said, yawning with her mouth open like a python's. 'In any case, it's not like we disturbed you or something. You have been playing solitaire since morning.'

'Yeah, and I think I suck even at this game,' he said, closing the application. 'I just can't seem to play this anymore.'

'OK, then listen to the latest scoop from Kohinoor's Korner,' I chuckled. 'Do you know, this dude kept a single pair of his yellowed vest and half-torn undies on full spin in the washing machine for six straight hours yesterday?'

'Shh,' Vishal cautioned. 'He sits in the adjoining cubicle, boss. How will he feel if he listens?'

'Don't bother,' I said. 'He has his headphones on; he is listening to some CD that contains a sermon on self-actualisation.'

'What?' Lekha burst out laughing.

'That's what,' I said. 'Yesterday he put these pieces of his bare essentials in the machine, and then left home to attend some self-actualisation programme conducted by some *swami*. I kept waiting for my turn to dump my heap of clothes for washing.'

'So what did you do then?' Lekha asked.

'I waited till ten,' I replied. 'When he still didn't return, I went out and broke two twigs of a tree, and then forked out his . . . er . . . garments out of the machine. Then I put my own in.'

'This guy's quite a specimen,' Lekha said, laughing louder. 'Thanks Nakul, you bring in so much entertainment during these dull days!'

'I second that,' Vishal said. 'The management has also blocked Orkut now.'

'What?' I asked aghast, like the world had crashed down on me.

There . . . that's where the clock's ticking gets reduced by a tenth of its rate. It had been about a month and a half since our team was 'on bench', the common euphemism for IT resources who had no work to do and were daily made to feel they were but a liability on the organisation. Our training on Xabre had ended long since, and we had installed the application on our machines too. We had 'got our hands dirty' on the application a zillion times, had our Canadian trainer almost pull off his hair in frustration with our stupid questions, and we had got our certificates stamped 'Xabre Qualified'. But the project was still in the dock, and we were rendered workless once again.

'Don't keep sitting waiting for projects to come your way,' Anand would often be heard instructing his resources via his snazzy video-conferencing technology. 'Work on organisational initiatives.

Add some value to your learning. That's the only way you move up the value chain.'

Well, as far as I was concerned, I was never ready to touch anything that would not pay me extra. I tried the initiatives jazz a couple of times in my initial days of enthusiasm, but then realised that after you do the ground work on the initiative, you are conveniently forgotten at the time of receiving accolades for it. I was happy to let my 'value chain' rust away then, but I would rather spend my time on scanning Orkut and all other social networking sites. If nothing else, they were at least good stress busters.

'Why the hell have they blocked Orkut?' I asked in disbelief.

'Some privacy issues, I guess,' he replied. 'So give a count at the end of the day on how many flies you swatted.'

'Damn it.'

I resorted to the next option – downloading the latest songs from the net. Again, for some reason, this was in violation of the company rules. The company didn't want employees to mix entertainment with work as it hampered productivity. But we were smarter than they thought, and had found a proxy through which we could access the music downloading URLs. Vishal resumed playing solitaire. The remaining team had gone into oblivion. They were still in their college mode, and welcomed the concept of bench. To them, it was akin to bunking a class. I waited to see how long they enjoyed their honeymoon period.

Kohinoor, in the meanwhile, looked completely unconcerned too. He went on listening to the swami's sermon over and over again with closed eyes, and every few minutes, he would take in a deep breath of self-satisfaction. Lekha took to the phone, very obviously to her friends who seemed a tad busier than her. This is what her one-sided conversation sounded like:

'Hi, babes . . . talk to me, I am bored.'

. . . . . .

You are always busy . . . you don't have time for me.'

. . . . . .

'I know, you don't love me . . . boo hoo . . .'

. . . . . .

'OK, at least listen to this one joke. . . .'

Slam! And the tortured recipient would hang up on her. An unfazed Lekha would then dial another friend.

I must have been on my tenth download, when Cheapo tapped me from behind. 'DJ-ing, are we?'

'I. . . .'

'That's OK,' he smiled. 'I can't blame you. I've been trading online since morning too. We're in the slumps as far as work is concerned. But I've news for you.'

'What? We got the project?' I asked excitedly.

'Not exactly,' he replied. 'But we are in the shortlist. The client has sent another request for proposal, asking for our cost estimates on testing their application. So we need to send them a report on our resource and billing requirements.'

He called the three of us to his cabin and showed us an intricate chart that was supposed to detail out the client's business requirements from the project.

'You need to read through each of these processes,' he explained, 'and compare them with Xabre's vanilla processes to check for the delta effort that will be needed in testing them. I want all three of you to come up with an effort estimate by tomorrow evening.'

'How do we differentiate vanilla processes from the customised ones?' I asked.

'Read between the lines,' he said in one line. *I obviously don't know*, he meant. 'Any other questions?'

We shook our heads dutifully and marched off.

'I can't start any new assignment without a fag,' Vishal nudged me. 'Let's go.'

My phone rang as soon as we reached the ghosla.

'Where would you prefer shopping for me from?' I heard Kavya's chirpy voice from the other end. 'D&G or Guess?'

I gulped at the mention of the names. 'How about Linking Road?' I tried a smart one. 'It's a romantic place to hang out, too.'

'Who cares about romantic?' she giggled. 'I want quality brands *na*, Golu!'

'Those brands are for the classes,' I said. 'I belong to the masses.'

'OK now cut the slack,' she ordered, 'and walk over to Phoenix Mills. I'm waiting for you.'

'What? You've reached already?'

'Yes.'

'But Kavya, I can't come right now,' I said. 'I'm in office.'

'So why can't you just leave office and come now?' she demanded. 'You only told me yesterday that you have no work in office these days.'

It's moments like these that make you repent for being honest with your girlfriend (OK, girls who are very good friends!).

'Yes, but I have to finish eight hours of work,' I explained. 'Else a day's leave will be deducted.'

'How costly is that, Nakul,' she asked, 'as compared to having me wait here for hours?'

'More than two thousand bucks,' I laughed, trying to ease the tension that was forming. 'That's my loss of pay for a day's leave!'

'Very well,' she said coldly. 'You've made your decision. I'll see you when you have the time.'

She cut the phone. I tried redialling a number of times so I could apologise, but she cut my call each time.

'Tell me again,' Vishal asked, lighting his second cigarette. 'How did someone like Kavya fall for a boring IT guy like you?'

'What do you mean?' I asked in an offended tone.

'This is no match, to be plain honest.'

'I can't decide my profession based on Kavya's interests, can I?'

'Alright, leave Kavya aside,' he said. 'Talk about yourself. I am just curious – you had specialised in marketing during your MBA, right?'

'Yes.'

'Then how did you manage to get into this rut?' He laughed aloud, louder than I had ever heard him laugh. It was like he was laughing at his own hapless reflection that he saw in me today.

I got defensive. 'Yeah, it's not like it was my first preference during placements. I simply took what I got, and I'm learning to adapt now.'

'Whom are you kidding, buddy?' he asked. 'Take it from me, a person who has slogged here for five years – it's going to get very boring in time to come. You're wasting your creativity as well as your precious MBA degree here.'

'So where do I go?' I asked. 'I'm a year old in this industry already, I'm sure I'm branded for life now.'

'If you wait and ponder for too long,' he added, 'you'll certainly get branded. You're still fresh from B-school. At worst, you will miss a year's growth.'

'Are you making an assumption here,' I asked amusedly, 'that I *want* to change my job?'

'Be the boss,' he said. 'I was just giving an opinion.'

'Why are you not contemplating a change?' I finally asked.

'I have limited options and location constraints too. Otherwise I would be somewhere else. Unfortunately, from what I hear, all software companies have the same story to cry on – low salaries, low motivation, and a snail-slow growth.'

'Time to make peace then, big man,' I said, patting him on the shoulder. 'Let's go complete that effort estimation.'

Just for the heck of it, as we prepared to go back in, I typed a message to Aryan: *How much money do you make at your banking job? What's the profile?*

The single source of inspiration in going back to my cubicle was always Kavya's gorgeous face I had set as wallpaper on my laptop. Not only did that cherubic smile offset the gloom friends like Vishal radiated around me, but it also gave me some motivation to aspire for something in life. A gleam in her eyes, hair falling sideways across her face – she was so beautiful she didn't need to cuddle with a teddy bear for the pose to add to the cuteness factor. In fact, I did not keep with us even the pictures that had both of us in them. Her beauty was too majestic to dilute, even with my own self-love. I hated admitting it, even to myself, but yes, I was falling in love with Kavya. Maybe I already was. And I wanted to go and give a piece of my mind to the guys who came up with this obnoxious rule of completing eight hours of 'work', because someone very important to me was waiting for me just three blocks across the road.

We got on to the effort estimation exercise, which, to everyone's surprise, was not much of a phantom. All it required was some logical analysis and some moderate number-crunching, which quite explained Cheapo's resistance to get himself involved in it. I downloaded some hundred more songs, and browsed news sites that talked of everything from Barrack Obama to the marriage vows exchanged between a bull and a cow in some corner of the country.

Strangely, the clock's ticking kept getting slower by the hour. In that last hour of vegetating for the day, a sea of thoughts flowed through my mind. I thought of the cramped one-room apartment I lived in. I thought of the work I had done in one year and the status quo after that. My heart sank when I thought of the meagre six percent hike I got at the end of it all. Vishal's suggestion that I was caught in the wrong job now hammered my mind hard. And all of a sudden, when I looked emptily at the wall in front of me and the two-by-two cubicle around me, I felt trapped. I felt alien, and I felt like calling for help. One afternoon of advice, and I suddenly felt I belonged somewhere else. The Bytesphere brand value, the swish office and the luxurious amenities it offered – all the lures that kept me going so long suddenly seemed to have lost lustre.

What's wrong with me? I tried to think of something else, and got up from my seat. But all I saw were Cheapo's face and a clock that ticked like tomorrow would never come. The depressing feeling was just getting stronger. My phone got a message beep. It was from Aryan: *I make around 70K a month – take home. Profile is . . . well . . . who cares!*

That's it, I'm out of here, I decided, and stormed out of the office.

∞

By Jove, soothing a livid Kavya Mehra was tougher than working on ten effort-estimation exercises put together. She ignored me as I pursued her among the floral skirts she casually perused, even as the store attendants sniggered at my perseverance.

'Look at me, Kavya. I am talking to you.'

No response.

'Look, you're making me look like a fool. Everyone's laughing.'

'And what about me?' she finally spoke. 'Mustn't I have looked like a fool waiting forever here for you?'

'OK, I'm sorry.' There was no point explaining the attendance concept anymore. Her temper was past that stage.

'You know, Nakul,' she went on. 'Sometimes I really feel you are just too insensitive.'

'I'm sorry.'

'I travelled all the way from Pune just for you. How would you have felt if you were made to wait?'

Frankly, I wouldn't have made a big deal out of it. But no, this was a dangerous answer to give. 'I understand,' I said. 'I'm sorry.'

After some dozen 'sorries' more, I said, 'Now stop sulking. Let's make the most of the rest of the evening. I'm going to make it up to you.'

'How?' she asked, a little cheerfully this time, suggestively looking at the prohibitively expensive outfits by her side.

'No, we are not shopping.' I led her away from the store. 'But you like candlelight, don't you?'

'Yeah. . . .'

'Come on then.'

I took her to Sheesha, potentially one of the most romantic restaurants in Mumbai. We sat on a *machaan* on the rooftop restaurant, soaking in the evening breeze. The candles were lit, and the weather was perfect.

'Leave some space after dinner,' she warned. 'I have a surprise for you!'

The food was served and consumed, but it was a secondary object of attention. All that mattered was a pair of soft hands ensconced in mine, a comforting situation that assured me it would ward off all my worries in life.

The midnight walk along Bandstand was a long one, but we didn't feel tired. We walked across the length of the road, till we reached the Bandra Fort at Land's End. At that hour of the night, the serenity was too beautiful to be real – this magical setting could surely not be Mumbai. It was a dream. The water flowed gently down the Mahim creek.

'What's the surprise?' I asked her.

She gingerly opened a bag wrapped neatly in paper foil, and showed me a bowl of *khasta kachoris*.

'I remember you telling me once you love them.'

'I adore them,' I said, picking one. 'Thanks!'

'I prepared them myself.'

'That makes me double-adore them!' I spoke between mouthfuls. 'I love you!'

'What?' she asked, shell-shocked.

'I mean, I love you for this!' I said, trying to cover up. I leant forward to pick up the second one.

'Easy, tiger!' She slapped my hand. 'They are fattening. So you get just one in a day. You need to keep check!'

'Why does the world bother about a few extra kilos?' I asked. 'And anyway, I go jogging everyday.'

'Yes, you jog in the mornings, and then eat kachoris for breakfast! What an effort! I'm going to call you Jogging Kachori from now on, Golu!'

'One nickname is enough,' I said, only half-angrily. I kind of didn't mind her calling me anything actually.

We sat through almost the whole night, keenly watching the line of lights around the horizon that lit some of the finest buildings of the city.

'I want to live in something like that,' she said, pointing to the same high-rise that was very much my object of pursuit too. 'Only that, my friend, is life!'

I always knew Kavya to be a person whose expectations from life were of extravagant measures, and that she could never settle for a second favourite. But when she said this today, it sent a never-felt-before surge of inspiration within me.

'Don't worry, we'll get it,' I said unwittingly, wrapping an arm around her.

It was only when she looked at me quizzically that I realised I had only assumed the 'we' factor in this dream. I blushed uncontrollably in spite of myself. As she laughed and came forward to affectionately stroke my hair, I instinctively pulled her towards me by the waist and kissed her. To my relief, she did not resist, but instead locked her hands around me. About a few hundred feet away, we could hear a pied piper playing the tune of *Baatein Kuch Ankahee Si* on his clarinet. After a minute, she looked up at me with moist eyes. Our lips collapsed into each other once again, and our worlds were as complete as they could be.

be-compassionate.com

'Not bad, mister!' Lekha whistled as I came into office the next morning with a gym bag flung over my shoulder. 'So finally Golu is inspired!'

'Shut up!' I said.

'Don't worry, darling.' She patted me. 'I'll get you looking like a hunk in no time. Today, 5 p.m. after work – come on, give me a high-five!'

I gladly obliged. Finally, some motivation to shed my stubborn flab! I had a gorgeous girlfriend; I needed to look a little presentable too. And in the last six years, I had made my body a huge storehouse of lipids for want of any kind of physical activity. All in the name of making a career.

'By the way, Anand stopped by at our cubicle,' she said.

'Why?'

'He is on his usual employee satisfaction survey,' she replied, yawning the early morning sluggishness away. 'I'm pretty sure he is not going to return a happy man, at least from our pod.'

'So what did you say?'

'Ah, the usual humdrum – it's been a great challenging experience . . . we're getting to mature with every new deliverable . . . blah this and blah that. . . .' She got up to get herself some coffee.

'Hey, that's not fair,' I retorted. 'You got to be the spokesperson for the entire team. And what you said is far from what I feel.'

'Yeah, right,' she said, rolling her eyes dramatically. 'And you think I must tell him what we actually feel? Sorry, I'm in no mood for a *bhaashan* early in the morning!'

'What did he say then?'

'The usual humdrum again,' she continued. 'Keep it up . . . keep innovating and improvising . . . our company rests on your abilities . . . blah this and blah that. . . .'

'Come on, yaar, Lekha. If we want some betterment, we ought to make some noise,' I cajoled her. The fact was I did not want to go to Anand alone and have a one-on-one chat. I preferred some support.

'Very well,' she said, flipping lazily through *Bombay Times* as she sipped her cuppa coffee. 'Go make some noise. Anyway he was asking for you.'

'He was?' I asked, hardly able to contain my joy. 'How come?'

'No, I mean he asked me who all were in my team, and I mentioned your name. And then he was like, "oh OK, that burly guy who wears green checks".'

'Very well,' I said crossly, 'thanks for explaining. I'll go and meet him. I hope he recognises me though – I am in blue today.'

I decided to be the lone crusader for our cause. The idleness was not funny anymore, and Anand owned the responsibility to do something about it. But oddly, my steps began to slow down as I approached the lion's den. There was an eerie silence, an aura around his suite that made us want to keep off limits. His assurance of an 'open-door' policy was quite a joke, really, because not too many employees savoured the prospect of entering through his open door too often. I peeped in quietly. He was buried in some research as always, twirling the overgrown strands of his unruly beard with his fingers. It was queer how he commanded so much respect and awe even from the international clients he visited despite his shabby appearance. I mean, all of us had a dress code and decorum to follow in order to look civilised, and here was a telecom vertical supremo who looked like he had not bathed for the last decade. Maybe the grey matter beneath his tropical Savanna hairdo was what allowed him to forgo the dapper-look details. His Einstein look was appealing enough.

I knocked hesitantly at his door. He strained his eyes, lowering his reading glasses. 'Come in,' he ordered.

'Good morning, sir,' I began, 'I hope I didn't disturb you.'

'Go ahead,' he nodded.

'I wanted to discuss with you my career path. . . .'

'Aha,' he exclaimed. 'I'm happy. Most people who come to me complain about frivolous things like insufficient salary and cancelled leaves.'

Great, so now I have two less things I can talk about.

I smiled. 'My case is more around the kind of work I'm doing.'

'And what's that?' he asked.

'That's the problem,' I said. 'I'm not doing anything these days. I've been on bench for the last two months.'

'Tch tch, that's pathetic.'

'Yes,' I concurred. 'We've been told to wait for Britcell to happen, but it's been long since we've got any work whatsoever.'

'Who's your project manager?' he asked.

'Cheapo . . .' I blurted like a fool.

'What?' he asked again, raising his voice a bit.

'Chirayu . . . Chirayu Chaudhary,' I said this time coolly, pretending he had heard me wrong previously.

He paused to say something, but then thankfully let go. 'Very well,' he said, shifting topic. 'I have something to engage you on.'

My face lit up. 'What's that, sir?'

'There's a three-week training on Java starting next Monday,' he said. 'I'll have you enrolled on that.'

'Java training?' I asked, disappointment clearly ringing in my voice.

'Yes,' he affirmed. 'It should be good for you.'

'But I just got off the Xabre training recently,' I attempted weakly. 'And frankly, I've spent most of my time only on trainings in the last one year. I was hoping to get on some project now.'

'So what?' Anand didn't mind 'healthy arguments', but he always ensured he won them nonetheless. 'Isn't continuous learning something you believe in, sonny?'

The 'sonny' term didn't sprout out of affection, just to clarify. It's just because my name was not important enough to be remembered. 'Sonny' was a sweet substitute, and Anand Pai had a thousand sonnies in the company.

'I do believe in that, sir. But implementing the learning somewhere is equally important!' I thought I had pulled a fast one. But Anand was smarter, and was bound to have the last laugh.

'Good, so learn Java, and I promise I'll put you somewhere you'll be able to implement it.'

'But Sir, I'm not even a coder. I'm on a business analyst profile.' I finally got to the core of the matter. Code programs unnerved me. Those nested conditions in ominous looking curly brackets, the millions of lines of script, were all like the evil characters in Aesop's Fables. I had heard stories about them, but had thus far been lucky enough not to encounter any of them. And now someone was expecting me to breathe codes.

'Business analyst!' he echoed, erupting into voluptuous laughter. 'Sonny, in one year of experience, you must hardly know what it means!' He paused and then added. 'You are an MBA, aren't you?'

I nodded sheepishly.

He shook his head in disgust. 'Same tantrums,' he muttered under his breath, but loud enough for me to hear. 'All you guys have the same problem. I don't know what B-schools teach you before sending you here, but somehow all of you from this cult always seem to want to get to the top without understanding the basics of a business. Now what could possibly be wrong with learning a bit of coding?'

'Just that I'm not a coder,' I said bluntly.

He heaved a sigh of frustration, and after a minute's thought, he threw in his final stroke. 'Tell me something, do you know how to drive a car?'

'Yes, sir.'

'Why? Are you a driver?'

I shook my head. I understood where this was going.

'Then?' he said triumphantly. 'You learnt so that you can drive in case your driver doesn't come to work someday, right?'

'Right,' I submitted.

'So similarly, you learn coding not because you are a coder, but so that you can handle a day's work even without the coding team.'

'Sure, sir.'

'Good, so I'll have you enrolled there,' he said, opening a spreadsheet. 'What's your name?'

'Nakul Kapoor, sir.'

'Are you a new employee?' he asked, curling his eyebrows into a deep frown.

I was too tired by now to even get angry for not being noticed. 'No sir, I've been around for more than a year.'

'Great then, I'll inform the training anchor that you're on.'

'OK, sir.'

I left the cabin wondering why I entered it in the first place. If anything, I had only landed myself in deeper muck.

'The only way you can escape,' Vishal advised, 'is if Britcell comes through in the next five days. Otherwise, enjoy!'

I reclined in my seat in dismay. 'Damn it.'

'Attend it, boss, how does it matter? You're not doing Archimedean research here anyway.'

I didn't reply. A new message in my inbox had caught my attention.

From: Shamit Mukherjee
Subject: Mom's dream

Bondhu,

Hope you are doing well. It was a great pleasure catching up with you after so long.

What I'm going to write to you now is something I've not discussed with anyone in the last three years. Maybe it's the camaraderie I've shared with you, or maybe because I know how close you were to mom. But please remember, what I'm writing is in no way an imposition. It's at best a fleeting thought I want to share with you.

Like I mentioned to you that day – mom had invested her life in social service, a field that many preach about, but few dare to toil in. She always said that the truest means of self-satisfaction is to give to society all you can in your best measure. Then, as a callous average teenager would, I dismissed her advice as an oft-heard sermon in our moral science textbooks. But now, with each passing day as I miss her, I ponder over the compassion with which she must have strived for the underprivileged till the very end.

When I look into the mirror, I feel guilty and ashamed for having turned into a complete waste in the last three years. Her words reverberate in my mind and beckon me to take up the ownership of her dream. Now I hope to make amends. I can't claim I have done much so far, but I've made a modest start. Attached is a link to a website (still in draft form) that I'm creating, and I plan to invite as many people as possible so that they can provide their inputs on what little things we, the educated masses, can do for the impoverished.

Trust me, I know nothing about your current profession. I don't even know if your profession permits you the bandwidth to think about such initiatives. But I was just wondering – is there a way

you can leverage your skills and learning in the IT industry and enable them to bring some value to my effort?
Do think about it and let me know – I'll be glad to get some rave ideas from you, mate! And even if you can't, it's perfectly fine. I'll still look forward to your wishes. Forever yours. . . .

Fondly,
Shomu da

I clicked the URL of his website that read www.be-compassionate.com. My contribution to social service was limited only to the ideas sprouted during tea-stall chitchats, or at best, elocution competitions. Now I was being asked to implement all of them for real. Frankly, if I were to weigh the expectations from my family and Kavya on one side, and unknown, epidemic-affected villagers on the other, the equation was lopsided – no contest at all. But on the other hand, I felt I had a chance of redemption from the guilt I harboured for not staying in touch with Shomu da in his time of distress. More so, it was my single chance of expressing my gratitude to Mukherjee aunty for all the love she gave me.

So, yes, I wanted to contribute, but not at the cost of my own personal aspirations – which, sadly, were far from fulfilment yet. I was convinced that I had to first ensure my own financial stability before I took up charity. After all, even Andrew Carnegie retired at 35, and he became a superstar in the eyes of society. I'd have my day of fame, too. So I typed a hurried mail to Shomu da, giving a wordy promise, and then shoved his mail back in the dock.

'What are you doing on Friday evening?' Vishal asked me after lunch.

'Nothing different from what I do every Friday evening,' I said. 'I'll sit at home or maybe catch a movie. Why?'

'Anita has asked me to invite you over for dinner.'

'Oh, that's sweet of her.'

'I don't know about sweet,' he warned. 'She's just bought a cookbook and is trying out some fancy dishes. You are going to be the guinea pig, for I've been made that once too often.'

'I don't mind being one,' I said. 'Thanks, I'll be there on Friday.'

∽

Your body fat is like an irritating Sunday lunch guest. You decide to invite it home, but it decides when to leave you. And if you are not smart enough to act in time, there are good chances it will never leave you. The track pants I was trying to put on in the gymnasium's changing room were a pair of comfortable, baggy sports tracks two years ago, which I had bought more with the intent of using to sleep at night. Today, they were tight as leotards, and I looked like a plump, middle-aged gymnast who was trying to find his way back to the acrobats club. I stood like a fool in the room, waiting for the crowd to clear out before I exposed my chubby trunk in order to change my shirt. But the room was continuously being refilled with dudes who would stop by at the mirror and examine their n-pack abs and bulging biceps in self-satisfaction. I was not keen in making the paradox too obvious by going Full Monty. I finally slid into the bathroom and changed into a t-shirt that I had bought eons ago. I had thought the purchase would be my inspiration to work out, but that had never happened.

'Remember one thing,' Lekha instructed as she took position on the exercise floor. 'Getting into shape is no big deal. It's made harder only if we think more than we do. Simple workouts everyday and a bit of diet control – that's all that's needed.'

'Sure,' I said, stretching my legs apart to get into some action. 'I can't wait to get started.'

'Wait,' she stopped me. 'I'll first prepare a workout plan for you. But before that, we need to check your weight.'

She began to drag me to the weighing scale, which already was in a slightly dilapidated condition. And if my weight were to be thrown on it, we would see the last of it.

'Hold on, easy, easy,' I said, pulling her back. 'We don't need all this, Lekha. It's wasting our time. Let's get started.'

'It just takes a second, idiot! Come on.'

Either Lekha was very stupid or sheer sadistic to want to put me through this embarrassment. For, the reason for my resistance was more than conspicuous – two girls stood right next to the weighing scale, practising some vigorous callisthenics. If they would get a peek at this little very personal detail of mine, it would be the headline in the company's newsletter the next morning. I stood reluctantly on the scale, blocking their view with my bulky frame. I got down in a flash of a second.

'Oh, my God!' Lekha exclaimed, loud enough for the whole gym to be drawn to the subject of amazement, thus relieving me of any effort to keep my personal detail personal. 'You are L-A-R-G-E!'

'Thanks for making this public, Lekha!' I growled. 'That's so sensitive of you.'

'Sorry *baba*, but I'll make it up to you. Come on now, let's start.'

She led me to the aerobics room and instructed me to follow her steps. 'Stretch your legs apart, as far apart as possible.'

'More!' she demanded after I followed suit. 'More, you moron!'

'Are you kidding me?' I said. 'My legs are not detachable. This is all I can do.'

She reconciled finally and made me swing some strange jigs with my waist in that position. In five minutes, I could feel the tear in my muscles (if I could be permitted to call them so). But it was too embarrassing to complain so early into the regime. So I obliged by following her then to the weights section.

'I usually prefer this seven-kg one for the bicep curls,' she began, hurling the dumbbell up and down as if it were a ping-pong ball. 'So let's see, what would you like?'

'This should be good,' I said promptly, trying to pick the ten-kg monster, more in an attempt to salvage my male ego. I tried a few curls with it, but then suddenly I felt a ligament snap. It was so loud, I swear everyone around must have heard it.

'Ouch!' I screamed.

'Delicate darling!' she mocked. 'Pick this one.' She handed me the five-kg one, and then ordered another hundred curls with it.

By twenty, I was famished and had begun panting like a poodle.

'Do you want to hold a pencil instead?' she teased.

I pictured Kavya watching me, collecting all the machismo I could to finish the rest of the workout.

'That's it,' I murmured at the end of one hour, and lay down prostrate on the ground.

'OK, let's call it a day for now,' she said, much to my relief. 'Tomorrow we'll practise kickboxing.'

'What's that?' I asked faintly.

She pointed to the room behind me. I turned around weakly and saw a bunch of fitness enthusiasts jumping around like maniacs, punching and throwing their legs around at nothing, grunting loudly.

'I feel faint,' I said. 'I need some glucose.'

My kind instructor then dropped me off back home on her Pulsar. But by then my limbs were dead. I even needed support to get off the bike. When I crawled up two flights of stairs and entered the house, I saw Kohinoor looking out of the window gravely. I was a seasoned campaigner by now; I could tell he was about to cry. I was too tired to strike conversation, and quietly came and lay down on my bed.

'Hello, dear brother!' Kohinoor began. 'I am having a small question.'

'Shoot,' I said, without opening my eyes.

'What is the full form of the short form SOB?'

'Son of a bitch,' I said without applying much thought. 'Why, whom did you hear use that short form?'

'Nothing brother,' he now said between whimpers. 'I am not feeling like performing discussion over this.'

I didn't respond. I was too tired to probe. I just flopped over to one side and went off to sleep. The whimpers lasted till I was completely asleep.

Symbiosis

'Team, big news!' Cheapo's voice echoed in the meeting room. We looked at him, then at each other. 'We've got Britcell!'

We heard a few hurrays and yahoos in the team. After the clamour died down, I jumped to the point. 'So what's the resource allocation going to be?'

'There are some extrinsic factors that will be instrumental in deciding that,' Cheapo declared. This meant he did not know. 'Leave that for now, today it's time to celebrate. I've booked a bay for all of us at Enigma tonight. So we'll see you all there at nine.'

'I want to go onsite,' I jumped excitedly as we walked back to our pod and discussed our prospects in hushed whispers.

'You might just be better off here,' Vishal said. 'If you stay offshore, the positive is that you'll at least get to work independently, without Cheapo nosing around. For he is going onsite, and that's certain.'

'How do you know?'

'It's obvious.'

My phone rang. 'Hello?'

'I want you in my cabin, right away.' I heard Cheapo speak agitatedly from the other end.

'Talk of the devil . . . ' I said. 'I'll be right back.'

I entered Cheapo's cabin to find Kohinoor standing there already. He was on his sobbing spree again. This guy was too good at it. Maybe the TV soap guys should consider casting him in their next soppy flick.

'What's the matter?' I asked, bewildered.

'You tell me,' Cheapo scowled. 'What do you read here?' He pushed his laptop in front of me to make me read one of his 'sent items'.

Kohinoor,

Mail me your bio-data which I can forward to the client team in the event of us winning the Britcell deal. I would like you to send me the same by tomorrow, SOB.

Chirayu

I was flabbergasted. So this was the SOB Kohinoor was asking me about. Hold on, this idiot actually went and asked Cheapo if he called him a son of a bitch? I looked at Kohinoor questioningly.

'What does SOB mean, Nakul?' Cheapo asked me.

'Start of Business,' I said in embarrassment.

'And what did you tell him?' he demanded.

'He didn't give me the context,' I argued meekly. 'And what I explained to him is the common expansion of the term SOB.'

'How could you, Nakul?' Chirayu asked, exasperated. 'How could you not know what SOB means?' He spoke as if his defined parlance had been accepted by the Queen of England herself.

'Your terminology confuses me at times,' I finally said. I saw him fuming, and then quickly added, 'But I'm sorry anyway.'

'That's better,' he said, and turned to Kohinoor. 'I hope it's clear now?'

Kohinoor nodded happily. I felt like kicking him.

'Please don't defame me like that again,' Cheapo warned. 'I have a reputation to protect.'

I nodded. There was nothing out there for him to protect, if you asked me. But I let my opinion be.

'And oh yeah, your appraisal review is due, ain't it?' he asked casually, like an afterthought. My appraisal review was three weeks overdue, but he had plenty to use as cover in the name of P 1 tasks. Today, Rip Van Winkle had finally woken up and decided to oblige.

'Yes, it is.'

'Stay back, then. Let's do it now.' He then turned to Kohinoor. 'You can leave.'

'So, Nakul,' Cheapo chirped after Kohinoor left. 'How's life treating you this financial quarter?'

'Nothing's changed, Chirayu,' I smiled my widest, fake smile. 'I'm still broke!'

He shook his head. 'You always talk money, my friend. That's because you don't view your career through Maslow's eyes!'

'What?'

'Have you heard of Maslow's hierarchy of needs?' he asked with an air of stupendous confidence.

'Yes.'

'Good! So do you realise that money is but at the bottom rung of that hierarchy?'

'Yes.'

'Well, what I'm working on for you is something higher than that – satisfaction at work, a level of self-satisfaction which makes you proud of yourself when you go back home. Now isn't that what you want?'

'I'm just looking for some quality work.'

'I've something interesting lined up for you, provided you are willing to cooperate and be a little patient.'

I sat still and stared at him in anticipation.

'Do you know why you got a grade two instead of a one in your previous review?' he asked.

Cheapo was finally reading my mind. Or maybe, it was his guilty conscience finally poking his fat brain.

'Why?'

'Because in this whole race of personal goals, you did not keep in mind that superior performance happens only when you understand that you need to work in a symbiotic relationship.' He spoke in a single breath, intentionally leaving me with no time for comprehension.

'Huh?' I was left open-mouthed, gasping for words to respond.

'Do you know what symbiosis means?'

Yes, I bloody well knew what symbiosis meant. I had studied in school that symbiosis was the mutual dependence and receipt of beneficial reinforcement between two organisms. We were given the example of a fly and a buffalo to understand this concept. But excuse me, what was symbiosis doing here? What was he trying to get at? Was I the fly and he the buffalo? Or was it the other way round?

'Yes, I know what it means. . . .'

'So you see,' he continued with purported élan, 'you'll never grow unless you proactively take up work and responsibilities from your seniors.'

'I'm absolutely ready to take up such activities, Chirayu,' I said agitatedly. 'I've expressed as much to you before also.'

'I'm very happy you said that,' he smiled. 'Now I can see that hunger in you to grow!'

Right now, I was hungry enough to chop off his head and make minced meat out of it. This madman was eating into my lunch time and talking jabberwocky.

'Look, I'm planning to launch an initiative to prepare a model on implementation frameworks,' he said. 'Once we are into Britcell full swing, we will leverage our learning from there to prepare this model. This initiative will have tremendous visibility across all verticals of Bytesphere. It can take us places.'

'So how exactly does this help me grow?' I asked.

'I'll want you to work on it single-handedly. I'll limit myself to offering my domain inputs to you. But you will be the champion of this model – the lone crusader.'

Alright, so now I understand symbiosis. I am the fly, he is the buffalo. And he is going to land a pile of crap on me which has no certain future, but I'm supposed to receive beneficial reinforcement from that crap. This was a risk, for, given his propensity to be a total jerk, there was a large likelihood that he would be the crowned champion of whatever model he was talking about, and I would be his second-fiddle stooge. But I thought it might still be a risk worth taking.

'I'm ready to start right away,' I suggested. 'We don't need to wait for Britcell to start. I can take inputs from other implementation projects across verticals. This should help in preparing an initial framework.'

'Good,' he said, patting me on the shoulder. 'We'll discuss further on this soon.'

I smiled. 'Sure.'

'So do you have any other questions regarding the appraisal? Any woes and concerns?'

'Uh-huh, no.' I said.

'Good then, see you at the party tonight.' He waved. 'And please, wear something other than green checks!'

I was fed up of this nagging about my green checks. I liked this shirt, but for some reason it had been tagged to my name like Jughead's crown cap was tagged to his. I finally relented and decided to buy a new shirt for the evening party. Kavya also would get a breather from the green checks when she met me next. I went to Phoenix Mills, and consulted my designer girlfriend on phone on what colour and style I should buy in order to look less fat and more youthful. She finally voted for a fluorescent yellow, which personally I found very kitschy. But then, who would bother arguing with her?

'Would you like me to buy you anything, sweetie?' I asked finally.

'Yes,' she said. 'Buy me a Gucci gown, will you?'

'How about down-scaling your demands?' I said in jest. 'I can't buy you a Gucci gown. Right now what I can surely give you is my heart and soul.'

'Why can't you buy me Gucci?' she asked in disappointment.

'Because I'm stuck in a job that doesn't pay me so much.'

'Then take up a job that gives you so much money that you can buy me these gowns every month!'

'What do you mean?' I said angrily. 'This is not like selling bangles in a flea market. Getting jobs is tough.'

I suddenly felt a shadow behind me. I gawked in fright when I saw Tisya standing right behind me with half a dozen shopping bags thrown over her arms and her office i-card around her neck.

'Hey, I'll call you later,' I said hurriedly.

'OK, first say you love me.'

'I'll call you later,' I repeated.

'First say you love me, Nakul,' she raised her voice.

'Hello? . . . Hello?' I shouted.

'Don't act smart, you ass!' she shouted from the other end. I hung up.

'I thought you keep busy at work,' I mocked as I turned to Tisya. 'What's with the detour to the mall?'

'I'm handling the company's retail division,' she explained gleefully. 'I am here because of work. But I just saw some good collection here, so decided to pick up some.... I presume this was your "just a good friend" Kavya who was asking for a Gucci gown?' Tisya quizzed me.

'Why were you eavesdropping?' I demanded.

'I just happened to hear it,' she said. 'I'm sorry if I shouldn't have.'

'It's OK,' I said. 'But what's wrong anyway? Don't you buy fancy stuff for Rajeev?'

'Rajeev is my husband.' Tisya frowned. 'Is Kavya your wife?'

'No,' I said, biting my tongue and avoiding eye contact.

'So, are you seeing each other now?' she asked.

'Yeah, we just started.'

She raised her eyebrows even more. Elder sisters presume they have the licence to regulate their younger brothers' lives. And if this has to do with a girlfriend, the girlfriend has to pass the litmus test with the guy's elder sister. 'Have you thought well about it?'

'Yes, I have,' I said. 'I've known her for long now. Moreover, she's all set to make her career now.'

'And what's her career?' Tisya asked.

'She's going to assist a couple of Bollywood fashion designers on some big projects, I guess. Big money involved.'

'More money than what you make?'

'I'll be delighted if so!' I chuckled.

'You think so?' she asked, tilting her head sideways. 'Will you be happy if she gets home more than you do?'

'Why would I object to that?'

'Male ego,' she said matter-of-factly. 'You might know better. But have you ever wondered, there might be a day when she might want to just sit back and expect you to bring in all the money? There will be a hundred Gucci demands then every day.'

'I know,' I said. 'I'm not up to that mark yet, but I'm trying. I'm also open to exploring a new job that offers a better life.'

'Is that going to be a yardstick for her to marry you?'

'Not really,' I said. 'But it is a necessity nonetheless.'

'Says who?' Tisya retorted. 'Remember this forever, Nakul – love is a function purely of faith and passion, not a function of finances and stature.'

'What? I didn't get you.'

'You are wise enough to understand me, Nakul,' she said coolly. 'If you think this is meant to be, I'm very happy for you. But before you take the leap, just ponder over what the love between you both is a function of.'

She hugged me and began walking away. 'And, oh yeah.' She turned to me again. 'Come home someday for dinner when you have the time! We still stay in the same city.'

'Of course, I will,' I smiled. 'Give my regards to Rajeev.'

'Bring Miss Gucci along if you like!' she added while walking away.

'Run along now!' I said, waving her off.

∾

Cheapo Chaudhary's taste in clothes was as tacky as his own demeanour. He had forced upon himself an extra bright lavender shirt, which was surely not his own size. Or maybe it was a shirt he wore two decades earlier in college, and this was his first opportunity in twenty years to act young again. The trousers were of a shade like . . . oh, forget it.

'OK, dudes and dudettes,' Cheapo quacked over his fourth peg of whisky. 'Let's hop on to the dance floor, and rock this night! Yoo hoo!'

Thank God for the fact that he was high, so he did not notice us grinning at his antics.

'Come, come, everyone!' He led one of the new girls by the hand. 'No excuses today for anyone! Let's party!'

The younger kids joined him on the dance floor, even as Lekha, Vishal and I continued slouching on the sofa, waiting for Vishal to finish his drink.

'What a comedian!' Lekha remarked, pointing at Cheapo, who was now inflicted with some sort of trance-mania. He was jumping uncontrollably at one place and raising his fists in the air. 'He must have springs under his shoes to be able to jump like that!'

'Gravitational force acts well on his heavy weight,' Vishal said, tenderly dropping cigarette ash in his whisky. 'He comes down faster than he goes up!'

'I just wish he stops drinking before he is smashed,' I said worriedly. 'I need to talk to him about that implementation framework jazz.'

'Then you'd better go right away,' Vishal warned. 'One more drink, and he'll be out.'

'Yes, he doesn't understand much even when he is sober.' Lekha giggled. 'You just can't take chances with him tonight!'

I walked towards Cheapo. I wanted to talk to him, but not about the framework jazz. I meant to speak to him about what I had promised Anita – giving Vishal a meaty role in this new project. If not for Anita's sake, at least for my own; it could give Vishal some break from spreading his contagious depression around our working pod. And maybe, while advocating Vishal's case, I could get a chance to push something for myself too.

But Michael Jackson the Second was in no mood to listen that night. 'Hey, Nakul,' he shouted, grabbing me by my collar. 'Come on, don't be an oldie! Shake some booty!'

I thought it wise to entertain him for a while, though after Lekha's gym classes, I was not even in a position to walk straight. I swayed around for a while and decided to make small talk before coming to the point.

'You dance pretty well, Chirayu!' I said, crossing my fingers secretly.

'Ah, yeah? Thanks,' he beamed, and then turned to the DJ. 'Hey DJ dude, play some fun music, not this Hindi holler! Come on, play some Pink Floyd stuff!'

He then began thumping his feet dramatically on the floor, chanting 'Pink Floyd, Pink Floyd' over and over again. The DJ got psyched out and immediately switched to *Another Brick in the Wall*. This really got Chirayu going.

'So, Chirayu,' I said, firm at my attempt at making small talk. 'Where did you learn dancing?'

'I learnt it by myself,' he said, winking. 'I'm self-trained.'

That explained the idiotic steps. 'But why didn't you bring Madam along?' I asked, referring to his never-heard-of wife.

All of a sudden, Cheapo froze. He looked at me with vexation. I wondered what I had said wrong. I was just about to apologise, when he took another large swig of whisky from his glass, and started jumping like a retard again. Maybe it was a good idea to skip the small talk after all, and get down directly to business.

'Chirayu, I need to talk to you,' I shouted into his ear. 'Can we take some time out from the dance, please?'

'OK,' he said, albeit a little reluctantly. It was like disturbing a hermit in the midst of his meditation. 'But let's get ourselves another drink.'

'I'll get it for you,' I volunteered. 'You can sit there.' I pointed to a sofa slightly away from where Vishal and Lekha sat in animated discussion. I marched off to the bartender and ordered a coke for Chirayu, which would pass off as a cocktail. I really needed him to be in his limited stock of senses if I were to bring this discussion to some constructive purpose.

'Here's your cocktail,' I said, offering him the glass of fountain coke.

'Thanks,' he said. 'Now tell me, what is it?'

'I wanted to talk to you about Vishal,' I began slowly. 'I feel he has not been keeping very happy of late.'

'Why?'

'Work stagnation,' I said. 'We've been doing very mundane work for a long time now. I was wondering if he could be offered a meatier role in Britcell, something like a client interface.'

'That guy doesn't speak a word here,' Cheapo resisted. 'What could he possibly speak in front of a client? We need glib people there.'

'He maybe an introvert, but he is surely a genius,' I corrected him. 'I'm sure he can pull off that kind of a role.'

'But why are you pitching for him?' Cheapo eyed me suspiciously.

'Actually, I'm pitching for both of us,' I said sheepishly. 'Even for Lekha in fact.'

'Leave Lekha aside,' Cheapo dismissed. 'I know for a fact she does not want to travel onsite. She has mentioned her constraints. Talk about you two.'

'Alright,' I said. 'I just wanted to ask you if we have scope to travel to London.'

He looked at me with a dazed expression. The whisky was beginning to take effect. 'Yeah sure, let's go.'

'No, come on, Chirayu, seriously,' I prodded. 'Tell me.'

'Yes, Nakul, you're both on my radar,' he admitted candidly. 'While I don't know what's in the fray as of now, I can assure you something good will turn up. Now can we get another drink?'

He hobbled over to the bartender and picked another peg of whisky. He could crash now if he wanted though. I had told him what I had to.

'Oh, by the way, a hypothetical question for you,' he said. 'What if only one of you gets to go onsite? Whom would you like to be sent then?'

He had me stumped. For the first time in one year, Cheapo had asked a really smart question.

'I guess Vishal should go first,' I said hesitantly. 'He's been here longer than me.'

Cheapo roared into a laugh. 'Sweet gentlemen like you can't survive here!'

'Why, did I say something wrong?' I asked.

'No, you were right,' he said dreamily, trotting back to the dance floor. 'But sometimes, you can end up being wronged by the right too.'

90 A Romance with Chaos

I followed his wily smile till it faded into the fluorescent lights of the disc. The music in the room suddenly became unbearably jarring. I wanted to get out of there. I saw Vishal and Lekha beckoning me to come and sit, but I could not hear them anymore. I just felt like going home.

Eagles in the Air

'My, someone's looking hot!' Shirley said to Lekha, pointing at my sweat-drenched shirt sticking to me like glue as I walked into office on a humid morning.

'Stop it, you two,' I said crossly, and turned to Lekha. 'And what are you doing here, running the gossip mill again?'

'Oh yes,' Lekha said excitedly. 'There is indeed some gossip!'

'What?'

'It's coming right behind you,' Shirley spoke quickly and lowered her gaze.

I turned behind to see a completely bald man with skin as white as snow and a weirdly designed beard walk past quick as a whistle.

'Hello, gorgeous day, nay?' he cheered, waving merrily at Shirley.

Shirley waved back dutifully.

'What about him?' I asked a minute later.

'Don't tell me you didn't recognise that hunk!' Lekha exclaimed.

I stood blank for a moment and then my mouth opened wide involuntarily. 'That was not Chirayu Chaudhary!'

They giggled in unison.

'That just wasn't him!' I repeated. 'Was he?'

'Your boss has gotten into the skin of a Briton, quite literally!' Shirley laughed. 'I caught him on Sunday at the Hazel beauty salon in Juhu, getting his dense vegetation scraped off his chest and . . . whatever!'

'Don't tell me!' I screamed out loud.

'That's not all,' Shirley continued. 'He told me he was going in for a facial after that!'

'No wonder,' I said, 'his face looks like a snowed-under igloo. But what's with the sudden desire to look cool?'

'I don't know.' Lekha shrugged her shoulders. 'But he's been acting extra sweet since morning. He even came to me this morning and said he wants all of us to get on a one-on-one chat with him and give him feedback on his leadership abilities.'

'Fantastic.' I grinned wickedly. 'That keeps me engaged for the whole day. Can I write him an essay on this?'

'Why, he isn't that bad!' Shirley came to his rescue.

'Listen, please don't make me run into that explanation again,' I pleaded. 'Maybe it's just that all bosses are supposed to be hated. So it comes naturally to me. Anyway, you ask him to a) let me go home on time daily, b) be non-interfering in my deliverables, c) give me a good appraisal next time, and I promise you I'll equate him with some demi-god of sorts.'

'That reminds me,' Lekha said. 'He has asked for a meeting. We need to head upstairs.'

As I met Chirayu near his cabin, I suddenly took a step back in fright when I saw his dark blue lenses. As if he didn't already look like a demon. The Hazel Salon effect was really showing, I guess.

'Dark blue today,' he said, pointing one finger to his lenses and another to his blue shirt. 'I plan to put on a different pair everyday, something that goes with my shirt's colour. What say?'

'I say, I hope you don't have a pink shirt!' I burst out laughing.

'Funny,' he grumbled, obviously not amused. 'Now come to the meeting room. We have updates.'

'Hello, team!' he addressed all of us. 'There are some important ramp-ups happening in our team with effect from today.'

He paused, waiting for us to enquire. When no one did, he continued, 'I'm travelling to London tomorrow night.'

Lekha and I looked at each other and smiled. No wonder he was making trips to Hazel.

'It's a good move for all of us,' he said. 'For me, it is so because I will be moving to the client location and will get to do some meaningful work. For you, it is so because there will be an obvious escalation of responsibilities that each one of you will have to manage in my absence.'

So, he was subtly alluding to the claim that he was the sole harbinger of our team's performance thus far. Wow, now that's vanity for you.

'Have you been to London before, sir?' one of the kids in the team asked excitedly.

'No, this is the first time,' he remarked with arrogance. 'I've been to Seattle, Norway and Melbourne on previous assignments, but London it's the first.'

'That's gross,' I whispered, almost to myself. We've never gone outside Lower Parel on any assignment, and here he was, rubbing it in. I looked at him expectantly, hoping he would remember what I mentioned to him recently at the party. He met my gaze briefly and then conveniently ignored me.

'Vishal, I want you, Nakul and Lekha to drive the testing efforts of the team,' Cheapo went on. 'You will be the lead test engineer from offshore, unless some travel plans are made soon.'

'And what about us?' Lekha asked. 'What will our designations be?'

'You will be senior test analyst,' he said. 'And Nakul, you will be the test requirement lead analyst.'

'That's a fairly long designation,' I said, smiling. 'What's the difference between these three roles, though?'

'What's in a name, really?' he quipped. 'These titles are only to present to the client for our billing. Don't bother about them, you are all in equally important roles. Now I want us to quickly go through this presentation sent from the client office – it has the detailed testing timeline and delivery dates.'

My phone droned with an urgent throb on the table. 'Mom calling'. I disconnected.

'Let's skip directly to slide three,' he said, flashing his laser on a complicated graph showing simple details of some testing delivery dates. 'Starting 5 August, we will begin the requirement analysis. . . .'

The phone droned again. 'Mom calling', again. I disconnected again.

'I want the offshore team to begin analysing the design documents,' Cheapo resumed. 'And do a requirement gap analysis by comparing it with Xabre. . . .'

The phone drone interrupted him again. Mom's a fighter, she just won't give up.

'Just take it,' Cheapo ordered, extending his hand towards the door.

There could be only two urgent things when mom called: either she had met Payal, or she wanted to check if I was eating on time. I dismissed the second possibility because she had asked me that question only twelve hours ago.

'Nakul, guess what?' mom shouted joyfully. 'I met Payal today.'

I've got foresight after all. 'Is it?'

'She came home today to ask for curd,' mom explained. 'There was no curd at their place, that's why. She was so courteous and sweet, I can't tell you. My eyes welled up.'

'How does a bowl of curd stir up such emotions?' I asked.

Admirably, my mom even had an answer for that. 'Yes, just see. Fate plays such kind games sometimes. Of all places, she came to our house and asked for curd, and we ended up having a nice, long conversation!'

'Mom, she is our neighbour,' I sighed. 'It's only logical that she rings your doorbell to ask for curd.'

'There are other neighbours too,' mom argued. 'Why did she come only here? Maybe it was an excuse to meet us. I found it really sweet! And anyway, the good news is that she was blushing when I mentioned your name.'

'You must have embarrassed her by saying something,' I reasoned, 'like the thousand times you embarrass me.'

'Mind it, Nakul,' mom admonished. 'I've not called you to listen to your nonsense. There is something I had to tell you.'

'Is it urgent?' I asked. 'I'm in the middle of a. . . .'

'Yes, it is,' mom interrupted me. 'Payal asked for your email address! I gave her your office id.'

'OK, I'll check,' I promised.

'Listen,' Mom continued. 'What salutation will you give her in the mail when you reply?'

'What?' I asked, surprised to the core. Mom is a case study in micro-management.

'I suggest don't write something like "Dear Payal . . ." – it sounds unduly intimate. A 'Hello Payal' would be much more apt. But make sure the initial line you write is warm enough.'

'Mom!'

'Do ask her about her paintings, etc.' she went on nonchalantly. 'And do give your regards to her parents, that's basic courtesy. . . .'

'OK Mom, I really need to run now,' I said hurriedly. 'I'll do the needful.'

Cheapo greeted me with a sardonic laugh when I entered the MR. 'Oh hello, Nakul! Sorry, we just got done, you are a trifle bit late.' While leaving the room, he added scornfully, 'Get the updates from Lekha or Vishal.'

Sitting in our work pod was now something comparatively more worth looking forward to. The networking sites had taken a much needed sabbatical, and all sorts of project tasks were welcomed with hungry anticipation in order to shake off the rust that had formed on us over the past few months. If there was still some entertainment that we permitted within the pod, it was our favourite Messenger Service.

Nakul: Beware, London! The dumb coot is arriving. . . . ☺
Vishal: What? As in?
Nakul: Arre baba, I'm talking about this item called Cheapo Chaudhary going global. I wonder what he'll babble in front of the client. What say?
Vishal: I wouldn't bother discussing these frivolities as long as my work isn't affected. Anyway, who are we to comment on his productivity? He has reached a level where his capability can't be questioned.
Nakul: What's wrong with you?
Vishal: Nothing, in fact am surprised to find myself a little happier now. I feel I've got some work now.
Nakul: I'm happy to hear that, dude! I really am. Keep that cheerfulness on.
Vishal: Yup
Nakul: But still, how did that backless pachyderm get so high in his career? He's a bird brain, yaar!
Vishal: Chuck it, *na*. To each his own.
Nakul: True. Oh, by the way, I am seriously contemplating a job change now.
Vishal: Is it? When did you decide?
Nakul: I've not decided yet, I am still considering. I do feel now that things are getting very mundane out here.
Vishal: So have you applied anywhere?

Nakul: Not yet, but I'm planning to talk to a friend from college who works with InvestZone bank in Delhi. I heard there are some openings.
Vishal: Cool, all the best.
Nakul: Thanks
Vishal: By the way, remember the dinner tonight, don't you?
Nakul: Of course, I'll be there by eight.

I was much happier now with some work, except for the Fridays, when my concentration was torn apart between a heavy load of completing the week's work and planning my weekend with Kavya. Today was particularly a drag, because I had to additionally oblige Cheapo with a pending presentation on 'Best Practices in Telecom CRM' to be submitted for the monthly newsletter, while he excused himself with some 'social obligations' he needed to complete the night before he flew.

While my late hours were a rarity, Shirley D'Souza was always the one to turn the office lights off – and often, the one to turn them on in the morning too. She must not average less than fifteen hours a day in the office, and yet she found time for indulgences like the health spa, downtown pubs and what have you. I envied her; I needed days to consist of twenty-eight hours only for my basic chores.

'Gosh, you're late tonight,' Shirley said as I prepared to leave. 'So what plans, are you partying?'

'Not really,' I replied. 'Just going over to Vishal's for dinner.'

'How about coming over to my place some day?' She winked suggestively. 'I'm sure I'm more interesting company than Mr. Vishal Boredom Tiwari!'

'I'll come some day,' I said, embarrassed by her boldness. 'I have promised him tonight.'

'I'll wait,' she said, blowing a kiss in my direction.

Anita and Vishal have a small but beautiful flat in Lokhandwala. The interiors of the house, I was told, were done by Anita herself, when she was on maternity leave sometime back.

'You are a genuine all-rounder, Anita,' I enthused as I examined the furnishings, even as Vishal smirked at my comment.

Anita ignored him. 'Thanks! This was a while ago, I hardly get the time now. You guys sit, I'll just get the food ready in ten minutes.'

'What kept you late in office?' Vishal asked, jiggling his infant in his lap like a dutiful father.

'The usual offloading,' I replied, picking up the nachos laid on the coffee table as starters. 'Cheapo had a party to attend.'

I moved forward to pick up the baby in my arms, but he started wailing immediately, and I had to hand him back. He was clearly not a happy child. He was clearly Vishal's son. He did bear some of Anita's pretty features though.

'That rascal!' Vishal said. 'He really needs to be sized up, man. How long should we be his clerks?'

'What's wrong with you, Vishal?' I asked, genuinely amazed at the way his mood swung. 'Not more than eight hours ago, you were all praise for him!'

'I wasn't praising him,' he explained. 'It's just that I'm tired of criticising him all the time. Moreover, you mustn't meow much when there are eagles in the air!'

'I don't get you.'

'I mean, we should avoid bitching about people like him in the office,' he said. 'There are always people like Jassi around who would love to give him gossip over a cup of tea.'

'I know, but today was different,' I said. 'It was only the two of us chatting. I was a bit surprised when you began singing Cheapo's praise.'

'Chatting is worse,' Vishal said. 'You leave a written proof of your hatred for your boss: strict no-no.'

I stopped eating and kept the bowl of nachos aside. 'So you mean you don't trust me enough to keep a conversation between us?'

'Come on, Nakul!' he laughed. 'It's not about you, it's a basic principle I follow. You never know when someone decides to screw you with tools like these. If you have grievances, we always have the ghosla to purge them out, don't we?'

I kept quiet and looked down. He patted me on the knee and said, 'I do trust you, Nakul. So don't get me wrong, OK? It's just that not everyone around us is as trustworthy as you and me.'

'Whom are you talking about?' I asked. 'Lekha?'

'Just about everyone, Nakul,' he said gravely. 'Just about everyone.'

'Dinner's ready, guys,' Anita shouted from the kitchen.

'I smelt it!' I said hungrily, striding towards the table.

The sight of the sumptuous food immediately made me forget about the 'eagles in the air'.

'What cuisine is this?' I asked excitedly. 'None of this looks familiar!'

'It's Greek stuff – called Piroski,' Anita beamed. 'I just learnt it today from my cookbook.'

They both sat and watched me, waiting for me to fill my plate.

'What about you?' I asked.

'Do the honours.' Vishal grinned wider than he ever had. 'And give me the sign-off. If it's edible, I'll binge!'

His comment was greeted with a nasty stare by Anita, which I chose to ignore for my benefit. I filled a spoonful into my mouth and was relieved to find that it tasted as nice as it looked.

'Sign-off conceded!' I said, raising my thumb in the air to Anita.

She smiled back and nodded.

'So where have you progressed so far on your job hunt?' Vishal asked, munching merrily on his Piroski.

'The job market seems to be dull,' I said. 'Requirements are coming in trickles.'

'What kind of job are you looking at?' Anita asked.

'Marketing,' I replied. 'Media marketing, preferably. Do you have contacts?'

Vishal pondered for a minute and spoke. 'There might be some openings in your company, Anita?'

'Why not?' Anita said and turned to me. 'Will you be interested?'

'I can give it a shot,' I said. 'I'll need to know more about the profile, the money, the mobility factor. . . .'

'Relax, relax!' Anita smiled. 'Just send me your CV first, and we'll catch up some other time to discuss the rest. No talking about work while we eat!'

I smiled back in gratitude. 'Thanks!'

'We will also pass your CV to our other friends in various companies,' Vishal assured me. 'So now stop worrying, and enjoy your food.'

'Thanks,' I said again. 'I sometimes feel very lost. I'm still not sure if I want to shift, but it looks like I am beginning to get bored. I am at this crossroad of an important decision and I guess it's times like these when you hate being away from home.'

'You're not away from home, Nakul,' Anita said softly. 'We are here with you. You are very much at home.'

I nodded gratefully. Actions speak louder than words, yes. But sometimes words that precede the action are sufficient to let you know that you are not alone. When you wander the streets of a lonely city and the dark shadows on the sidewall frighten you, you look for such words to escort you until daylight appears. And when you do meet daylight, these words still remain imprinted in the recesses of your mind, becoming the benefactors you remain perpetually indebted to. That night, I had found my benefactors.

Two Strawberry Shakes, Cutting

Kohinoor's pranayama histrionics were a commonality now. In fact, they had become a necessity of sorts, especially on Sunday. If not for his self-volunteered alarm clock service, I had the ability to sleep through the entire holiday like a log.

'Good morning, brother,' he spoke between an extended inhalation, opening one eye to look at me. 'Would you like to join me in this exercise?'

'Good morning and no thanks,' I said groggily, picking up the newspaper from the doorstep. 'I've alternate ways to spend the day.'

The paper was filled with the usual stories of the chaos in the assembly, the break-ups in tinsel town and civilian woes in the city.

'Any important news, brother?' Kohinoor asked, not moving from his hermit stance.

'NGO stages peaceful *dharna* on city roads to protest against the abject living conditions of Mumbai's slum-dwellers,' I said, reading out loud.

'Tch tch, how sad!' Kohinoor mused.

'Why are you sad?'

'I'm sad for the poor people,' he said. 'Aren't you? Don't you think something should be done?'

'Yes, I'm sad too,' I said. 'But what do you want to do?'

'What can I do?' he defended himself. 'I can only suggest, rest is up to the NGO.'

'Then why feel sad?' I mocked. 'If you can't do anything, you mustn't sit and brood. You'd rather invest your time in something you *can* do.'

I fished out a CD and inserted it into my laptop, and plugged on the stereo system, readying myself for a home-screened matinee of *Borat*.

'What are you watching, brother?'

'*Borat*,' I replied laconically.

'What is it about?'

'Comedy,' I replied, even more laconically.

'What does *Borat* mean?' he went on like I was Google Search or something.

'Why don't you just watch it with me, Kohinoor?' I suggested angrily.

He happily came and began watching the movie, which, incidentally, was not the best fit for him. Within minutes, the movie had got inundated with lewd gestures and scandalising scenes that could unsettle someone even with the crassest sense of humour. And then, Kohinoor Pratap Kesari was but a mild goat. It sent him into fits of hysteria.

'How can you make me watch something like this, brother?' he asked in horror.

'Take it easy, man,' I said, gesturing with my palm to calm him down. 'I didn't force you to watch it; you have a choice.'

'Even you can't watch it!' he said firmly.

'What?' I almost couldn't believe my ears. 'Why can't I watch it?'

'Please brother,' he pleaded, 'I keep photos of the goddess in this room. This is a holy place, so please don't pollute it.'

'I understand,' I said submissively, looking behind at the photos pasted on his cupboard. 'But isn't God omnipresent?'

'Still,' he persisted. 'Don't watch in this room, it's not good.'

I saw the firm eyes of the Goddess glare me in the eye. I was left with no choice but to consent to his command.

'But now I've nothing to do the whole day!' I complained.

Suddenly, my phone rang loudly. I looked at the screen flashing 'Private Number Calling'.

'Or maybe I have,' I said as an afterthought while answering the phone. 'Hello?'

My guess was right. 'Hey Nakul, young fella!' Cheapo's voice echoed from the other end. 'How's the weekend been?'

'It's been kind so far,' I said. 'How about you?'

'It's been great,' he said. 'London is a nice place, Nakul. You should come here some day.'

'That's quite up to you!' I said matter-of-factly.

'Ha ha, good one!' He laughed and then ended that discussion abruptly. 'Listen, what are you doing right now?'

'Chilling.'

'Dude, I need both you and Vishal to run to office and do a quick task for me.'

'On a Sunday?' I asked with disappointment.

'Yes, I am in office too, ain't I?' He got stern. 'And we work in a team, remember?'

I grunted reluctantly. 'What work is it?'

'Last evening I got a call from our Programme Manager,' he explained. 'He said he needed the exact number of test cases we have planned in the Campaign Management functionality. He also wants the split of how many of these cases are vanilla Xabre functionalities and how many of them need external interface with other applications.'

'OK. . . . ' I waited.

'So, go and do this analysis, boss!' He was beginning to get panicky now. 'The psycho needs this on the table by tomorrow morning 8 a.m.'

'It's simple, Chirayu,' I said coolly. 'I can explain on the phone how to go about it. Do you have the test tool and Xabre open in front of you?'

'Yes, yes!' he replied frantically.

'Alright then,' I continued. 'Just follow my instructions. Open the excel sheet attached to the test tool. It has the list of test cases we have identified for Campaign Management.'

'Done.'

'Now open Xabre,' I instructed. 'Click the navigation icon.'

'What icon?' he asked.

'The navigation icon,' I repeated. 'Do you see a round, green-coloured button on the top left side of the screen?'

'Where? I can't see.'

'It's right there, Chirayu, it has to be there,' I said. 'It looks like a pear.'

'Pair of . . . ?' he asked dumbly.

'Not pair,' I said, now beginning to lose my patience. 'OK, leave it. Just open the "Campaign Forum" sub-view below the Home screen tab.'

He gave up. 'Listen, there are just too many tabs here. And anyway, this is not my domain of expertise, you see? You guys are trained on Xabre.'

I sighed. 'Alright Chirayu, we'll go and do it.'

I called Vishal. 'Cheapo wants us in office. He needs an analysis on the Campaign Management test cases. Can you make it?'

'I don't know, Nakul,' Vishal said. 'After ages, Anita and I finally decided to take the baby out. We're planning to go to Amby Valley. Why did that moron have to call us today?'

'It's urgent,' I said. 'And he doesn't have the capability to do it himself.'

'Ass!' Vishal grumbled. 'Just when I thought Anita and I could have some time out. . . .'

'Listen, don't bother,' I said reassuringly. 'You guys go ahead, you don't get this chance everyday. I'll handle it.'

'You think so?' Vishal asked. 'It doesn't seem right on my part, *yaar*.'

'Shut up!' I reprimanded. 'Don't indulge in these formalities. You can pay back some day.'

'I sure will,' he said. 'Thanks, pal.'

'No worries.'

And so here I was, all alone in the office on a Sunday noon, analysing a boring spreadsheet. Maybe it wasn't a bad option after all, given the alternative of spending the rest of the day listening to Kohinoor and his lectures on morality and spiritualism. Kavya had been calling me every second hour to ask my whereabouts, so I didn't really feel alone and bored.

'Are you still in office?' Kavya called for the fifth time that day, barely an hour after I had begun work.

'I've only just started,' I said. 'Why?'

'Come and get me from downstairs,' she ordered.

'What?' I asked in disbelief. 'You are in Mumbai?'

'Yes, sir!' she said. 'I'm in Mumbai and I'm right outside your office.'

'What are you doing in my office?' I asked worriedly. 'If someone finds out I have let in a stranger. . . .'

'I'm not a stranger, Nakul Kapoor! I am your girlfriend. And no one will find out anything. You are the only donkey who's likely to be working on a Sunday.'

'But office rules don't allow. . . .'

'Now are you getting me in or should I leave?'

'OK, wait.'

I went down to fetch her. I swiped the door and let her in, and suddenly the office rules, or the world, for that matter, didn't concern me anymore. She looked drop-dead gorgeous in a red tie-n-dye wraparound skirt and a black spaghetti-strap top.

'You're looking . . . good!'

'I love it when you praise me!' she beamed, grabbing me by the arm. 'Now show me your office.'

I took her up to the pod, which was nothing much to boast about in terms of acoustics.

'That's it?' she asked with a tone of dismay. 'You don't have a separate cabin to yourself?'

'What were you expecting?' I asked with a smile, returning to my seat to finish off the analysis.

'Nakul, you've been here so long,' she said. 'They should at least give you a cabin.'

'Shut up, Kavya,' I laughed. 'Now let me finish my work in this average, damp, squat cubicle, so that we can get the hell out of here.'

'Hold on,' she said. 'First tell me, why are you working on a holiday when there is not a single soul besides you who is just as dedicated?'

'These are ad hoc requirements, Kavya,' I said. 'It's difficult to explain. Not everyone is screwed everyday.'

She cupped my face in her hands and spoke. 'Nakul, you've been working your life out for the last one year – so much so that you have even kept me as a secondary subject of attention. Then, after all the hard work, all the sincerity, smartness and sacrifices, you are still at the same level in the hierarchy and you still have the same money and the same one-room apartment. How long will you let this go on? And to top it all, you don't even have a cabin!'

I couldn't understand her fetish for a cabin. 'Stop rubbing it in now! I think of this enough myself; I don't need you to poke me any further.'

Her eyes got moist. Her nose turned ruddy red and began to quiver.

'Alright, I'm sorry, I know you said it out of care,' I said, mellowing down a bit. 'But please, it just adds to my worries. As of now, this two-by-two enclosure and a low salary is all I have, so accept me the way I am if you can.'

'I accept you the way you are, my Golu,' she purred, pulling me closer with the i-card string around my neck and kissing me gently. 'Nice?'

'No!' I said awkwardly. 'Behave yourself, Kavya. This is my office!'

'But didn't you say I looked good today?' she raised an eyebrow.

'So? What does that mean?'

'That means . . . ' She winked, placing one foot on my shoulder and leaning back against my desk.

'Don't even think about it.' I pushed her foot back. 'Listen, please let me finish my work quickly. Then we can go out somewhere and you can do whatever you want. I am a little scared of acting funny here.'

'OK . . . ' she began and then swiftly turned her face to my laptop as something caught her attention. 'Show me, show me, what's that?'

I flushed in embarrassment as she caught sight of her picture I had set as my wallpaper.

'So sweet!' she exclaimed. 'That's so romantic.'

She started going into her intimate mode again and drew her face close to me. Now while I must admit this was very thrilling, the choice of venue was really bad. Per force, I had to push her back again.

'OK, but I'm not getting off your lap,' she declared. 'Hope that is fine with you.'

'You will have it your way anyway,' I said helplessly. 'So why ask?'

'You know me so well,' she said, curling my hair with her hands as I grappled with my incomplete analysis.

'That's a damn expensive watch you are wearing!' I exclaimed, looking at a new watch dazzling on her wrist. 'Where did you get it from?'

'Dad brought it from Switzerland last week,' she said. 'This is the third watch he has got me from there in the last five visits.'

'Why?'

'I lost the first two,' she giggled.

'You are spoilt silly,' I remarked.

'Indeed I am,' she quipped. 'But I guess that's how my parents are. They treat me like a princess. That is why they are so finicky about finding a guy for me.'

'As in?'

'As in, they want that the guy I marry is able to continue spoiling me silly!' She laughed louder this time.

'Are you dropping me a hint?' I asked. 'I know I don't buy you Gucci, but I still love you, don't I?'

'Of course, you do.' She tugged at my cheek. I loved it when she did that. 'But I keep dropping this hint so that you are motivated to make it bigger in life.'

'By the way, I am looking at a job change,' I said in passing. 'I'm looking at a marketing role, possibly in a company that pays me better and in a best-deal situation – if it gives me a cabin too!'

'Nice!' she said. 'So have you applied anywhere?'

'I'm going to talk to Aryan soon for a position in his bank,' I said. 'In fact, maybe I should speak to him now itself. He is rarely free on a weekday.'

'OK, speak to him now,' she said. 'The earlier, the better.'

I dialled Aryan. 'Aryan, are you free?'

'Bro!' he shouted into the phone. 'Is this called telepathy or what! I was just about to call you.'

'Why?'

'Buddy, I need your help,' he said in an urgent tone. 'Is there a job opening with Bytesphere?'

'You must be kidding!' I said. 'I called you for the same purpose!'

'You . . . you want to join InvestZone?' he asked and then broke into laughter.

'What's funny?' I asked.

'You are a fool,' he said, still laughing. 'You want to quit a comfortable, respectable job and make cold calls to lousy HNI customers!'

'Sometimes, too much comfort also makes you uncomfortable,' I said. 'You know there are phases when I am so without work I begin to doubt if I am considered a useless jerk.'

'Well, you won't exactly be treated royally at InvestZone either,' Aryan mused. 'But OK, if you are keen to try your luck, all the best! Send me your CV.'

'Great,' I said. 'I'm sending it right away.'

'But hold on, Nakul,' he said as an afterthought. 'I have a suggestion. Why don't you come and spend some time here with me, while I walk the field? You might get second thoughts about the job once you see me doing it.'

'How bad can it be?' I insisted. 'There's good money and it's a marketing job. All said and done, it's *some* work at least. Trust me, walking the field and gaining some meaningful sales experience sounds better than mechanically writing test cases on an excel sheet and then analysing the same thing again on a Sunday!'

'You sure sound harried! Alright, send your CV. But what's the harm in coming here anyway? You'll get a break from the excel sheets too.'

'Not a bad idea at all,' I said. 'I'll plan my visit this month itself.'

'Adieus, then,' Aryan said. 'Let me know once you finalise your plan.'

'Sure, ciao.'

Kavya looked up at me. 'Is there an opening?'

'He doesn't know,' I replied. 'He said he will find out. I might go to Delhi and meet him once. I hope this clicks.'

'I hope so too, darling,' she said. 'But remember, I love you even if you don't have a cabin!'

She kissed me again. Her kisses were an enchantment alright, but acting funny in office was a fine line between guts and folly, and I was scared to my bones.

'I really think you should get off my lap, Kavya,' I said a little firmly this time. 'And please stop kissing me.'

'You are right.' She looked at me. 'We've been seeing each other for long enough now. How long should we just keep kissing?'

'What do you mean?'

'I mean . . .' She smiled at me mischievously, and took my hands in hers, slipping them under her spaghetti top and guiding them through previously unchartered territories.

'God!' I exclaimed. 'That sure feels good . . . but don't you think you are putting my job at risk?'

'What fun is making out without an element of risk involved?' She looked at me and winked. 'If we can pull this one off without you getting so scandalised, we will remember this day for the rest of our lives.'

'Did you say "making out"?' I looked at her with disbelief. 'What exactly do you have in mind?'

'The wildest that your mind can conjure,' she chuckled, as she dragged me by the arm and led me to the stationery store opposite my cubicle.

'Ouch, this thing is hard,' she squealed as she tried to position herself on the photocopy machine.

'You never know when it will give way,' I said, pulling her and taking her to the floor. 'Let's stick to the floor. I don't want them to come asking for explanations as to how the thing broke.'

She laughed and began to unbutton my shirt. As my body met hers, I went into a tizzy. She clutched me in her arms and pulled me closer towards her.

'Gosh, Nakul, are you heavy or what!' she spluttered, as she struggled to breathe under me.

'As if you didn't know it before!' I shot back.

'Today I know it like never before!' she gasped, tilting her head upwards to kiss me again.

I took in the warmth of her breath, the scent of her skin and the smooth caress of her lips over and over again. The clock ticked by as the passion heightened.

'Let's not go too far with this,' she said, albeit a bit reluctantly.

'What is too far?' I asked.

'You know,' she replied.

'That's a difficult proposition,' I laughed. 'After all, you are gorgeous!'

'You've said it before!' She smiled.

'Today, I know it like never before,' I smiled back. 'I particularly like that butterfly tattoo on your lower back.'

'Of course,' she said, stretching her hand to pass my shirt lying on the floor behind her. 'I got it done specially for you.'

'I see that you like planning things in advance,' I said, helping her to her feet. 'But I guess you are right. Some things are best left to afterwards. Now let's get out of here.'

I opened the door of the room cautiously, with Kavya peeping from behind me, struggling to set her hair straight. Sadly, trouble had already arrived. My pulse shot up suddenly when I sensed a figure looking at us from a corner of one of the cubicles. It was Jassi – the perfect antithesis to the bliss of the moments just gone by. I froze.

'Hi . . . hi Jassi,' I said.

Kavya kept her hands from trembling as she feigned a casual glance at Jassi.

'Kavya, this is Jassi, he works with me here,' I stuttered with the formal introductions in this highly awkward situation. 'And Jassi, this is. . . .'

'Hello, *bhabhi*!' Jassi folded his hands in earnest greeting, still not shifting his overt gaze from Kavya.

'Bhabhi?' I asked uncomfortably. 'Her name's Kavya.'

'Man, Nakul, you didn't tell me?' Jassi asked with a tinge of sadness. 'It's a pity that I, of all people, didn't know that something was on.'

'She's a friend,' I defended helplessly. 'She was visiting Mumbai, so I thought I'd show her the office.'

'But why were you showing her the stationery store?' Jassi insisted. 'That's hardly a place to show to a visitor. Why don't you take bhabhi to the Bytesphere lawns? Show her the landscaping, na!'

'That's exactly where we are headed now,' I said hurriedly, leading Kavya by the hand. 'So long, Jassi.'

'Stop trembling now,' Kavya said as we walked out of the office. 'Whatever has happened is over now.'

'Whatever has happened should never have happened,' I said frantically. 'That Jassi is a bloody magpie. He won't stop chattering about this episode.'

'Don't worry.' She smiled at me. 'It's not like he knows everything. The best secrets will stay well guarded within the four walls of your stationery store!'

'Funny!' I retorted.

We took a cab to Marine Drive, strolled along for a while holding hands, and in minutes she made me forget about the embarrassment we had gotten into. Call it the power of her smile or the conviction with which she held my hand, but I no longer seemed to be flustered by anything around me.

'I'm going to make up to you for the office fiasco.' She looked at me cheerfully. 'We will take a long walk down Marine Drive and then we will have dinner at the Hilton. Sounds good?'

'The walking down Marine Drive idea sounds good,' I said. 'But what's Hilton got to do with making me feel any better? I am also happy with a *pav bhaji* at Chowpatty.'

'Please, that's tacky!' She wrinkled her nose. 'And you'd better upgrade your tastes too.'

That would be quite an upgrade for me, but I was insanely in love and couldn't help but agree.

'Alright, then,' I nodded. 'Hilton, it is.'

The buffet was scrumptious, but it all got well nullified when we were presented the cheque.

'We didn't ask for it yet, did we?' Kavya admonished the steward and then looked at me. 'What will you have for dessert?'

'Didn't we just have dessert in the buffet itself?' I spoke to her in a whisper.

'Yes, but there was nothing in strawberry there,' she pouted. 'I wanted strawberry shake.'

I glanced at the menu to check the price and somehow held myself. God damn it, why couldn't they have just added a strawberry something in the dozen desserts they had laid out? But then again, what was a five hundred bucks strawberry shake against an already existing bill of four thousand?

'OK, order it.'

'I won't have it alone,' she said. 'You also must take one.'

'What kind of condition is this now?' I asked, irritated. 'I'm full, I can't take anything more.'

'Actually, even I am full,' she declared, tossing the menu back on the table in disgust.

'OK, OK, I'll order,' I said. 'Let's share one. Is that fine?'

'Yeah.'

I turned to the steward and said, 'Two strawberry shakes – cutting.'

The steward looked at me, bearing a baffled expression. 'Sir, we don't have that option. We serve the entire glass.'

'But . . . OK, just bring one strawberry shake,' I said, 'and an extra straw.'

The steward suppressed a smirk and walked off.

'This is really embarrassing,' Kavya said with a red face. 'What will he think of us, ordering cutting shakes in a five-star hotel?'

'Why should I care what he thinks?' I reasoned. 'We both know we are not hungry enough for an entire glass.'

'Still, it is so low society. . . .'

'Kavya,' I looked into her eyes. 'I am not high society. This is what I am. Money wastage concerns me. Is it fine?'

She didn't look at me and instead kept fiddling with her expensive watch as she muttered: 'Yes, it's fine . . . I guess.'

Erratica Erotica

'What's the urgent meeting about?' I looked up from my screen as Lekha came in to collect some printouts. 'Team shuffling again,' she said. 'We are forever dynamic.'

The team assembled in the meeting room and called Cheapo through the speaker phone.

'Guys, there are developments,' Cheapo began in a hurry. 'The client has come up with the tentative resource allocation to both the onsite and offshore locations. So, under the current scheme of events, we need one more from you guys to move here in order to share my load.'

He paused. Vishal and I looked at each other. I don't know about him, but to me the pause seemed to last forever.

'Vishal,' Cheapo continued after a brief silence. 'Are you OK travelling to London next weekend?'

I can swear I saw Vishal's face light up just then. But he expressed little, or rather nothing. 'Yeah, I can,' he said casually.

'Excellent,' Cheapo said. 'Pack your bags then. And get your tickets ready. You will join me here by Monday.'

I am not sure how instrumental my request to Cheapo for Vishal's travel was, but I was glad anyway that the mission was accomplished. Well, half the mission was accomplished.

'What about the others?' I asked, covertly alluding to myself.

'The others stay there for now,' Cheapo said. 'As of now, the client is looking at minimising costs, so it wants an offshore-heavy team. We will let you know in case of any updates.'

'Is there a team expansion in the pipeline?' Lekha asked. 'I'm not sure if these many of us will suffice during the test execution.'

'Expansions will obviously happen,' he said. 'But that will be once the project evolves into a more mature phase. Until then, Nakul will be the offshore execution lead.'

'So in the expansion process, there could be someone senior who would join in?' I asked blatantly.

Cheapo fortunately got the hint. 'Don't worry, even if there is someone, you will continue as the offshore execution lead throughout.'

Offshore lead throughout??? That didn't sound too good. Was he suggesting indirectly that I was to stay grounded at offshore? I decided not to rake this in front of everyone and to take it offline with him instead.

'How are things otherwise?' he asked. 'Is work running smooth?'

'We are facing an issue,' Kohinoor said. 'The application shows "DFX server error – unable to retrieve data".'

'Huh?'

'There are some server issues,' I said, making things simple. 'To put it simply, the application is showing erratic behaviour. It times out repeatedly, probably due to overload. That's disallowing us from navigating through the application during execution.'

'Well, whatever that is,' Cheapo said impatiently, 'get it resolved. Call a meeting with Brenda. She is the chief technical coordinator for Britcell.'

'Yeah, Kohinoor and I will call her after this call ends,' I said.

'Good,' he said. 'I think the others can drop off the call now. Vishal, can you stay back for a few minutes? I've to give you a list of things I need from India.'

'OK,' Vishal said as curtly as possible.

Lekha pressed the mute button and slapped Vishal on the back while going out. 'Enjoy, courier boy!'

Kohinoor and I went to the adjoining room to call Brenda. The application was behaving funnily and our work was stalled for the last seven days. Strangely, the client members never seem to understand such technical mumbo-jumbo. All they do know is to stand on our heads like Satan when the day's deliverables are not met. And they can be damn nasty when they do that.

'Hey, brother,' Kohinoor said, biting his fingernails nervously. 'I've never spoken to Englishman before. I'm feeling scared.'

'OK, a few tips,' I said as we took our seats in the conference room. 'Number one – never, ever address them as 'brother' or "sister". More importantly, never say "dear" while talking to them, OK? It sounds too intimate and they don't appreciate it at all. Just call them by first name.'

He nodded his head fervently.

'Number two, you need to cut the ice with them in the first conversation. Don't just start off with the issue at hand. Begin by talking something else first.'

'For example?'

'For example, the first time I spoke to them, I asked them a bit about their country and their culture.'

'What else can we talk?'

'There are many topics to break ice with,' I continued, 'depending on how much time they have on that particular call. They like discussing sports, weekend trips, the weather, etc. It makes them feel you are ready to be cool and friendly with them.'

'OK, I think that looks easy,' Kohinoor said, much to my relief. 'Let's call.'

The phone rang exactly three times before we heard Brenda Audrey's cheerful voice singing from the other end. 'Hello there, this is Brenda Audrey.'

'Hi, Brenda,' I said. 'This is Nakul from the offshore team here at Bytesphere.'

'Oh hi *Nay-khool*,' she said. 'How are you doing today?'

'Pretty well, thanks,' I said. 'I have also my colleague, Kohinoor Kesari, online with me.'

'Hi, Brenda,' Kohinoor said jovially, 'how are you doing?'

'Good, thanks,' she replied. 'Hope the same for you too. So how can I. . . . ?'

'So how is it in London?' Kohinoor continued, determined to strike a chord with her in the first conversation. 'Is it very cold? Is it snowing?'

'Uh, yeah it is cold,' Brenda said, unsure of where this interrogation was heading. 'It's beginning to freeze up a bit, but it's not really snowing. So what brings us on this call. . . .'

Kohinoor was in no mood to stop. 'So what are you doing on the weekend?'

I put my finger on my lips, signalling Kohinoor to stop. But he was on a trip of his own.

'The week's just begun!' She laughed a little, trying to cover up the irritation building within her. 'It's too early to plan for the weekend!'

Even I was getting flustered now. I prayed he would stop.

'Did you see England vs. India ODI on Saturday?' he asked of her. 'India defeated England badly by 139 runs!'

'Yeah, I know,' Brenda said, her voice positively rising in decibel now. 'We saw the game at Lord's.'

'Oh, you must have gone with your kids?' Kohinoor quizzed yet again. 'What are their names?'

This really shot up the mercury. 'I don't have any kids,' she said crossly, 'if that query helps you in any way. Nakul, what's going on?'

I froze in my seat. I muted the phone and said hurriedly to Kohinoor. 'Tip number three. When you get the hint, stop the frivolous chat.'

'Hey Brenda,' I un-muted the phone. 'We actually had to discuss a technical glitch we are facing since morning. The application has been timing out every few minutes due to a server overload.'

'Yes, yes,' Kohinoor butted in, determined to make his point with a fancy word. 'It is showing very erotic behaviour.'

I felt myself go numb. I thought I must have been brain dead by now.

'What the hell?' Brenda was shouting now, very offended.

'Sorry, he meant "erratic",' I said, covering the goof-up. 'It just closes down without warning. This is preventing us from creating new data in the system for testing purposes.'

'Ah, sorry, I guess it was not communicated to your team,' she said after a pause. 'There is some migration of data happening in the system for the next two working days, so the system is going to be in flux.'

'So should we eschew testing until migration is complete?' Kohinoor asked.

I turned to him with a stunned expression. The usage of that fancy word 'eschew' by Kohinoor looked like an oasis in a desert – a welcome delight, but something totally out of the blue.

'Chew what?' Brenda asked after him, failing to comprehend his even fancier accent.

'Eschew, eschew,' Kohinoor repeated excitedly, and then looked at me and smiled proudly.

'Oh well, yeah, you can *eschew* testing until tomorrow end,' Brenda replied, stressing on the word 'eschew' in obvious mockery. 'I'll send out a mail to everyone once testing can resume.'

'That's nice, Brenda,' I said, urgently trying to close the call before Kohinoor could create more trouble. 'Thanks so much.'

'My pleasure,' she said rather tersely and hung up.

'Brenda was very abominable, brother,' Kohinoor announced after the call. 'Very acerbic tone.'

I smiled. 'Don't worry, you can eschew paying attention to her!'

Kohinoor blushed with smugness and walked away. Vishal signalled for a smoke break.

'So, 'tis the last week before you pick an *Inglis* brand?' I remarked in jest.

'I'm feeling a little bad,' Vishal said slowly, 'that I am going alone.'

'Why? You're allowed to travel with family, right?'

'Not family, duffer,' Vishal said. 'I'm talking about both of us. I mean, we both have worked together throughout, as a team. Now I'm travelling and you don't get to. See, I always said life is a bitch.'

'Hey, that's perfectly alright,' I said. *Come on now, whom am I kidding? It's anything but alright!* 'This is how things work. You don't have to feel sorry about this.'

'Still, it's unfair towards you. . . .'

'Vishal, you have felt upset about plenty of things in your life,' I said, patting him on the back. 'Now this is a beautiful opportunity for you to see the brighter things in life. So please, stop bothering about me. You need to understand that life is not meant to move our way all the time.'

More importantly, he needed to understand that it was no good peeling someone's wounds and rubbing salt over them. His words of sympathy were doing little good to me; in fact, they were sharp blades cutting through my nerves. I wanted to cry, I wanted to shout and scream. But all I could do was stand dumbly and lie to him that I was damn happy about his career development.

Like shit I care about his career, man! Why can't I go too? The answer kept ringing in my mind in the form of Cheapo's words to me the other night at the party: *Sometimes, you can end up being wronged by the right too.* Damn my philanthropy. Damn Anita's teary-eyed story. I wanted to take my request back. But it was too late. Vishal was going to be the emerging stud of the team, while I was to stay put, handling a team of newbies and a moron who was now addicted to using incomprehensible words!

I went back to my seat and messaged Aryan:

Coming to Delhi Mon morning. C u there.

Happy Hours

I swatted Aryan on the head as soon as I saw him outside the New Delhi station. 'Why the hell do you need to hold a placard to find me?'

'Bro, that's because it's been a year too long.' Aryan hugged me. 'Moreover, given that I have changed quite a bit myself ever since I started working, I presumed your job must have treated you equally badly. So I wasn't sure if we would recognise each other.'

'The eternal dramatist!' I mocked in jest. 'In what way have you changed by the way?'

'Look at this!' he said, pushing back his fluffy hair and pointing at his pate. 'This is a consequence of the tension this good-for-nothing corporate life has given me. Not to mention the muscle loss over my body. I haven't got to see the face of the gym in one year.'

'You are absolutely alright,' I said reassuringly, as I struggled to arrange my luggage trolley in the backseat of his Santro. 'If you compare it with what has become of me.'

'I don't want to make that comparison, buddy!' he spoke between giggles. 'You look like an uncle alright!'

'Ass!' I snorted. 'I'm trying to do all I can to knock off some weight, so I won't entertain any fun being poked at my pudgy body.'

'What are you doing, if I may ask?'

'I'm a regular at the gym,' I said, and then slowly added: 'For the past one month. That's the difference between us – you don't have the time to work out because your office keeps you busy, and I have built a virtual base in the gym because my office treats me like a piece of broken furniture.'

'Bah!' he dismissed. 'Chuck the gym and just join InvestZone. Your field visits will get all that darn fat off you in ten days – something your gym won't be able to do in a lifetime.'

'Fantastic,' I smiled. 'I can't wait to get started.'

'Sure,' Aryan muttered, shaking his head in pity as he swerved the car over an empty New Delhi road.

'So what time are we off to work?' I asked.

'Not before 10,' Aryan said, 'today I am making visits to my dear clients who don't get their fat bums off their deluxe beds that early. So it's suicidal to even try calling them before 10 a.m.'

'Who are these clients?'

'The wealthy merchants from all over India who are sitting on pots of gold here,' Aryan explained. 'The work-from-home types, or worse, the no-work-only-eat-n-drink types.'

'Oh, the poor dumb rich guys?'

'You bet,' he said. 'They are so dumb they don't know the difference between a debit card and a greeting card. But they bring in the *moolah* to my company, so my company likes it if I treat them like the Sultans of Delhi.'

'Talking of Sultans,' I interrupted. 'I can't forget the way you effortlessly strummed *Sultans of Swing* back in college. Do you still have your guitar?'

'Nakul, I am a salesman now,' he said bitterly. 'These things are a dream for me now. I need to face it. I regret having rejected the Flash Consumer Durables option and taken this one, just for a few lakhs extra!'

'A few lakhs is a lot of lakhs, boss! Don't dismiss them as something so trivial!'

'Yes, but a point comes when the burden on you becomes heavier than your wallet,' he said, 'and that's when you begin to fall.'

He spoke volumes of how he had struggled to survive amidst the high-pressure environs of InvestZone, where hurling abuses at young professionals was the order of the day, where nobody ever got a word of acknowledgement or a pat on the back for the long hours of drudgery spent in a day, and where he got constant threats of being transferred to the Rann of Kutch to sell investment solutions if his underperformance continued over the next quarter. To an average mind, his recount in that half-hour drive would be influence enough to take a U-turn and catch the next train back to Mumbai. But my mind was now no longer in sane confines. It might be in keeping with the adage that the grass is always greener on the other side. But somehow, I felt the entire grass at Bytesphere was burning into hay. Each day was a new story of frustration and boredom, and a typically staid routine that I was getting fed up of. Add to that the undesired responsibility of understanding technical modalities in an IT job and Kavya's unmatched expectations of a Gucci lifestyle, and I knew my life in Bytesphere was a mess.

'You at least have an identity here for all the slog that you go through,' I argued. 'As in, even if your management abuses you, they first call you by your name and then abuse you. Here, my telecom vertical manager doesn't even know my real name. On the few occasions that he has felt the urge to ask for me, he has been like "where is that guy in green checks who always has that what-am-I-doing-here look on his face?"

'What would you rather choose?' he asked. 'Being ignored in a mélange or being singled out in front of an entire staff and told that you suck?'

'Don't brainwash me now,' I said firmly. 'I've made up my mind.'

'Cool,' he said, as he pulled the car into the garage of his apartment. 'You have two hours to bathe, eat and look around. We leave at sharp ten for Connaught Place.'

At sharp ten, we plunked ourselves back into the Santro, and were out on the mission. Aryan flicked out his flashy PDA and began scrolling through the names he had to call. He let out a brief grunt on reading the first name.

'Tahir Moolchandani,' he read out. 'A *seth* who runs a diamond business. He sits out of his primary office in Connaught Place. Doesn't know crap about investments, but does know to splurge money at the city's pubs and gambling dens every night. Rascal of order one – let me relieve myself of his burden first.'

We drove down to the parking lot at CP's inner circle, where Aryan pointed to Moolchandani's office, a dark shanty dangling precariously over a sweet shop.

'Can I come in too?' I asked.

'Yes, but let me call him first,' Aryan said, getting his number on the PDA. 'The jerks have short memories, and then they accuse me of disturbing them without appointment. I'll leave it on speaker, so you have a treat for your ears.'

The phone rang about ten times before a gruff voice answered it. '*Haaloo?*'

'Very good morning, sir, this is Aryan Nair from InvestZone,' Aryan began in an earnest, sugary tone. 'If you remember. . . .'

'*Ha bol, kya hai?*' Yes, speak up, what's with you?

'Sir, we had an appointment. . . .'

'*Kedi appointment?*' What appointment?

'Sir, regarding your investments with us. . . .'

'*Kal aana call karke.*' Come tomorrow after seeking an appointment.

'But sir, I already have an appointment for today. . . .'

'*Toh kya sar pe bitha loon?*' So what, shall I seat you on my head?

'Sir, I don't mind waiting outside your office till you are free. . . .' The desperation in Aryan's voice was peaking.

'*Bola na kal aana, samajh nahi aata kya bhen* . . .' I told you – come tomorrow; do you not get the point, you son of a. . . .

'I get it, sir,' Aryan replied. 'No problem, sir. Wish you a good day.' Slam!

I looked at Aryan's face in horror. Knowing him and his ego, he should have flown into a mad rage after that call. Instead, he maintained a stoic expression as he calmly looked for the next customer's number.

'Don't look at me like that,' Aryan said, looking up from his PDA. 'This is precisely what you have come looking for all the way to Delhi! So you'd better get tuned.'

I gulped. 'Fine, who is next?'

'The next is some Manoj Dubey, owner of a chain of restaurants here,' Aryan said, reading out the details on this handset. 'I've called him once before, but like is usually the case, he ignored me. But he is slightly more human than Moolchandani.'

'Hello?' we heard Dubey's voice.

'Very good morning, sir, this is Aryan Nair from InvestZone,' Aryan parroted off once again in a fixed template format. 'If you remember. . . .'

'Yes, Aryan.'

Aryan heaved a sigh of relief. 'Sir, can I meet you now to discuss your investments?'

'OK,' he said hesitantly. 'But come immediately, and you have only ten minutes.'

'Ten minutes is good, sir! And I'll be at your door in five minutes.'

In less than five minutes, we were facing Manoj Dubey, a thirty-something client slouched in his armchair.

'Sit,' he beckoned to us. 'Begin.'

Aryan rattled off at jet speed on multiple permutations and combinations of investment options with his company that would make Dubey richer than what he already was. Dubey, in turn, obliged by sleepily nodding his head intermittently and looking impatiently at his watch.

'Leave your brochure with me,' Dubey interrupted in less than two minutes. 'I'll read it and let you know what I want. For now, I have another problem if you can solve it.'

'Sure, sir, anything,' Aryan said enthusiastically.

'Your useless bank's ATM has been giving me trouble since morning,' he complained. 'It's not user-friendly. Can you just come along to the ATM and tell me why it's so out of whack?'

'I'll try my best, sir. Let's go.'

We entered the InvestZone ATM right next to Dubey's office. Dubey struggled to locate the right keys to activate the machine, and then began bungling further by trying to insert the debit card in the wrong slot.

Aryan suppressed a snigger. 'No Sir, that's from where the cash comes out. The upper slot is where you swipe the card.'

'Oh-ho,' he exclaimed, and then swiped the card followed by a furious entry of his pass code. 'Look, this bloody machine tells me I am not authorised to make any transactions. It doesn't allow me to take out my own money.'

'Take it easy, sir,' Aryan lost control over his tone for the first time. 'It must be a minor problem. Let me see.'

'Why are you looking at my card?' Dubey asked hysterically. 'I can't show you my card.'

'Excuse me, sir,' Aryan tried to keep his cool, but he was going off the lid. 'There is no privacy issue here, is there? I can't do anything with your card without knowing your pass code.'

'Don't act funny,' he replied unabashedly. 'I know that the pass code is printed right at the back of my card.'

Aryan and I gasped in unison. 'Sir, that's not your pass code!'

'Then what's my pass code?'

'Sir, you must have received your pass code when you opened an account with us.'

'I don't remember getting any such code. How do I trace it back now?'

'Don't worry, sir,' Aryan explained. 'You can call the customer care centre, they will take you through a verification process and then issue you a new pass code, which you must ideally reset immediately.'

'What verification process?'

'They need to do that to ensure you are a real customer, so they will ask for details like your verification password. . . .'

'Again password!' Dubey was getting flustered now. 'Why are you after my password?'

'Sir that password is just a . . .' Aryan stopped. He had given up by now. 'Sir, let's do one thing: I'll send you an email with stepwise instructions, so it will make things more lucid for you.'

'If you just had to send me an email later, why did you waste my time?' he complained. 'I told you I had only ten minutes, but you took more than half an hour. And my problem's still not solved.'

'I'm sorry, sir,' Aryan apologised, visibly fuming. 'My mistake.'

A visibly annoyed Manoj Dubey grumbled something and huffed his way back to his office.

'Do you need a break?' Aryan asked. 'Or should we go ahead?'

'Let's carry on,' I said, smiling. 'This is entertainment at its best.'

Aryan smiled and dialled the third guy. 'Good morning sir, this is Aryan Nair from InvestZone. . . .'

'Please don't disturb,' the irate voice shot back. 'I don't need anything.'

He was off the phone line in a second. 'The bastard!' Aryan got wild. 'Now look at this!'

Aryan snatched my phone and kept a handkerchief near the mouthpiece. He dialled the same guy again, this time from my number.

The phone rang, and Aryan began under a seductive feminine voiceover. 'Very good morning, sir! This is Alisha from IPIM bank.'

'Good morning!' a totally contrast sweet voice spoke from the other end.

'Sir, can I disturb you for a minute? I need to talk to you about our investment solutions.'

'Yeah sure, go ahead, Alisha!' the voice went on in the sugary tone. 'I am free.'

'Thank you, sir,' Aryan returned to his original voice. 'This is Aryan Nair again from InvestZone!'

'Don't act smart, you rat!' the voice shouted again. 'You do that one more time, and I'll complain against you to the police!'

Slam! There went the third customer.

'That does it,' Aryan said. 'These three idiots are dealt with. It now makes the rest of my day easier, as I know things can't get worse than this.'

'So what's next?'

'A few more calls to close some deals,' he said. 'And then, it's happy hours.'

'Happy hours?'

'I'll tell you,' he said.

We got done with the remaining calls and squeezed in five minutes for a quick lunch at McDonald's. At three, we began driving to Aryan's office.

'This, my friend, is happy hours,' Aryan explained. 'When I give the day's status report to my manager in the three-thirty meeting. You know the Happy Hours concept in restaurants, right? When you get free combo meals in an hour?'

'Yeah, so?'

'On the last day of every month, I am given special treatment by my boss,' he said. 'He calls me to his cabin and abuses me left, right and centre for not having met the month's unrealistic targets.

In that one hour, he gives me the bonus of the entire month with his kind words.'

'That bad?' I asked.

'And worse. I'm taking you for a demo so you can see for yourself.'

His manager met us in the hallway leading to Aryan's cubicle. 'I'll be right back,' he said. 'Wait for me right here.'

He looked at me questioningly and then turned to Aryan.

'He's my friend,' Aryan told his manager. 'He is staying with me for a day or two. I just tugged him along to office, else he would have got bored at home.'

The manager nodded and muttered something with brevity before walking away. He returned soon, and asked Aryan to follow him in his cabin.

'Wait here,' Aryan whispered to me.

He held his file in hand and followed the lion to his den. Seconds later, I began hearing the heated conversation. Embarrassingly for Aryan, the acoustics of his manager's cabin were not designed sufficiently well to seal the sound of the invectives. Portions of the manager's speech found me as an unintended recipient. I tried hard to comprehend the dialogue until my attention got distracted by an object that flew out of the cabin's open top in a projectile motion, landing near my feet. I bent down to see it was Aryan's file containing his month's report. His manager had quite a signature style of conveying his appraisal remarks!

A few minutes later, Aryan came out and coolly picked up his file. 'Let's go. I am done for the day.'

That night, we sat on the terrace of his apartment, trying hard to indulge in the kind of nothingness we did in our college days. But every few minutes, our worries would gnaw at our minds menacingly.

'My manager told me that an ordinary salesman could get him double the business of what I do, at one-third of my salary,' Aryan spoke after a long silence. 'He suggested I go back to college.'

'If wishes were horses,' I mused. 'That would be something I'd love to do. Life sure treated us better there.'

'Oh, really? Didn't we then hate the life we had out there – the tension of the low grades, the heaps of assignments we could never finish?'

'Yes, but. . . .'

'And the funny thing is that all of that tension we took was in order to get a good job, which we have now. But we are not any happier even today. I think it's just that we are too conditioned to hating life.'

'That's not true,' I said. 'It's just that we are still in the process of settling down. It's all about finding the right job and the right lifestyle.'

'Bullshit,' Aryan said. 'I'll tell you what; our minds are like gas. They are always in flux, and they can never be at ease – even if we become the CEOs of our companies some day. The CEOs also surely think their lives suck.'

'I know what's lacking in my life,' I said after a while. 'Which is why I came seeking help from you. It's the excitement – the challenge that's missing. Things are too straight-jacketed in my job.'

'And the money?'

'Yes, the money is important too,' I added. 'You get much more than I do.'

'You did see what all I had to go through in a single day, right?'

'Yes, I did. That's precisely the challenge I am talking about,' I said. 'If I can withstand the initial torment and gain some worthy experience in the long run, that torment is worth it.'

'So do you want to send your CV?'

'Yes, I do. And I'm going to send it to you first thing when I reach Mumbai.'

Aryan smiled. 'Sure. I'll forward it. And I'm sure you will be called for an interview, for they are now heavily on the lookout for some new scapegoats.'

'And what about you? Do you want to try Bytesphere?'

'I'm not sure yet,' Aryan said. 'I'm beginning to wonder if jumping jobs is the solution to my problems. What if the new job makes me even more miserable? I might rather deal with the unhappiness I am used to, till the point where it can no longer affect me. After that I might as well settle down in one place and learn to reconcile with all the negatives.'

We sat through most of the night without talking much. Only once did Aryan point to a bungalow lined in the row opposite to his apartment. He told me it belonged to a rich industrialist who was all of forty years of age. We gazed listlessly at the bungalow for hours. We were usually prone to giving in to fancies of seeing ourselves in such mansions someday in life. But today, that fancy did not seem to work any magic on us. The simple inspiration that could stir us up but was still eluding us was a warm, satisfying smile when we went to sleep each night.

To Each His Own

'Nakul, this is Bhavna Munshi from InvestZone, Mumbai,' a female spoke in a stern tone. 'I got your reference from Aryan Nair.'

'That's right, ma'am,' I said, my heart beating wildly.

'Can you come down for an interview tomorrow at 10 a.m.?' She asked. 'Have you seen our office near Flora Fountain?'

'Yes, I have,' I said. 'I'll be there. Thank you very much.'

I suddenly began to feel elated, and I was already cajoling myself to call Cheapo and hurl abuses at him just for cheap thrills before I called it quits to Bytesphere. Maybe I could send him a hate mail and call him names therein. Or I could dial him some whacky crank ISD calls, all at the expense of the company. Somehow, sanity got the better of me and I composed myself. But the bubble of elation suddenly burst unannounced when Lekha thrust a paper containing a strange diagram and a lot of wordy text up my nose.

'What is it?' I questioned.

'A directive from Cheapo,' she said ruefully. 'Read it yourself.'

Dear Team,

With a view to streamlining our processes as well as our reporting mechanisms, we are going to follow a fixed format of hierarchical reporting (explained below in the pyramid diagram). Under the ambit of this new structure, it may please be noted that the work allocation between the offshore and onsite members be evenly and judiciously distributed. Simply said, this will mean that all the execution activities, test planning and rework will be administered by the offshore team (led by Nakul Kapoor), and the client interfacing, gathering of requirements from the business, review co-ordination with the client, and task delegation to the whole team will be handled by Vishal Tiwari, here onsite.

It may also please be noted that no offshore team member will escalate issues/concerns, send reports or advise review comments on achieved deliverables directly to the client team. If this is not followed, it can create serious trouble or embarrassment as it will reflect insufficient communication between offshore and onsite. These should be routed through the proper channel (Vishal and then me), who in turn, will talk to the client.

In case of any issues, please revert to me.

Best,
Chirayu Chaudhary

This did not feel too good. I felt a little queasy, and my worst fears came true when I glanced through the embedded image at the bottom. For most parts, it was an incomprehensible figure with multi-coloured sections supposedly depicting each hierarchy. All that came to my restless mind's notice was that Vishal Tiwari's name appeared above mine in that pyramid. Suddenly, I felt my heart was being mangled from within. I looked closely again. Sure enough – the pyramid dictated that the new kids would report to Lekha, who was designated senior test analyst. Lekha, in turn would report to me, the offshore test lead, and I would report to Vishal, the onsite test lead. . . . Hello! Holy Cow! What the hell was going on? This was ridiculous. I decided to attend to the matter immediately and called Cheapo.

'Yes, Nakul,' Cheapo said calmly. 'How is life?'

'Not very good, frankly,' I replied bitterly, 'after reading your mail.'

'Why, what's wrong?'

'Everything's wrong!' I shouted. 'How can you ask me to report to Vishal? We have shared similar responsibilities all along, and, though I hate to bring this up, but at the organisational level I am at a higher profile than he is.'

'So what?' he asked coolly. 'The hierarchy I am talking about is only for this project.'

'Whatever,' I insisted. 'It's still unacceptable.'

'Listen, you are overreacting,' he said, 'because this hierarchy is only on paper, to present the team structure to the client. Internally, we are all equally important. Both you and Vishal are like the brothers I can trust.'

'OK, let's leave the hierarchy aside for now,' I said. 'Please tell me what do you mean when you say none of us get to interact with the client directly?'

'I mean what I say,' he said. 'And I think I've explained the reason for that in the mail as well. In any case, if there are any issues or suggestions, you can always raise them with Vishal or me. So what's the problem?'

'I can't explain this well, I know,' I said, 'but I am beginning to feel an identity crisis now. When I was completing my education, doing back-end clerical work like a mute mule was not how I had envisaged my future. I also aspire for something meaningful.'

'Nakul, you are crossing your limits now,' Cheapo growled. 'Don't forget I am your boss.'

That was the problem. Even if I wanted, I could not forget that this donkey was my boss. What sense does it make to have five levels of hierarchy in a team of ten? Crazy moron!

'Fine,' I relented. 'In that case, I assume we don't need to attend the daily 2'o clock meeting with the client?'

'What makes you make that assumption?' Cheapo asked in surprise. 'Of course, you have to attend it. The entire offshore team need not, but you should – so that you know what deliverables are lined up for you and for your team.'

'But that I can always find out from you or Vishal,' I argued, 'as in any case I am reporting to both of you and not to the client.'

'If you can hear the instructions from the original source,' he explained. 'You will save us the effort of explaining them to you for the second time. We need to always remember we work in a team, right? So we need to be as supportive towards each other as possible, right?'

'Right.'

'Good,' he said, 'so I'll see you during the 2 o'clock call. Just remember to keep your phone on mute during the call, that's it.'

His last line pricked the life out of me. I felt like picking the same prick and deflating his fat body to the size of a chewed bubble gum. But all I could manage was a dumb 'OK' even as he dropped off the call.

I decided to speak to Vishal about this. At least he would understand my issue with reporting to him.

'Yes, I read that silly hierarchy mail he sent,' Vishal confirmed when I called him. 'I wonder what's with him!'

'Vishal, he is asking me to report to you,' I started on a cautious note. 'I know you are the only person I can talk to about this frankly. Do you think this is right?'

'It's absolutely wrong,' Vishal said sympathetically. 'But, tell me, would you want to rub him the wrong way by fighting for something as trivial as this?'

'Trivial?' I asked in disbelief. 'Would you call this trivial if it happened to you?'

'You're not getting it,' Vishal explained. 'Consider yourself lucky it is only me you are reporting to. I know we are both at par, so I'll ensure that the work between us will be shared, rather than being delegated. Effectively, it is you and I together who will take most of the decisions on behalf of the whole team. Cheapo himself is looking only into the overall project management.'

'Then why that stupid idea of offshore staying on mute during the daily status call?' I asked. 'What is he trying to tell us?'

'That's stupid indeed,' Vishal concurred.

'Then can you please try talking him out of this dumbass plan of his?' I begged. 'Seriously, Vishal, this is thoroughly demeaning.'

'I'm sorry, Nakul,' he said. 'I understand your angst because I have seen a lot of it myself before coming to this onsite position. But there is nothing much I can explain to Cheapo regarding this, for he will anyway do what he feels like. And beyond a point, there is no sense in locking horns with him. He gives us our bread.'

'He doesn't give us our bread,' I said angrily. 'And I don't know why you have suddenly started respecting him like he is some god. Is it just because your needs are met?'

'Needs are like a perennially flowing river, buddy,' he said, 'they never cease. And no, that's not the reason. It's just because I realised that a day comes when you need to kill the rebel in you and live with the reality of hierarchy. Even jerks need their egos to be massaged.'

'I don't believe you are saying this,' I said dejectedly. 'Anyway, I'll be off now.'

'Dude, you are getting me wrong.'

'No, I'm not,' I replied wearily. 'And I am not blaming you either. It's just like you said – to each his own.'

I sat for what seemed like hours, gazing blankly outside the conference room window. I could not remember the last time my mind went through such tribulation. Scott Adams might want to give Dilbert some rest and make cartoon strips based on me. I wanted to scream, but I had only the walls to hear me out. And an extra-curious Kohinoor.

'Dear brother, why are you looking so abject and despondent?' Mr GRE asked. 'Is there something I can do to alleviate your affliction?'

'That's very kind of you, Kohinoor,' I said with complete honesty. 'But I'm fine. Can you please send Lekha in?'

Lekha knocked on the door moments later and peeped in. 'What's up?'

'You tell me,' I quipped. 'You've been reading the papers. What do my stars predict today?'

'Not too bright?'

'No stars would be more like it,' I said, and suddenly fell silent. 'Someone seems to have tossed my stars out of orbit.'

'Did you speak to Cheapo?'

'I spoke to him, and also to Vishal,' I said. 'And I need not talk about Cheapo, I know. But even Vishal did a volte-face.'

'Oh, so finally,' she said, 'he showed what friends are all about.'

I shook my head. 'Let's not doubt Vishal. He isn't like that usually. It's immature to make a judgement on him.'

'And it's maturity to understand the reality. When opportunity knocks even on your best friend's door, you play second fiddle to the opportunity.'

'Lekha, let's not discuss this,' I begged, 'or I'll puke.'

She cringed. 'OK, relax. What have you thought of now?'

'I'm going to quit,' I declared rather openly. 'Listen, don't discuss this anywhere, but I have an interview with InvestZone tomorrow at Flora Fountain square.'

'What time?'

'10 a.m. Will you be able to handle the workload?'

'The workload is OK,' she said, 'but are you aware of those "peaceful protests" the NGO is carrying out against the living conditions of the Mumbai shanty owners?'

'Yes, what about them?'

'They seem to have blocked many roads in the city to carry out their dharna,' she warned, 'so you'd better leave margin for those roadblocks.'

'These are routine things,' I said, 'I always leave margin for them. But hey, can I take your bike to the interview tomorrow? It will be easier to weasel around rather than sitting in a rickshaw.'

'Sure,' she said. 'I'll be coming to office early tomorrow. So come by to office and I'll give you the keys near the parking lot itself.'

My phone beeped. It was an SMS from Kohinoor:

Let your smile be brighter than the sun, so that even your worries have to face the glare before they face you. ☺

The poor chap was sincerely trying to lift my spirits. But frankly, right now my spirits were down in hell somewhere. I went over to his desk nonetheless and thanked him for his effort.

'That's very nice of you, buddy,' I lied. 'You made my day.'

'Oh anytime, brother,' he said. 'Just tell me what I can do for you so that you are jolly.'

'I am jolly, thanks,' I replied. 'All I can request you to do is attend the 2 o'clock meeting and take down the minutes of that discussion, as I won't be able to attend it today.'

'Why?'

'I have some work to finish,' I said, 'that's why.'

'OK, no problem, Sir,' he said jovially. 'I'll take down the minutes.'

Lekha, who had overheard the conversation, came up to me. 'What work do you have?'

'Nothing much, actually,' I shook my head. 'It's just a revolt against Cheapo's senseless directives for offshore to keep its mouth shut.'

'Then why us?' she asked.

'Relax, Lekha,' I assured her. 'I'll join from tomorrow. Just for today, I am not up to it.'

'OK, no issues. Take care and don't let it bog you down too much.'

In the one hour that followed, I tried preparing for the next day's interview. But I was getting increasingly pissed off with each beep of my phone that went off with a new SMS from Kohinoor, even as I struggled with financial terminology I had hardly ever heard of. *How the hell was he managing to note down the minutes of the meeting while sending these philosophical one-liners? Was the team concentrating on the call at all or was it goofing off? Gosh, I would have been better off attending it. . . .* Slowly and surely, my mind began to drift off the financial journals. And it fell totally off the cliff when Kohinoor returned from the meeting room and began singing in front of me in a cacophony.

'Have you got a sunshine S-M-I-L-E, have you got a sunshine S-M-I-L-E,' he yowled, stretching his lips with his fingers into a sunshine smile. 'Wherever you may be, whatever you maybe, have you got a. . . .'

'Kohinoor, will you do me a favour?' I stopped him. 'Please shut up! Please! I need some concentration out here.'

It was probably my volume, or maybe the devil had gotten inside me, but I realised that I had upset Kohinoor beyond repair. His mouth began shaking like a piece of blubber, and his nose turned cherry red. I almost wanted to plug my ears in anticipation of a hysterical howl. But for the sake of tranquility, he thankfully managed with a few sniffles and walked away – but not before giving me a look of disgust. I tried to dig myself into my screen once again, but from the corner of my eyes, I could see my entire team give me that famously recognisable 'you-are-such-a-pig' look. *That does it*, I decided, *so much for an interview preparation.*

I left home early that evening, hoping to tuck myself into bed before being faced with the prospect of handling Kohinoor's sobbing once again. I was too beat to eat, so I changed into my shorts and slumped into bed. Shortly after, and sure enough, I was woken up by his whimpers. I tried ignoring them for a few minutes, and tossed over to the other side of the bed. But the noise, or probably my guilt, got the better of me, and I finally decided to confront him.

'I'm sorry,' I said meekly.

'Oh, don't say sorry, brother,' he said, crying all the louder. 'I think I indeed vex everyone ad nauseum.'

His GRE mania didn't let go of him even in a bad mood. Now that's what you call diligence.

'What do you mean by "everyone"?' I asked out of concern. 'Whom else have you vexed?'

I pressed the trigger at a wrong time, and thus began his story that lasted through much of that long night:

'I am the single child of my parents whom I love a lot. For most of my childhood, I was brought up with a lot of affection in our ancestral house in Pali. Do you know, brother, our house is the grandest in the whole of Pali! My friends also used to feel jealous that I had such a big house, two cars, three plots of fertile land and one big successful factory. . . .

My problems started once I finished Class 12. My father wanted me to join him in the family's business immediately after school, but I wanted to go to college and study. I curse that moment when in school I participated for fun in a contest related to computers, which I won. My interest in the field was formed and I decided to make it my career. . . .

My parents told me they would disown me if I decided to study further instead of joining the family business. Mummy said that I was a disobedient son and was disgrace to Pali culture. One day I wept and wept so much, I felt I did not know where my life was taking me. I just wanted to run away to the jungle. . . .'

That depression explained his fondness for crying. 'Then? What changed your mind?'

He gave me a sore look. I don't know what I said wrong. I was only trying to sound participative in the story. Maybe the way I structured my question was not apt.

'Somehow I managed to finish my engineering studies and get a nice desirable job with Bytesphere. When I told Mummy-Papa that I have got my job in Mumbai, they chastised me instead of feeling happy. Papa said that the doors of the house would forever be closed for me if I left Pali that day. But I still touched their feet and came here. Can you imagine?'

No, I could not imagine. This sounded straight out of the films. But his now uncontrollable tears said otherwise.

'Brother, this is why I was asking you to give a sunshine smile because I know how painful it is to be lachrymose.'

'I'm sorry about the way I shouted at you, Kohinoor,' I said. 'It's just that I was a little stressed then.'

'Who is not stressed, dear?' he asked, still wiping his tears. 'See how much stress I have faced in life.'

'I understand,' I said. 'But why forgo an easy path and withstand unnecessary pain? I mean, don't get me wrong, but compare your grand villa in Pali with this one-room studio in Mumbai. . . .'

'We all worry about the initial pain,' he mused, 'but we forget that sometimes this pain is what makes the success sweeter!'

I suddenly fell silent and sat up straight in bed. *Good Lord, he is so right! Doesn't this so well explain that my predicament is but a passing pain?*

'What happened?' he asked.

'Nothing,' I replied. 'It's quite late. Let's sleep.'

I muttered silent thanks to Kohinoor for showing me the value of what we call pain. And admittedly, what I was going through could hardly qualify as pain, if I compared it with what he had seen in life. But then again, pain can never be relative. It is always superlative when it is your own, and a mammoth that only you can combat. That night, Kohinoor showed me the trick to combat it. His last comment helped me sleep easy as I drowned my fears for that night. But sadly, the comfort was ephemeral.

Cheapo Chaudhary the ogre is towering over me and laughing his guts out. His gigantic shadow sprawls all around me and all I can see is darkness. I am feeling snuffed out and I am looking for an outlet. I fish out a needle from my pocket and jab it hard in the ogre's stomach, hoping to deflate him so that I can breathe. But to my dismay, I don't see anything happen. When I observe carefully, I notice a big hole in the middle of his head through which a huge pipe runs out. The pipe connects to a hand pump, and I find Vishal pumping furiously into it. 'I told you, bro, even jerks need their egos massaged,' he shrugs helplessly and says to me. The ogre is inflating faster than I can deflate him, and I resign myself to my fate and cower under his shadow. He bends down and growls, 'Do as you please, Nakul, I'll always be bigger than you!'

I am getting increasingly uncomfortable, and the ogre's breath, which is no less than a hot furnace, is almost ready to burn me to death. 'Just the initial pain, brother,' Kohinoor eggs me on, and I steel myself to weasel out of the trap. Kavya is standing on a pedestal two steps ahead of me, and is stretching her hand towards me. 'How long are you going to stay down there, bozo? If you can't climb this pedestal, how will you ever be able to hold my hand?'

I woke up with a fright, half an hour before my alarm went off. It was one of the queasiest nights I had spent in recent times. For starters, I had the goosebumps about the interview. Secondly, Kohinoor had unsettled me by running me through a reality check of life and success. No less than three cups of strong coffee with breakfast could drown my anxiety.

I sped in a cab to office at the time decided with Lekha. I reached the company gate a few minutes earlier than scheduled and was ill-destined to meet Jassi at the parking lot. Seeing me in dapper formals and a cleaner-than-ever look on a Friday, he coned his eyebrows quizzically. 'Oye hero! What's up with the good boy look?'

'I am going to attend a friend's wedding.' I lied helplessly.

'Who in the world gets married at 8 a.m.!' he asked in bewilderment.

'The marriage is at lunch-time,' I explained. 'But it's far from here. So I need to leave now.'

'Aren't you too soberly dressed for a wedding?' he asked suspiciously. 'Why have you worn a white shirt?'

'That's my favourite colour,' I said without making eye contact with him. *Hell, why was Lekha taking so long?*

'And what's that file doing in your hand?' he went on relentlessly. He was caught in the wrong job. He should have been with the CIA.

'I have my friend's wedding gift in it,' I replied. That was the dumbest lie I had ever told.

'Strange!' he mumbled.

'Jassi, why must you always ask so many questions?' I finally reprimanded him.

Thankfully, I saw Lekha coming running towards me, her bike keys dangling from her mouth as she adjusted her hair with her hands.

'All the best!' she said as she handed me the keys and hugged me.

'Why are you wishing him good luck?' Jassi's inquisitiveness shot up exponentially. 'It's his friend who is getting married!'

'Good luck for the long drive on the bike!' I shouted, as I roared the bike's engine to a start and raced away from the scene.

While Flora Fountain was not really far from our office, I had left sufficient buffer time keeping in mind the legendary Mumbai morning traffic. But today, I was in store for something more than just the traffic. I saw hordes of NGO activists lined up on the corners of several city streets, shouting slogans against the sloppy municipal initiatives that were not taking care of the slum-dwellers in Dharavi. I got alarmed. As I went a little ahead, I saw the road was blocked with activists sitting on the road. The cops had placed barricades on the road, and the traffic was being diverted to another route. I could feel my heart throbbing right in my mouth even as I took a sharp

U-turn to the alternate route. I must have driven half a mile into it, only to find the same barricades placed there as well. My hands had now begun to tremble. The traffic was getting increasingly chaotic, and the commuters increasingly irritated. I chased down the third route, then the fourth, and then the fifth. Before I could realise that I had landed myself in this web spun by the activists, the time was well past 10 a.m. At 10.30, I got a call from Bhavna.

'Nakul, we are expecting you since the last half an hour.'

'I'm sorry, Bhavna,' I spoke nervously. 'I am caught in traffic.'

'That's a lame excuse, Nakul,' she scolded gruffly. 'How long are you going to take?'

'I'm afraid I can't say,' I said.

'Very well,' she replied. 'I suggest you retreat from wherever you are, because the interview now stands cancelled.'

'But. . . .'

'No buts, Nakul,' she said sternly. 'Our company doesn't wait for anyone. So long.'

My view was now getting hazy. I'm not sure if it was the smoke emission on the road or my pent-up emotions that were welling up in my eyes. But through that haze, what I could clearly see was a huge hoarding put up by the activists, with their chief's mega-size poster on it. Through the picture, his eyes met mine, and his face twisted into a sadistic grin. Below his poster, were the words written in gigantic font:

IF YOU DON'T HELP THE SOCIETY PROSPER, YOU CAN NEVER PROSPER EITHER!

He kept grinning at me with his whole heart. He had reiterated his promise and proved to me that he was right. He had had the last laugh.

Smart Ass

After about a month's turmoil, I finally smiled the sunshine S-M-I-L-E. All thanks to a late night phone call that asked me to finally pack my bags for a flight to London in forty-eight hours.

'That's sudden!' I cried.

'This company is always full of surprises,' Cheapo said.

I called up Kavya excitedly and informed her of the development.

'I'm so happy,' she squealed. 'Let's cancel the plan of that house on Bandstand. I now want a house in Wimbledon that overlooks the tennis courts!'

'One step at a time, please,' I laughed, struggling to dump my belongings randomly into my suitcase. 'I have not yet set foot there.'

'When is your flight?'

'Tomorrow night,' I said. 'Sorry, we didn't get time to meet.'

'No problem,' she said. 'I'll come to Mumbai tomorrow and see you off.'

'Just a caveat,' I warned, 'my parents will be coming too.'

'So what? You can introduce me as a "good friend".'

'Fine,' I said. 'I think I'll meet you directly at the airport.'

Kohinoor stood a few feet away, waiting patiently for my conversation to end. He had something tightly clasped in his hand.

'Yes, Kohinoor?'

'Brother, this is my farewell gift to you.'

I was moved. 'Thanks, buddy. But it's not farewell. I am just going for six months.'

It was an envelope with a letter in it.

Dear brother, you are leaving tomorrow,
Knowing this, my heart's filled with sorrow.
But I am happy that you have finally
Discovered your sunshine S-M-I-L-E.

I wish you all the very best in life,
May you get a beautiful English wife.
But always remember me when you are in need,
I'll prove to you that I am a friend indeed.

Guilt churned up within me. I had always only found reasons to be annoyed with Kohinoor, but my selfishness never allowed me to see the goodness in him. It was a mistake I'd committed much too often in life, and probably one that a lot of us commit: we get so obsessed with the desire to draw love from a long-sealed well that we tend to ignore the vast ocean of love that beckons us. But twenty-four hours before my flight, all I could do was hug him and let him know that I acknowledged and respected the gesture.

'But I don't want an English wife,' I complained.

'Oh, no problem,' he assured me. 'You can have more sexy fun if you are a bachelor there.'

'Sexy fun?'

He paused and then fidgeted with embarrassment. 'I mean, naughty things. . . .'

'Ah, I see,' I exclaimed. 'Thanks for the tip, I'll keep it in mind!'

I went to sleep that night with a stomach full of butterflies, which were not entirely because I was going abroad for the first time. My anxiety was more because mom told me that an entire platoon of my relatives was coming to see me off at the airport the next day. For the sake of my peace of mind, I assumed she was kidding. But the fear of a family drama embarrassing me to death at the airport stirred me up no end.

The next evening, I met Kavya at the airport more than four hours before the departure. That left us with some time out before my parents would meet us. We took a corner table at a cake shop near the departure terminal.

'You are dressed very sparsely,' I commented quietly, examining her near-see-through netted sleeveless top and denim shorts that were shorter than short.

'Yeah, but isn't that how you like me?' she hummed, playing footsie with me.

'Don't!' I admonished, pushing her foot away. 'Mom and dad could be here anytime.'

'So what?' she asked. 'Anyway, it's time now that they know about us.'

'It is?' I asked, bewildered.

'Of course, honey,' she said. 'Now that you are going to London, you can also start analysing the prospects of us settling down there in a while. Then I can also mention about us to dad.'

'What does my going to London have to do with your talking to your dad?'

'It's an indicator that you are settling well in life,' she replied promptly. 'And that we are fit to get married.'

'And if I stay put, just the way I have been?' I asked bitterly.

'Come on, sweetie,' she placed her hand on my cheek. 'Why are you getting me all wrong?'

'No, tell me,' I said, pushing her hand away. 'I want to know.'

'Look Nakul, I know we have discussed this before and it has offended you then as well. But all my parents want is that after I get married, I see the same affluence and comfort that I have seen all my life.'

'So you will be ready to push me to the wall so that I fit the family bill, won't you?'

'Stop it, please,' she raised her voice. 'You know I have been coaxing you into doing better only so that when you meet my parents, I don't want them to say anything we would not want to hear. I am scared, Nakul.'

I hugged her for the last time before I flew out, but I felt my grip on the hug a little slippery. If love were to be understood by its literary definition, we were far from being in love. For love was always supposed to be unconditional, wasn't it? Then what were her Daddy Dearest and his list of good-boy-parameters doing between us? I should have felt repelled after what she just told me. But her ever-lovable scent and the brush of her soft face against mine simply knocked me off all sanity and logic as always.

That hug might have lasted for hours or maybe for just a few seconds, I do not know. I was lost in another world, another time zone, and was woken up only when my phone beeped with dad's message, informing me that they would reach the airport in another ten minutes.

'Let's head back to the front gate,' I told Kavya, releasing myself unwillingly from the grip. 'Folks are on their way.'

'I am so excited to meet them!' she beamed.

We stood at the departure gate for about twenty minutes before a noisy Matador came to a screeching halt in the parking space. Noisier than the engine though were the passengers of the vehicle: an infinite number of middle-aged aunties playing *antakshari*. Evidently, they knew nothing about harmony, and worse, their high pitches emanated in unison through the half-open windows of the Matador, commanding eyeballs from all over the airport.

'Look at that bunch of noisy women!' Kavya laughed.

'Those noisy women are my relatives,' I hung my head abashedly. 'Welcome to the family!'

Kavya's face turned pink with embarrassment. 'I am so sorry, I didn't mean offence. Which one of these is Aunty?'

'The one who is half a degree quieter than the others.' I pointed at mom as the passengers began getting down from the vehicle. Even now some of the unrelenting aunties were still at their singing. 'And there, the quietest of all, standing in the blue shirt, is dad. Go and wish them.'

'Can I?'

'Of course,' I said, pushing her forward. 'But just take extra comments and whispers from relatives with a pinch of salt, please.'

'Don't worry, I understand.'

Kavya strode confidently towards dad, with me in tow, hiding my blushing face behind her.

'Good evening, uncle!' she bowed in greeting. 'I am Kavya, Nakul's friend.'

I wished she would not bow too much, for some of my curious aunts had already made Kavya the object of their interest, and were examining the tattoo on her lower back. The design got a rather disparaging look from one of them. If I were to have my say, I loved that tattoo. But who was going to listen to my opinion anyway?

'Good evening, Kavya.' Dad patted her on the head. 'It's so nice to see you.'

She then turned to mom, who was flanked by her trusted lieutenants, Bindiya *maasi* and . . . gosh, why do I always forget the other one's name? I was prepared to see mom throw a fit, but was pleasantly taken aback by the contrary. mom held her hand and kissed it.

'You are so pretty, beta!'

Kavya gushed with pride. I guess any girl was fine with mom as long as I was willing to get married.

Mom turned to me. 'Look, son, we were all so excited about your going abroad that half the family has come to see you off!'

I examined the bevy that comprised a couple of *chachis*, a couple of *maamis* and half a dozen *maasis*.

'They came all the way to Baroda and then took the train with us,' mom added.

'I am touched.' I looked at all of them and nodded respectfully.

I then turned to dad and met him in the eye. He looked at me with a hassled expression. Dad and I had an amazing chemistry, and I am sure he understood my I-know-what you-have-gone-through expression. Now, just when I was about to heave a sigh of relief for no display of histrionics on seeing Kavya, one of my *chachis* threw in the first bomber.

'Look at her knickers!' she whispered rather loudly, in true blue Punjabi accent. 'They are so short!'

My legs began to tremble and I could feel beads of sweat running all over me.

'And did you see her top?' another one commented. 'Low cut!'

I wished the earth below me would cave in. Or I could hold the pilot at gunpoint and force him to get my plane to take off immediately . . . I knew Kavya could hear all the comments a few feet away, but she chose to ignore them and kept talking to dad nonchalantly.

I walked up to the gang of girls. 'Aunty, please. Kavya can hear all of you.'

'Tell me *na*, Nakul,' one of them persisted, 'do you like her?'

'Yes,' I replied, as briefly as possible.

'*Hawww*!' She was aghast. 'But look at her clothes!'

'There's something beyond those clothes also, isn't there?' I retorted.

'You've seen that also?' another one shouted.

'Please,' I said. 'That's not what I meant. Mom, please, what's happening?'

Thankfully, mom intervened. 'My son is going tonight. Don't spoil his mood.'

She came forth and lovingly hugged me goodbye, and then whispered in my ear. 'But to tell you the truth, I don't like that butterfly on her back.'

'That's a tattoo,' I sighed.

'Whatever that is,' she said. 'Anyway, it's a small thing and can be sorted out. Otherwise it's a go-ahead from me. Take dad's approval now.'

That was not a big deal. I was pretty convinced I would get the nod from dad, though he was not much into tattoos either. I spoke to my parents briefly, amidst intermittent questions from my aunts on what kind of accommodation I was to get there, whether my roommates would be all guys, and if relatives could come there on unending tourist visas. Kavya waited patiently for mom and dad to bid me goodbye before she accompanied me till ten steps ahead, just before I was to enter the check-in area. The next step was going to be a heavy one and I was not quite able to take it. John Denver's *Leaving on a Jet Plane* lyrics sailed through my mind in a painful melody. I wanted to say something mushy, but I could see the platoon of relatives gazing at me a few feet behind.

'I'm going to miss you,' I said after an awkward moment of silence.

She refused to let go of my hand. 'I hate this moment.'

'So do I,' I said, clutching her hand firmly.

'Come back soon,' she said, planting a kiss on my cheek. This was right in view of a dumbstruck audience in my family, and I can swear I heard all of them moan and grumble in chorus. But this time I chose not to look behind and ran towards the check-in line.

For the long duration that I stood with my luggage trolley in the line, I must have turned to look back at my parents and Kavya every alternate second – to see their faces beaming with pride. Strange as it might be, our society never ceases to associate a foreign work permit and a work stint abroad with an individual's success meter. For my own sake too, I was glad I was going, not so much for the excitement of visiting a new country as much for the prospect of gaining some value at work after all.

'Good evening, Mr. Kapoor,' the highly affable attendant at the desk addressed me when my turn arrived. 'May I have your photo ID please?'

I started fishing for my photo ID in my wallet when my phone rang. It must have rung about ten to twelve times before I could pick it. *Chirayu calling*, it displayed. I cut the phone.

'Those two to be checked in, please,' I said to the attendant, pointing at two huge luggage pieces I thumped on to the belt.

Chirayu called again. I picked it up this time, wondering what the emergency was.

'Nakul, where are you?' he asked.

'At the check-in counter,' I replied. 'Just proceeding for immigration.'

'Hold on, hold on,' he said. 'There might be some updates.'

This was unreal, man! I was in no mood for an anticlimax now. I had Kavya watching me from the gate, I had my parents waving me goodbye, and they had brought me an entire battalion of relatives who sang me *In the Wink of an Eye* with their whole heart and volume right there at the airport gate to bid me farewell. And now this jerk wanted to give me updates.

'What updates now, Chirayu?' I seethed. 'I am in the line. Others are waiting.'

'Get out of the line and wait for my call,' he said quickly and hung up. I was stunned.

'What's up, Mr. Kapoor?' the cheery attendant asked.

'I don't know,' I mumbled. 'I'll get back to you.'

Cheapo called back in two minutes. 'Nakul, your requirement has been put in abeyance for now. Stay offshore until further communicated to.'

'But. . . . '

'But what?' he asked rudely.

'My luggage has already crossed the belt,' I attempted.

'Retrieve it then,' he said. 'And let's have a word once you get back to office. These things happen. The client suddenly held a review meeting and decided they didn't want to incur expenses on another onsite resource at the moment.'

I didn't reply. I simply disconnected the call and brought my luggage back. When I retreated towards the gate, I could sense curious whispers amongst my relatives, a tinge of anguish in my parents' eyes, and disappointment in Kavya's. But I somehow couldn't gather the courage to look them in the face.

'What happened, Golu?' Kavya asked once I came out.

'You asked me to come back soon, didn't you?' I said, trying my level best to smile. 'This was thirty minutes too soon!'

My parents looked at me with a pitiful expression, which is something I just can never take. There was a clucking of tongues among the aunts. I contained myself and smiled to them.

'Plan cancelled for now,' I smiled. 'You can all probably plan an excursion trip near Mumbai some place.'

'We only want to be with you, Nakul,' dad said, holding my hand. 'We want to spend time talking to you.'

I looked the other side. Mom placed her hand on my shoulder. 'Whatever happens, we are always happy as long as you are happy.'

'I know,' I said, still looking the other side. 'Mom, why don't you all retire to the hotel for now? I'll come and see you in a few hours.'

They readily agreed, without too many questions this time. So that part was taken care of. I now turned to Kavya, who was almost ready to cry, God knows why. Today, at least, was my turn.

'What the hell was that?' Kavya finally asked. 'Is this how a top performer in your company is treated?'

'Good, isn't it?' I smiled. 'You got the demo.'

'Nakul, this can't continue. We can't think of settling down until you get settled yourself first.'

'I am settled,' I defended. 'These things happen. Don't I have a job? Come on, Kavya. You're making it sound like I am a wastrel or something.'

'It's not that,' she answered. 'But Nakul, let's get real. A marriage is not just about the union of two people. There are responsibilities that come with it, and unfortunately I don't see that stability in your career which gives me the assurance I need.'

'You're being incoherent,' I said, not ready to believe what I was hearing. 'Come, let's go sit somewhere and talk.'

I walked a few steps towards the taxi stand, and then turned behind to see her standing at the same place, motionless and expressionless.

'What?' I asked, irritated.

She didn't reply.

'So should I interpret your silence as something I would not want to hear?'

She turned the other way, still not willing to reply. I walked out on her. Or it was rather the other way round, I tried not to care any more. I plunked myself in, and as the car swerved out of the parking, I looked back to check if Kavya was still standing there. She was gone.

I headed to the office. The airport fiasco was very embarrassing and I truly felt Cheapo Chaudhary owed me an explanation for that. I got the explanation sooner than I thought when my phone rang as my cab buzzed around the traffic.

'Nakul Kapoor,' Cheapo sang in a rather caustic, sarcastic tone. 'The Smart Alec of my team! So how does it feel to be a hapless loser?'

How does it feel? How about I cut off your balls and put them through a paper shredder? You'll know how it feels.

'Those are not gentle words, Chirayu,' I said.

'You are talking about words, you twerp?' Chirayu shouted. 'I should actually be doing worse. You think you are too smart, eh?'

'What's wrong?' I asked nervously, trying in vain to stop my limbs from trembling.

'I know what you talk about me behind my back, you swine!' he barked. 'If you think you are so smart, reach where I am and then let's talk!'

I went into a spin. I must be dreaming. How did this little truth about my hatred for him reach him? I pinched myself awake. No, the call was still on.

'Now you see what I do,' he threatened, 'I am going to show you your true place.'

'Chirayu, let's discuss this at peace, please. . . .'

'Shut up, Nakul,' he said, 'and just plan on how you can save your career here. For your own sake, you'd better pray you get your goddamn banking job soon. For if you don't shove out of here, I'm going to make life hell for you.'

The banking job scoop should have given me the lead. I remembered Vishal's 'eagles in the air' warning, and instantly understood that it was our company's most notorious eagle, Jassi, who must have blabbered in front of Cheapo. I recalled the way I spoke a mouthful about Cheapo in the cafeteria a few months back right in front of Jassi. Lekha had warned me of its repercussions then, which were working their ill-effects on me today. I made a mental note to pay Jassi a visit on my way back from office to give him a piece of my mind, and if my energy permitted me, also to break a few of his bones.

I entered office at an opportune time of the night, when most of the office was empty, and the lights had been put off. Pretty convenient, I'd say, for I could howl and cry all I want, and the sounds of my distress would only ricochet against the wall. I went to my cubicle and did the needful. There, that felt better. But I was not ready yet to go and face my family in the hotel, so I decided to spend some time alone, trying to convince myself that the situation was not as bad as I was making it out to be. I opened my laptop and decided to check all my junk mails. And the first thing that caught my eye in the inbox is something I will not forget for the rest of my life. It was an email from Chirayu Chaudhary titled *Smart Ass*.

Nakul, you smart ass,

In case you are wondering where you bungled up and hit an axe in your own foot, refer to the mail below. I am grateful and you will surely be spiteful. But maybe jerks like you ought to learn their lessons the hard way. Be prepared to get screwed.

Chirayu

I read the mail chain below:
From: Vishal Tiwari
Sent: 29 August 2008 12:45 p.m.
To: Chirayu Chaudhary
Subject: Why Nakul shouldn't be called onsite.

For a brief moment, I felt compelled to slam my laptop screen shut. I was petrified to read the contents of the mail, because I was not quite willing to accept the level of betrayal I was going to witness. But the rapier of betrayal is lethal anyway, whether it stabs you in the front or in the back. Taking it in the face is a better bet, for if you turn your back to it, it kills you a million times over.

Hi Chirayu,

In view of the current project execution status, I think calling another resource onsite is an unnecessary overhead. All the deliverables alongside our meetings are being handled quite comfortably and an extra resource will be a waste of our time because we will have to acquaint him with the modalities of work here, when actually both of us can handle everything by ourselves.

I believe you plan to call Nakul onboard, but I must inform you that he has recently expressed his desire to quit Bytesphere and join a banking job. His motivation level is low and bringing him onsite might be a risk as we would not know how long he will be willing to stick around.

The other reason, though I hate bringing this up, is that he doesn't feel very comfortable working with you. I sense some friction of sorts, which I have derived from my discussions with him. In such a scenario, I am not sure if he will be able to appreciate the arrangement of working under your directives. Please read below an excerpt of my discussion with him not too long ago:

Nakul: Beware, London! The dumb coot is arriving. . . . ☺
Vishal: What? As in?
Nakul: Arre baba, I'm talking about this item called Cheapo Chaudhary going global. I wonder what he'll babble in front of the client. What say?
Vishal: I wouldn't bother discussing these frivolities as long as my work isn't affected. Anyway, who are we to comment on his productivity? He has reached a level where his capability can't be questioned.
Nakul: What's wrong with you?
Vishal: Nothing, in fact am surprised to find myself a little happier now. I feel I've got some work now.
Nakul: I'm happy to hear that, dude! I really am. Keep that cheerfulness on.
Vishal: Yup
Nakul: But still, how did that backless pachyderm get so high in his career? He's a bird brain, yaar!
Vishal: Chuck it, na. To each his own.
Nakul: True. Oh, by the way, I am seriously contemplating a job change now.

Vishal: Is it? When did you decide?
Nakul: I've not decided yet, I am still considering. I do feel now that things are getting very mundane out here.
Vishal: So have you applied anywhere?
Nakul: Not yet, but I'm planning to talk to a friend from college who works with InvestZone bank in Delhi. I heard there are some openings.

Please don't bear any grudge in your mind. Nakul is a highly capable resource, and I am sure he is very efficient in terms of handling the entire offshore team there. But maybe bringing him here at this point of time will not be the wisest move to make. It will also hamper the productivity of the team there. So do consider your decision.

I also request you to please not inform Nakul that I have discussed this with you as I share an excellent rapport with him and I don't want him to mistake my suggestion for anything inappropriate. This, I feel, is in his career interests too.

Regards,
Vishal

I read the mail over and over again, with an insatiable thirst to drink in every nasty word he had written soaked in sugar syrup. I safely vaulted every syllable of this mail in the archives of my memory so that I would be cautioned each time I decided to trust someone again. I could not cry any more, for I had already exhausted my tear glands. I could not shout, for my tongue was dry and parched. I could only manage the expression of a zombie as I stared blankly at my computer screen, until I felt a hand on my shoulder.

'I have nothing to say,' Lekha whispered in my ear as she took me in an embrace, 'except that I am there for you.'

'Even Kavya walked out on me,' I said, beginning to break down again.

'I said, I am there for you,' Lekha repeated.

I was surprised to find solace in Lekha's muscular arms, of all people. Maybe it was because I never got physically that close to her or maybe that the rest of the world felt so ugly right now, but tonight I sensed Lekha's beauty for the first time. Alright, so she loved riding her Pulsar, she wore men's deodorants and her biceps were bigger than mine. But anatomically she was still a girl, wasn't she? What was more, she was the only person tonight whom I could share my deepest fears with. Call it the rebound effect if you please, but getting a girl's affection no sooner than being jilted by another was a situation too comforting to be denied.

'Thanks Lekha,' I said. 'That felt good.'

'What?' She teasingly nudged my arm.

'I mean, thanks for being there,' I said and laughed awkwardly.

'I will, always,' she said. 'Only now I have to go home because it is late. I'll see you at work tomorrow.'

'Yeah, sure.'

'And don't worry about all this,' she advised. 'Everyone goes through chaos some time or the other in life.'

Saying so, she walked away, reminding me of Payal's sketch on *Eric in Chaos*. Understanding art was still impossible for me, but tonight I could finally understand the essence behind her sketch. I forked out her number from my mobile that mom had thrust into my message inbox before forcing me to speak to her as a 'courtesy call' less than a month ago.

'Hi Payal, I hope I am not disturbing you.'

'Hey, good to hear from you,' she said. 'What's up?'

'Nothing, just wanted to know what's happening with Eric,' I said. 'Have you shaped the sketches well yet?'

'Status quo,' she replied. 'I'm short of ideas to complete the series.'

'Do you think I can have a peek into your completed sketches?' I asked.

'Only on the condition that you help me complete the series,' she demanded.

'OK, I will,' I said.

'Wow! How come the sudden interest? You said then that you weren't remotely connected to art.'

'I still am not,' I replied. 'But I feel the connect to your theme.'

'How come?'

'Because I am Eric,' I said.

A World of Jackals

There is succour in strife, especially if the strife has been so painful that you are sure it can't get any worse. Then germinates a fighter in you, who prompts you to give back to the world in double measure what the world has dished out to you. After days of gloom, I returned to office with that fighter's vengeance, and I could feel that extra bounce in my gait as I barged right into the conference room to dial Vishal on a Monday morning.

'Bro!' I heard Vishal's extra cheery voice on the line. He had never sounded so happy. 'Where and how have you been?'

'I'm alive,' I said, 'if that answers your question.'

'What?' he asked. 'You sound kind of harried.'

'Oh, do I?' I mocked. 'That's a news flash!'

'Nakul . . . Nakul, what's the matter?'

'Don't act fake, Vishal,' I shouted. 'I know everything. So, over with the crappy acting.'

'I . . . I didn't get you. . . .'

'Oh, you very much did, Vishal,' I shouted louder. 'You are a rat. A fucking rat! You told on me, didn't you, you juvenile rascal?'

'No . . . no, Nakul, you must be mistaken!' he stammered. 'I haven't. . . .'

'Shut up!' I was screaming now. 'It's all out there in black and white, you pimp! You are nothing but Cheapo's stooge. And you thought I would never find out?'

'Nakul, I can explain,' he said calmly.

'Oh yes, you anyway have to,' I jeered. 'I can't wait to hear your explanation. So what was it – a mermaid swam out of the Thames and hacked into your account, did she?'

'No, it was me,' he said, still trying desperately to compose himself. 'But what you see is not all what is meant to be.'

'Yeah? Then what is it? Come on tell me, I am all ears.'

'Nakul, you can't imagine how difficult things are actually getting out here,' Vishal began. 'Working with Cheapo in a team of two is very tough. And knowing your hatred for him, I just knew you would not be able to tolerate it.'

'So you were willing to sacrifice for me?' I laughed. 'That's very touching, jackass!'

'I just thought working as a lead from offshore would at least give you better leeway and a sense of independence,' he said.

'And a directive to keep our phones on mute and only finish the mechanical work, eh?'

'Nakul, you are a lead there,' he stressed on the word 'lead' as if I had been made Bytesphere's Bishop. 'Here, I am living the life of a wretch.'

'OK, bunk that,' I said. 'Tell me what made you forward our chat transcript to Cheapo? What part of your benevolent plan was that?'

'See, I just wanted him to know that you were keen on looking for another job,' he struggled for the right words to lie. 'Because if he would bring you here, your job search back in India would have got stalled.'

'That's mighty thoughtful of you.'

'I'm serious,' he continued. 'In fact, now even I agree with you that it is time to look out. It's been quite a few months here and I think I am well settled now. So I plan to call Anita and my son here. Very soon, I might quit and try joining Britcell in an operational role.'

'Excellent!' I said. 'I wish you had written this to me. And I know the reason you didn't want me to come to London.'

'And what is that?' he asked.

'You were insecure, that's what,' I said. 'I was, after all, a competitor to you, and not a friend. And you wanted all the limelight to yourself.'

He was unmoved. 'Who doesn't want the limelight, Nakul? A day comes when you need to break free and fly. And in doing so, sometimes you have to forgo your personal emotions. You have always been like a kid brother to me, buddy. But I have my family to look after too, and I have a set of dreams. As a big brother would, I only want you to know that I have always wished well for you, and am always there to help you. . . .'

'Hey, big brother,' I interrupted him. 'Up yours!'

I banged the phone and stormed out of the room.

Lekha Rao's smile was not exactly something that could start off the second Trojan War, but it had surely begun to lift my spirits. Her friendly slap on the back when I entered the cubicle was the most striking antithesis there could be to my discussion with Vishal.

'Welcome back!' she said.

'Thanks.'

'You look like you haven't eaten for years,' she remarked. 'You've lost a lot of weight in these last few days.'

'So that's nice, isn't it?' I smiled.

'No, it isn't,' she scolded me. 'And from today, you are having lunch with me – no arguments.'

'As you say,' I said.

'I have prepared lunch for both of us today.'

Now just when I was beginning to consider that to be really sweet of her, she added, 'Boiled spaghetti and soya soup – it's good for the health.'

I cringed internally, but still accepted. 'OK, I'm sure I'll love it.'

A mail from Payal titled 'This is how the story begins' sat in my mailbox, occupying half the size of my inbox. I clicked on its attachment to view the contents. They were four images zipped into a folder. I opened and examined each image one by one. Each one was a scanned copy of a sketch, below which was written a brief description of the scene in exquisite calligraphy.

A team stands afar, with a mission to conquer a pinnacle, only the tip of which can be vaguely seen at the horizon. The path to the pinnacle is unknown, but the team claims its spirit is high and its determination strong. Eric is one of the many team members who have held hands and are gearing up to embark on the mission.

As the 'team' moves a step closer to the destination, the view of the pinnacle gets clearer and more alluring. The prospect of reaching it and taking in the view of the world from that height is enticing, and the prospect of having to share the space on the narrow edge of that peak is unnerving. All hands are freed and each person makes a dash for the goal – each man for himself.

Eric is a lamb who struggles to survive in a world of jackals. By the time he can realise that the team's mission has converted into a full-blown race, several people have

zoomed right past him, leaving him behind in confusion. Even his most trusted comrade, Derek, now views him as a competitor and busies himself with devising plans to get rid of him. For running fast is not sufficient to ensure that you win the race. You also need to ensure that the others are pushed as far behind as possible.

Eric is in chaos. He falls prey to the trap and reaches no man's land. But he must understand that this is the worst that can happen to him in this race. He thinks he is lost. He stares listlessly at a signpost that shows four arrows in different directions, clueless as to which arrow he must follow. A tornado is blowing over his head, ready to fling him away. But he must remember that the world is round, and everything in life goes a full circle. He can choose any of the options at this chaotic crossroad, and he can be assured that he will be able to make his way back. It's a long walk, but the destination is still within bounds.

Kudos to Payal Saxena! She had hit me bang on the head with her artistic view of life and the chaos it had to offer. But hello, what's the solution to the chaos? Or maybe, the solution is indeed so undefined that she could not articulate it well enough. She conveniently rounded it off by telling me that the world is round. Very well, that makes sense, I thought. Eric would rather blindly choose one of the paths and get back on the race track, rather than brooding his head off in no-man's-land.

I was thrilled to find a striking similarity between Eric's chaos and the chaos I had landed myself in. In the weeklong hibernation that I had gone into following my unpleasant encounter with Cheapo, all that I had done was to stare at the signpost. The arrows pointed to directions I could not comprehend, and I had almost submitted myself to the direction in which the tornado flung me.

But now I knew that this was not meant to be. I had to retrace my steps. I had to fight. I had to provide a solution to Eric's chaos, rather than seeking it from Payal. And I would, if it weren't for Lekha's lunchtime alarm.

'Let's go,' she ordered, shutting my laptop.

'That's cute,' I said and patted her on the head. 'The way you show you care.'

I was going nuts due to the stress. I was beginning to find her bossy stunts cute. I also found her bland spaghetti and soya soup as good as ambrosia.

'The food is great!' I said.

'Thanks,' she replied. 'I'm so happy you are getting back to your own self.'

'The wounds will take time to heal,' I said. 'But yes, I can feel it. I am coming back.'

'It's hard to believe that Vishal could be such a. . . . '

'There's no point thinking about that now,' I stopped her. 'He has done the damage and I have learnt my lesson the hard way. Now I only need to figure out how to come out of this mess.'

'It's a deep mess, Nakul,' Lekha said. 'I'm afraid it's not going to be easy to come out of. Cheapo can be nasty.'

'It's not easy, but it is possible,' I countered. 'For everything in life goes a full circle, Lekha. There will be a way out.'

'What do you plan to do?' she asked.

'I don't know yet,' I replied. 'But I will do something.'

'All I can say,' she said, 'is that I will be with you throughout.'

Saying so, she bent forward and kissed my forehead. And while I was quite pleased by her gesture, I secretly prayed she wouldn't do this, as I was still steeling myself against my first heartbreak and was not sure if I was ready to jump into another cycle of romance. But once the walls of a heart are weakened, they become so porous that even a whiff of affection permeates in like a gush of insane emotions, sweeping you off all your sensibilities. There is a fine line that divides friendship and love, and I was walking that line. It was up to me to not cross the line. But I was getting tipsy and could hardly keep balance. The view of that line was getting blurred by the day.

Payback Time

Nothing could get me happier than word being conveyed of Cheapo missing from work. It had been a week, and no one was aware of his whereabouts. To my mind, this news called for celebration, but I wanted to make sure before I partied, so I made some enquiries. Vishal and the client stakeholders had been trying his phone frantically for many days but to no avail. Vishal went to his apartment in South Hall, but there was nobody at home. His landlord was questioned too, but he did not really care. In fact he was reportedly relieved to know that Cheapo was missing because he had made his life really miserable by paying monthly rents in weekly instalments. The last option was to check if Cheapo had come back to India for some reason, but we couldn't do that either, because we did not know whom to check with.

I was ecstatic. My mind began throwing up fantastical ideas as to what might have happened. I suddenly wanted to believe in ghosts and witchcraft, and I desperately hoped someone had done voodoo on him and made him disappear. Or maybe an evil witch kidnapped him and drove him away on her broomstick, so she could use his enormously chubby body for ten hearty meals. How I wish! For all I knew, he might have been lying sloshed somewhere in some strip club and forgotten his way home. Nonetheless, even a temporary respite from him was heartily welcome. Only, now Vishal would be the stand-in reporting manager, and I hated that.

'Nakul, I want everyone from offshore to join the call five minutes before the regular time,' Vishal called and explained. 'I have some quick instructions for everyone.'

'I don't have the time,' I replied curtly. 'I am busy. I have to go take some interview. I won't even be able to attend the daily meeting.'

'Oh, I see,' he mused. 'OK, I have no issues with that.'

What the hell! I didn't even ask him for his permission, or if he had any issue with it. His position was indeed getting to his head now and his behaviour was going par tolerance.

'What interview, by the way?' he asked after a short pause.

'There's a new applicant,' I replied as briefly as possible. 'Anand asked me to interview her.'

'That's really cool, Nakul,' he said. 'Look, you are getting noticed there.'

'Off with it,' I got ruder. 'Come to the point.'

'Actually, I need your help,' he said sheepishly. 'Julian has asked for some inputs on launching their mobile phone campaigns to target market segments. Julian is the marketing solution head for Britcell. . . .'

'Yeah I know who Julian is,' I cut him short. 'I'll call him and discuss later in the day.'

'No, no. We have to follow Chirayu's reporting structure, remember? All communication with the client is to be routed through either him or through me.'

'So do one thing then,' I said. 'Help yourself to the problem and give him your own goddamn inputs.'

'Oh come on, buddy,' he laughed shamelessly. I felt like slapping him for calling me his buddy. 'How long will you keep sulking over that small episode? I am taking your help only because I know you have a good understanding of the campaign functionality.'

'OK fine, speak up,' I said. 'But make it really quick.'

'See, Julian told me they are seeking to build a market segment to target their new handset at. All customers in this segment must receive the advertisement for this handset through a campaign launched via Xabre.'

'It's simple,' I said. 'Just build the segment in Xabre and attach it to the campaign. Then launch the campaign through the email channel and the vendor should be able to send the campaign content to all customers within the market segment on their email addresses.'

'No, that's the problem,' Vishal said. 'He has actually specified that the campaign be launched through the SMS channel, and not the email channel. And we don't have the vendor facility within the SMS channel.'

'So what? We can. . . .' I suddenly stalled on my advice. What the hell was I doing? This was a golden opportunity for me to not only find my way back to the race track, but also to zip past Vishal. He was a dud when it came to the campaign functionality. And I, like the nice moron that I am, was helping him with each step of the solution!

'Yeah, you are right,' I said after some thought. 'There is no vendor facility within the SMS channel in Xabre.'

'So is this out of testing scope, you mean to say?' he sought to confirm.

'Yes, it's out of scope,' I lied. 'You can't launch a campaign when there is no vendor to send out the collateral. So the SMS channel does not have this capability.'

'Gosh, that's bad,' Vishal said. 'Julian told me this was a really important functionality that should be part of their business processes. Its absence might be quite an impact on them.'

'What a pity, I know.' I smiled to myself.

'So should I reply to him saying this cannot work in the current environment?'

'Yes.'

'I hope you are sure, Nakul,' Vishal said nervously. 'Because if they find out later that I was wrong, they'll have my neck for it.'

'Relax,' I said. 'You can have my word for it.'

'Sorry if I'm sounding nervous,' he said, 'but my rapport with Julian is really important. If I want to join Britcell someday, he is my gateway.'

'Oh, I see. Don't worry,' I said, now grinning a wide, devilish grin. 'You can trust me.'

'OK then,' he said. 'I'll reply to him in the negative.'

'Will you mark me on the mail as well?' I asked.

'I don't think that's needed,' he said with an air of undue confidence. 'What say?'

'Yeah, I don't think so either,' I said.

Wonderful, idiot! This is what I was hoping to hear. Now I'll fix you tonight. All the best.

'Thanks man,' Vishal said.

'No problem,' I said. 'I got to go now. I have another call waiting for me. Bye.'

I picked up the other line.

'Hi sweets,' Shirley spoke from the reception. She sounded hot even on call. 'There is a candidate for an interview here, by the name of Mehek Gupta.'

'Yeah, send her to my floor,' I said. 'Third cubicle from the right.'

'By the way,' she cooed next. 'It looks like you are forgetting something.'

'What?'

'You had promised long ago that you would come home some time. I'm still waiting.'

'I'll come some day.'

'Tomorrow?'

'I can't commit like this.'

'No, tomorrow evening it is,' she insisted. 'Otherwise you'll slip away again.'

'OK, I'll tell you by today evening,' I promised. 'Now please send Mehek upstairs.'

In about five minutes, a bright pair of eyes covered by thin-rimmed glasses greeted me cheerfully. She was a short girl, and only her face just about stuck over the edge of my cubicle wall. She rested her chin on the wall rather casually as she spoke to me, and somehow I sensed an odd familiarity in her appearance.

'You must be Mehek?' I asked, extending my hand.

'Yes, hello sir,' she replied, polite but confident.

'Our company's culture is to address everyone by first name,' I said. 'And I'm not that senior anyway.'

'Alright then,' she smiled, 'I'll keep it Nakul.'

'Good,' I smiled back. 'Please proceed to the meeting room at the end of the corridor. I'll join you there in a minute.'

When I got up and watched her walk towards the meeting room, I noticed her shabby khadi *kurta* and her flat-heeled sandals, which were ready to give way any moment. Her hair was messily tied into a loose bun. And it suddenly struck me – she was the same girl who had met me on the flight to Baroda a few months ago and had relentlessly given me unsolicited advice on how I should serve my countrymen rather than just think of my own interests. It looked like she finally had a chance encounter with life's realities and had decided to walk her way into the corporate world too.

'So, Mehek Gupta,' I said as I took my seat across the table in the meeting room. 'Do you by any chance recognise me?'

'Yes, I do,' she said. 'We met on a flight a few months ago.'

'Good,' I said. 'So I think you might know what my first question to you is going to be?'

She stared at me blankly, but absolutely unfazed by the fact that she was sitting in a tense interview atmosphere.

'I thought I would find you some day as an activist or something,' I laughed. 'What is a person as socially driven as you doing in the office of a company like ours, which is only interested in how much turnover it makes annually?'

'I grew a little more practical, you can say.' She blushed. 'I do understand it's important to make a living for yourself.'

'I'm glad you agree.'

'But I still maintain that you can be of use to the society even alongside the pursuit of your professional aspirations.'

'Keep that thought in abeyance for now,' I suggested. 'For I can promise you that if you come in, you are going to find very little time for your own personal interests, leave alone those of the society.'

She did not argue on that. Instead, she just responded with a stoic expression and a pleasant smile on her face. I asked her detailed questions on her technical expertise, her behavioural and soft skills, and what have you. But at not a single instance did her smile leave her face. And at the end of the interview, I knew she was a clear winner for the job.

'Excellent,' I said admiringly. 'I think we can have you.'

'Thank you.' She beamed.

'I'll get the HR to start your paperwork,' I said. 'You can expect to join from tomorrow itself.'

'That sounds good.'

'Do you have any questions for me?'

'Whom will I be reporting to?' she asked.

'Me.' I smiled. 'I hope that's going to be OK?'

She smiled. 'I'm sure,' she said and took leave of me.

Notwithstanding my miffed opinion of her after our first meeting, I gave her a nine-on-ten recommendation and passed it to Anand for his final approval.

'What's wrong with Kohinoor?' I asked Lekha when I went back to my working pod. Kohinoor sat sullen, his eyes moist as (almost) always.

'His father called,' she replied. 'He was lambasting the poor fellow left, right and centre. It seemed to be some argument over leaving this job and getting back home so that he can join their family business.'

'He needs to get into a good mood. A good movie or a dinner might work well.'

'Yeah, you are right,' she said.

Then, after a moment's thought, I added. 'Would you like to join us?'

'Yeah, why not?' she enthused. 'But I'm kind of broke, so I can't afford a fab place. Does something like *pav bhaji* at Chowpatty excite you?'

'You said it, Kavya!' I gave a high-five, and then suddenly fell quiet. 'Sorry, I meant Lekha. . . .'

She looked me in the eye and smiled. 'Hey, I understand.'

'Yeah,' I mumbled. 'See you tonight. I got to go in for a meeting now.'

'Great,' she said. 'I'm off for the day. Catch you later.'

I went into the conference room and connected to Julian. It was about time Eric played his cards right.

'Hello, this is Julian,' a thick, no-nonsense voice responded to my call after a number of rings.

'Hello, Julian,' I said. 'This is Nakul Kapoor from Bytesphere's testing team in Mumbai.'

'Oh yes, Nakul,' Julian replied. 'I've heard about you. But we haven't interacted before, have we?'

'We sure haven't,' I said. 'But I *do* want to talk to you right now, if you are free.'

'Sure Nakul, go ahead.'

'Julian, I heard you were enquiring on your application's capability to send campaigns to customers through the SMS channel,' I said. 'Is that right?'

'Oh yes,' he said. 'I checked with Vishal from your team on this, but he told me this could not work out in the application.'

'Oh, did he?' I feigned surprise. 'Why is that so?'

'He said there is no vendor facility within the SMS channel to send out the campaigns,' he said. 'I'm not really across the technical nuances of Xabre, so I presume he is right.'

'But that's not true, Julian,' I said as innocently as possible. 'You *can* send campaigns through SMS in Xabre.'

'What? Are you sure?'

'I'm positive,' I affirmed. 'We don't have the vendor facility there, but there is an auto dispatch option that can send an SMS to your customer without vendor intervention. Did Vishal not mention that?'

'No, he didn't.' Julian's pitch was rising in anger. 'I'm very disappointed with him. This could have caused serious business repercussions.'

'I understand,' I said sympathetically. 'But I'm sure it must have just slipped Vishal's mind. He is highly capable otherwise.'

'This was a major slip,' he shot back. 'I had a very high opinion of his capabilities so far. I'm afraid I'll have to reconsider my opinion.'

'So what plan of action do you have on this front now?' I asked eagerly.

'I'll have to think,' he said. 'I've already shared Vishal's response with all stakeholders. Your colleague has very unwittingly put me into an embarrassing position. And this functionality is very important from our point of view, so I'm sure we must talk frankly about it.'

'I think I can help you on this if you like,' I seized the opportunity. 'I am quite comfortable with the processes around this functionality. So maybe I can arrange a demo in the application for all your stakeholders, if that helps?'

'That will be excellent, Nakul,' he said happily. 'When can you do it?'

'As early as tomorrow?'

'Brilliant!' he exclaimed. 'Thanks, Nakul. I wish everyone in your team were as proactive and proficient as you.'

'Thanks for the compliment, Julian.' I punched my fist in the air. 'I'll send you all a meeting invite for the demo. I'll arrange for a video conference.'

'Sure thing, Nakul,' he said. 'Thanks a lot, and have a good day.'

'You too.'

I kept down the phone and looked at my face in the glass wall of the room; my face wore the evilest smile I had ever seen. It gave me a rush of sadistic delight that was more endearing than the most positive of emotions I had ever nurtured in life. I guess such is the intensity with which the devil in you kills your wisdom to differentiate between moral and immoral. Vishal's deeds were going to boomerang on him and I felt victorious.

I pulled out an A4 paper and sketched my response to Payal.

The world indeed is round, and Eric finds his way back. He scoots through a different route that intercept's Derek's path. He has a choice to run now, but the thought of landing Derek in the same chaos is more

exciting than just achieving the pinnacle. He lays a booby trap for Derek and sits to watch the fun. Sure enough, the trap gets Derek – which becomes Eric's point of elation.

I scanned the image and zipped it in an email attachment for Payal. I clicked the 'send' button and instantly felt my entire system getting purged of all the torture it had sustained over the last many days.

'Brother, when can we go home?' Kohinoor asked when I returned to the pod.

'Immediately, bro!' I said. 'Let's leave.'

I saw Shirley sitting at the reception, engrossed in some last minute work before she left for the day.

'Hi Shirley,' I stopped by. 'About coming to your place, I'd love to. But I really don't want to bother you with cooking dinner for me.'

'I wouldn't bother myself,' she chuckled. 'Just come for a cup of coffee.'

'That sounds good,' I said. 'How about Friday night?'

'Aha, perfect!'

'That's a promise,' I said. 'I'll block our calendars!'

I felt a little silly, feeling guilty about accepting Shirley's invite to her place. I mean, I wasn't answerable to anyone anymore, right? Kavya was out of the picture, so I was independent. Then why the hesitation? I decided to tell Lekha I was going to Shirley's on Friday night. Not that it would matter to Lekha, but somehow it felt like the right thing to do. Until next Friday, I met Lekha almost every evening for dinner or a long walk. Life was finally getting back on track and the evenings were beautiful again. I kept telling myself this was not love. They were just a few harmless dinners. But they turned out to be a few dinners too many.

Kisses have Variety

I learnt quite a few basic mantras of success over time, albeit very late in the day. One: if you are squirming for space in a maze of rules and processes, leap out of the maze and mend the rules. You will only be snuffed to death if you stay loyally grounded in the maze. I hence tossed Cheapo's reporting rules into the dustbin and followed my own protocol of communicating with people who would matter in my career development.

Two: If you think you are smart, flaunt yourself. Modesty is a virtue that the modern world hardly recognises. So, yes, I gave that demo to all the stakeholders in Britcell, and I must say, in thorough immodesty that I did a pretty cool job of the whole thing. Suddenly, I had risen from being a nobody to being Britcell's darling.

Three: Nobility is a luxury that few possess. So don't unnecessarily try and be noble if your nobility is killing you. You'd rather be the reactive villain who strikes only if struck at, but with an intensity that your opponent will never forget.

'Nakul and team, this is fantastic stuff,' Julian remarked on one of the daily team calls. 'You guys have turned around the SMS campaign testing fabulously!'

'Thanks, Julian,' I replied. 'It's the result of a lot of hard work put in by my team here.'

'It sure is,' Julian agreed. 'By the way, I have recommended your name to the Bytesphere senior management for the client satisfaction award. Trust me, you deserve it, Nakul.'

'Hey, that's super cool, Julian,' I couldn't contain my joy. 'Thank you!'

'Any time,' he said. 'Anyway, let's get started with the execution updates.'

'Well, we are through with the SMS campaign testing,' I began. Yes, offshore no longer kept its phone on mute. We were free now to be as participative as we wanted. 'We do have two defects in this functionality, but they are low in severity and won't impact business much. . . .'

'I've examined those defects,' Vishal interrupted me, 'and I believe. . . .'

'Hold on, please, Vishal,' Julian snubbed angrily. 'Let Nakul speak. Can you please mute your phone until then?'

Until a few seconds ago, I had thought this was the moment I was waiting for, when Vishal would get back what he had given. But now that it had happened, something about the whole dialogue did not feel right. I wished I could get hold of Adam Sandler's remote control and undo what I had done to Vishal. It's not like I had forgiven him or that I felt sorry for him, but the bitterness that was brewing between us kind of squared off the joy I ought to have felt on receiving the client's accolades.

I'm sorry, I must mention the fourth mantra of success right away: prolonging a personal duel at work is like trying to ignite a used matchstick. It's going to yield nothing and is only likely to burn your finger in the process. My conscience was suddenly more important than my ego and I had to do something about it.

'By the way, Nakul,' Julian's baritone jolted me from my thoughts. 'I have made an interesting recommendation for you to Anand. Do connect with him after this call and let me know what you think.'

'Sure, thanks.'

I went to Anand's den after the call ended. I saw him through the glass door, scratching his ever-growing beard, as though trying to fish something out of it. He had his glasses perched on his nose as usual, and he seemed to be mumbling something to himself when I interrupted him.

'Sir, may I?'

'Yes?'

'I believe Julian Morrison from Britcell discussed something about me with you?'

'Who are you?' He frowned.

What was his problem? How many more knocks on his door did he need to know who I was? Even Dr Manmohan Singh would have remembered my name by now.

'Sir, Nakul Kapoor.'

'New employee?'

This was it. I failed to understand how he could miss a person my size so often, especially when we sat on the same floor.

'No Sir,' I sighed. 'I've met you often before. If you remember, the last time we met, you had suggested I get onto the Java training schedule.'

'Oh yes, yes,' he remembered finally. 'Green checks!'

'Yes Sir, green checks.'

'Tell me, sonny, what can I do for you?' He looked up at me. 'That training's already over.'

'Sir, it's about what Julian Morrison discussed with you about me!'

'Ah, yes,' he said, fishing for something he had scribbled on his notebook. Yes, he still preferred paper sheets over the digital notebook. 'He told me about your performance on the project over the last week, and he is very impressed with the results. He wants you to work in liaison with him for a short assignment – on a contractual basis.'

'That's excellent!' I almost shouted in joy. 'What's the assignment?'

'It's basically the same project that you are working on currently,' he explained. 'Just that it is a small offshoot, and in this case you will be representing the client side in designing their campaigns rather than being in the Bytesphere testing team.'

'That sounds awesome!'

'Yes, it is awesome for sure,' he said. 'In fact, he told me he had initially spoken to Vishal Tiwari for this role. But apparently he has had some unsatisfactory experiences with Vishal in the recent past. So he wanted to know if you would be willing to join him instead.'

'Instead?' I choked on the word. 'Does that mean I'll have to replace Vishal?'

'Yes, that's what "instead" usually means, sonny!' He let out a short grunt which was supposed to be a laugh. 'Why, is there a problem with that?'

'Yes Sir,' I said assertively. 'Vishal is senior to me and is already a strong contender for this assignment.'

'He *was* a strong contender,' Anand said, shaking his head. 'Now he isn't. This is how the game is played. You fall lax for a second, and you lose.'

'No Sir,' I argued. There was no way I could live on with the guilt of screwing Vishal's prospects. 'I don't think we can judge a person's capabilities based on one bad day.'

'I am not doing that,' Anand said, raising his hands. 'But do you expect me to go and offer this advice to the client too? They never give a second chance.'

'Yes Sir, we do need to talk to them on this,' I pleaded. 'Couldn't this have happened to me too, or for that matter to you also? After all, Sir, every dog has its day!'

'Are you calling me a dog?' Anand's eyes went cold.

'No Sir,' I mumbled stupidly. 'I'm sorry, that's not what I meant. But my only request is that we give Vishal a second chance. I can guarantee that he will not let you down.'

'Hmm, OK,' he said, curling a strand of his beard into a tiny ball. 'Let me talk to Julian once again. So are you really willing to forgo this opportunity for Tiwari?'

I gaped at him. 'That's not what I meant.'

'Then what did you mean?' he asked irritably.

'I meant I'll go there too and work with Vishal on this,' I explained. 'We've always been together in a team, and I think it's our synergy that has always helped us deliver good results.'

'Well, I can't promise about both of you being on the same assignment,' Anand considered. 'But I'll talk to Julian nonetheless. But whatever be his response, I must say one thing, Nakul – I am truly impressed by your commitment to our values of team spirit!'

'Thank you, sir.' I smiled. 'Coming from you, it's the biggest compliment I've received so far.'

'You have already shown that your work is exemplary,' he said. 'And now you've also shown what it takes for a team to succeed. I really wish others would take a cue from you.'

'I'll always try my best to keep improving, sir,' I said, trying in vain to look modest. Hell, man, I was on cloud nine!

'You will go places, sonny,' he said, shaking my hands, which were trembling with excitement. 'You are going to be in my radar now, and I want to ensure you move forth with the same zeal.'

'I will do so, sir.'

'By the way, how long have you been here?'

'It's been a year and a half, sir.'

'Let me see if I can put in a word of recommendation during your appraisal,' he said. 'I think you deserve to move up now.'

Finally! There was a ray of hope now after all the smoke. Hopefully, this also meant he would remember my name now on, and that in itself was a big motivation for me. Today, I could smell the success I often dreamt of. Of course, the benchmark to define success keeps getting higher as you move an inch closer to it. But for now, it was reason enough for me to rejoice. And there are no prizes for guessing whom I wanted to celebrate with.

'Lekha.' I ran up to her. 'I think I'm in for a promotion!'

'Damn neat!' She stood up, giving me a high five. 'This calls for a treat!'

'Yeah sure, how about tonight?'

'No, tonight will be difficult,' she said. 'I've already committed to someone for dinner.'

I felt my hackles rise. This last line just murdered all the excitement.

'Oh, I see.' I paused, giving her time to speak further and tell me the name of the jerk.

'I've been postponing it for long now,' she explained, 'but I just couldn't say no today.'

Fine, so she wants to keep it a secret. Fair enough, Nakul. You must know your limits. Don't investigate. . . .

'Friends?' I asked in spite of myself.

'Friend,' she corrected me. *Damn it!* 'Probably one of my closest friends.'

OK, that sent the alarm bells ringing. These 'close friend' variety are the most dangerous ones. They capitalise on some godforsaken gloomy evening when the girl finds only their shoulder to cry on. After that you can do what you please to win her over, but the tell-me-your-sob-story dude always has the first-mover advantage.

Whatever be it, Nakul, don't let the desperation show. Pretend you don't care. . . .

'As in, the "special" kind of close friend?' Shit, the desperation was showing.

'Ahem.' She cleared her throat. 'Someone's getting curious.'

'Ha! Big deal, lady!' I laughed it off. 'Keep your secret to yourself!' *Come off it, just tell me who is he?*

She laughed. 'It's no secret, *baba*, it's just a small dinner! But I'm very happy for you today. You must be on top of the world.'

'Yeah, I am,' I said. 'After a year's long wait, I feel I am being recognised after all.'

I fetched another A4 sheet and sketched my next scene before sending it to Payal.

Eric finds the pinnacle and sits proudly on it. Yes, there is no way he can occupy it forever, as there will always be some force that will try and bring him down. But as long as it's there, it's all his. The view from the pinnacle is a surreal dream. He waves down to the world in ecstasy and he prays to God that the moment lasts forever.

It took me two hours before I could convince myself that my attempt at the sketch looked close to what I intended to convey. At

around 6 p.m., I sent to Payal what I presumed would be my last sketch to complete her story. I was just clearing up my pending deliverables for the day, when I saw Lekha come out of the ladies' changing room in an elegant blue top and low-waist denim. Even her short spiky hair and muscular build could not veil her subtle elegance that evening. I kept staring at her with my mouth open.

'What?' she asked, worried. 'Am I not looking good?'

'You're looking lovely,' I said. 'Your "close friend" is damn lucky!'

She laughed, cleverly evading the answer. 'See you later.' She waved as she picked up her purse. 'I'm off.'

'Where are you going for your dinner?' I finally asked. To hell with self-respect.

'Why?'

'I . . . er . . . I can drop you in a cab,' I stuttered. 'I don't know if you should go out alone after dark in such clothes.'

Yes, I know it couldn't get cheesier than that, but in the scheme of things that was the best shot I could give.

'That's so sweet of you,' she said, patting me on the head. 'But I've got my Pulsar.'

'Fine' I gave in. 'Go have a nice time.'

'Thanks!'

When I saw her leave, I got entangled in a web of thoughts and doubts. I'd rather get the answer to my question myself than live an entire night of unbearable anxiety. The devil gripped me, and I made a dash for the staircase at the opposite end of the corridor from where she took her elevator. I ran to the gate where she usually parked her bike and asked a cab to pull over. I plunked myself in it.

'Where to?' the cabbie asked.

'I'll tell you soon,' I said, looking in the direction of the parking. 'Just hold on.'

The driver looked at me with a confused look even as I ignored him and kept an eye on the gate. Lekha came out shortly, merrily sat on her bike and roared it to a start.

'Follow that bike,' I instructed the cabbie as she sped off.

The cabbie turned behind and grinned evilly. 'What are you up to, *sahib*?'

'Boss, there's no time for an explanation,' I said angrily. 'Please hurry up.'

The driver dutifully obliged and followed Lekha as swiftly as possible, weaseling his cab between the deluge of vehicles in the heavy traffic of the evening. But Lekha was no less than a blitzkrieg. Her bike raced far ahead of us and at one point I even thought I had lost track of her. But fortunately, about ten minutes later, I found her stuck on the same traffic signal as I was. That was probably the only time I must have thanked Mumbai for its traffic. As the signal turned green, she drove another hundred metres before screeching to a halt near the pavement on the left.

'Stop!' I shouted to the driver.

To my left was Spicy Grill, one of the fanciest restaurants of the city, located at Marine Drive – arguably one of the most romantic spots that Mumbai had to offer. My pulse rose sharply. It's the pav bhaji at Chowpatty for me, and a candlelight dinner for him! This was highly unfair. I had a good mind to barge in and throw Mr Closest Friend into the Arabian Sea.

I tiptoed behind her and entered the waiting area of the restaurant, keeping enough distance to avoid her view, yet close enough to watch the action. I stood behind a bunch of bushes kept for decoration at the threshold of the waiting bay, and peeped out every few seconds to see her engaged in animated conversation with the manager. Apparently, they were into some kind of debate relating to the table she was looking for. It must be some silly demand for a table at the remotest corner of the restaurant, or the table farthest from the noise of the pesky orchestra. Or maybe she was simply demanding that her table have a few extra candles to add to the romantic effect.

I was suddenly startled by a voice behind me. 'Can I help you, sir?'

I turned behind in fright to see a steward looking at me in astonishment.

'Er, nothing,' I stammered. 'I'm fine.'

He peeped into the bushes and then turned to me and said uncomfortably. 'Sir, the washroom's inside, in case. . . .'

'I am fine, thanks,' I scoffed. 'I'm expecting someone.'

I warded the steward off and turned back to the scene of interest. The debate had now ended, and I saw the manager lead Lekha inside. I followed her quickly. She marched right through the breadth of the restaurant and sure enough, she took a corner table decorated with four scented candles. I could feel the fire right inside my gut. I quickly scampered behind. The next two tables behind hers were already taken, so my best option was the third table behind her. I ran and occupied it, keeping my eyes on her as she waited for her date to arrive. The steward came and offered me the menu card. I pretended to flip through it, but I kept my eyes on Lekha.

After what seemed to be an endless wait of fifteen minutes, I saw the silhouette of a lady in her late twenties walk into the restaurant with a chic gait. In the dim lighting of a few hundred candles and amidst the clouds of *hukka* smoke, I could not see her face clearly from a distance.

As the silhouette approached closer, the face began to look a little familiar. She waded her way through the smoke and approached Lekha's table. And then, in what would go down as one of the most scandalising moments of my life, I saw Lekha get up and hold the hand of the figure, pulling her closer. In the brief second that I could see her face clearly, I noticed the shine on Short-Skirt Shirley's face as she cuddled with Lekha. The embrace lasted long enough for me to make up my mind to exit the scene before I got to see something worse. But the fool that I am, I needed more evidence to help it sink in my mind. So I sat open-mouthed and watched as they came closer and kissed – a kiss short enough for the people around to notice, but long enough to send me reeling into bouts of writhing heartache. I tried hard to convince myself that it was a dream, but no – it was all too real, and all too shocking. I would have rather liked to see a guy as her dinner date. They could have then kissed all day long, but I would have at least lived with a hope that I could still fancy my chances some day if she found him to be good for nothing. But here, I had gone tangentially far, far away from the target.

Not everything was as it seemed, I said to myself. This did not necessarily have to be the passionate kind of kiss that I was getting so hassled about. Kisses have variety too, don't they? And I couldn't really tell from a distance what variety this one might have been! There's the 'we-are-just-close-friends' kiss, which is but a light peck. It ends by the time you realise it began. Then there is the 'socialite kiss', where women just blow imaginary kisses near each other's face – a social obligation which is really not worth reading into. And then, there's the kiss of love, the kiss of passion, where . . . No, it could not be that for sure. *Wait and watch*, I voted.

The film was not for free either. The steward pestered me to death and told me I could sit only if I gave them some business, for my occupancy of that table was keeping four hungry monsters waiting outside. So I sat there for an hour, meddling with some expensive spaghetti pasta that felt insipid to my taste buds, as I watched my love story (if you may call it so) crumble before my eyes. For most part, I could only see their backs leaning on each other like Siamese twins. Thank God for little mercies that I could not hear what they were talking, but on a few occasions, I would see one of them reach for the other's body through rather overt actions. The other would then let out a mischievous shriek, following which they both would burst into a raucous laugh and fall all over each other again. That apart, the kissing never stopped, and for the time that I held myself to watch, their lips stayed locked practically continuously.

After they had thoroughly ensured I was stoned with shock, I saw Shirley take out her phone from her purse and furiously dial a number with one hand, playing with Lekha's spiky hair with the other.

My phone rang, shaking me up from the shock. *Short-Skirt Shirley calling*.

'Hey Nakul,' she said. 'I'm sorry I'm running a little late. I got caught up in a dinner.'

Yeah, she is caught up like hell indeed! And if my mood was anything to go by, I had no mind to visit her for coffee anymore. 'That's OK,' I said. 'We can do it some other time.'

'Or maybe we can meet right here if it suits you,' she suggested. 'I'm at Spicy Grill on Marine Drive.'

'OK, I'll meet you when you are done,' I said. 'I'm not far from there at all.' Now that I had seen what I shouldn't have seen, it wouldn't hurt to hear the story I shouldn't have been hearing.

Shortly, the two girls got up and got into the embracing act again. Why does this have to be a prolonged thing? I mean, I've hugged people all over the world, but my hugs never seem to last more than a second. And here, each of their hugs was like a lifetime of distress for me. As I watched Lekha leave, I quickly slipped in the cash – quite some heavy cash, as my bill for the pasta, and then walked over to Shirley.

'Hi Shirley,' I said, shaking hands with her.

'That was quick!' she said, smiling happily. I spotted a mark of lipstick on her right cheek, but for the sake of my own sanity, I tried to ignore it. Obviously, I couldn't.

'So how was the dinner?' I asked.

'Excellent!' She raised a thumb in the air. I could scream now.

'Good evening, sir, would you like to. . . . ?' The steward balked in astonishment on finding me again. He must think I was one hungry pig who just couldn't do with one dinner.

'Good evening,' I said, ignoring him and turning to talk to Shirley again.

He examined me for a moment and then hurled the bomber. 'Would you like to order something else, sir, or do you want to go for dessert?'

I glared at him hard. 'We'll let you know. Thanks!'

Shirley eyed me suspiciously. 'What did he mean when he said "order something else"? I thought you just walked in.'

I looked down. 'Actually, no. I have been here for long.'

'Oh, were you?' she asked in surprise. 'With whom?'

'With no one,' I said, still looking down. 'Shirley, there is something I want to tell you. But I don't want you to misunderstand me in any way.'

She cocked her ears. 'What's the matter?'

'I followed Lekha from office to this place tonight,' I said softly. 'I was sitting right behind you during dinner.'

Her smile suddenly disappeared and was replaced by a deep, annoyed frown. 'Are you trying to say you were spying on us?'

'That's not what it is,' I tried to explain. 'There was no ill intention behind it. It's just that. . . .'

'It's just that you felt insecure because Lekha was going out for dinner with someone else, right?' she interrupted me angrily. 'So you decided to carry out a sting operation!'

'I'm sorry,' I said. 'Maybe I shouldn't have. But I have just not been in my best of senses over the last month or so. I have been irrational, and have been trying to analyse too many whys and whats.'

She was unmoved by my plea for forgiveness. She took out a filter cigarette from her purse and lit it. 'So why are we here now, to analyse why we are what we are?'

'I don't think I have the right to ask the why,' I said. 'And I have no intent to intrude into your space either. But frankly, though I am thoroughly embarrassed at saying so, I was kind of broken to find Lekha like that with you. So I just thought I'll ask you if. . . . '

'Yes, you guessed it right,' Shirley said. 'What you saw was the truth. Sometimes circumstances mould you into becoming something you had never imagined you would be. I'd say that's what happened to me.'

'I don't understand,' I fumbled for the right words.

'It's something that you might have seen only in the films,' she quipped, 'but I doubt if you can connect to it. It's the typical story of a simple girl from a Goa village who had to make some "minor compromises" to try and live her dream in this city. And guess what – I am still just trying!'

'What compromises?' I asked.

'You're making me rake up stories I had buried long ago, Nakul,' she said, hooting smoke off her mouth as she spoke. 'But now that the wound is opened, I'd rather let myself bleed. Without taking too many names, some of which you will find familiar, I can only tell you that I have faced exploitation wherever I've gone. I alone know what I've had to endure just to get a plain wooden desk with a vintage computer, and continuous telephone calls for sixteen hours a day, with not a single one being to ask how I am doing. And at the end of it all, I get so much as to be an object of lewd discussions on how my interview was conducted by Kamal Kothari behind the closed doors of an interview room, and imaginary fables on what my latest sexual escapades have been. I first thought it was all a passing nightmare, but slowly I began to reconcile to the fact that these humiliating tags had become a part of me. When I stepped out of office, I saw that the world was no better outside either. I have submitted my identity to the filth of the male mind.'

'I never thought ill of you, nor did I ever engage in any such conversation with anyone,' I defended. 'I fully sympathise with you, Shirley. But I think you must not generalise.'

'That explains the second part of the story which you don't know, Nakul,' she said. 'And that is, I had a soft corner for you once upon a time. I always knew you were different. It's not that you didn't lust after women, but I could see the purity of your mind.'

'I lust after women?' I asked, offended.

She laughed. 'Yes, Lekha came angrily to me a few months ago, and asked me to stop wearing the suggestive clothes that I had kind of got used to. When I prodded her to tell me the truth, she said she had caught you checking me out with the look of a you-know-what.'

'That's bizarre!' I protested. 'You girls have the tendency to equate even a normal, harmless glance as a lusty eyeful.'

'No sweets, not me,' she corrected me. 'I, in fact, did not change my opinion about you even then. I just discarded Lekha's outburst and told her not to be so possessive about me.'

I felt faint and at a loss for words. I couldn't be blamed. I had never been faced with a situation where I would be expected to comment on one girl's possessiveness for the other.

'Oh, is that why Lekha had got ticked off with me!' I exclaimed, putting two and two together. 'And I interpreted something totally different.'

'You thought she was in love with you, didn't you?' Shirley laughed.

'I'm afraid, yes. I feel like a fool now.'

'But tell me,' she asked, 'why has the news of my relationship with Lekha blown the living daylights out of you? Don't tell me you were in love with her now!'

I didn't respond.

'Nakul, isn't it a strange coincidence that the girl who sat two feet away from you never appealed to your senses for as long as one year?' she asked. 'And then one night you looked around and saw you were all alone. You cried out for help and you found the same girl's hand on your shoulder, and all of a sudden she became the world for you?'

'Should that be translated as "you are a spineless loser who just needed Lekha to lean on for emotional support"?'

'I'm not saying that,' she said. 'Nor am I blaming you for falling for her. It's but natural that we look for love the most desperately when we do not have it. But I only wish you would have had the patience to pick the right sink for your woes. Now, you'll have to find a sink to drown two of your miseries – not just one.'

'I'm good,' I assured her. 'Don't bother about me.'

'But what about Lekha?' Shirley asked. 'Have you wondered how she will feel when she finds out that the friend she cared for so deeply in tough times is now spying on her personal life?'

'You are the only one who can give her this significant bit of information,' I said. 'And you have a choice to curb your feminine instincts and keep mum about it, right?'

She tapped her fingers on the table playfully. 'Do I have an incentive to do you this favour?'

'If you can't do it for my sake,' I replied, 'I'm sure you can do it for her sake! In any case, I am already sorry about what I did and I can't undo it now.'

'Hmm, I'll think about it,' she said. 'You only need to come home for coffee once!'

'Oh, is the deal still on?' I laughed. 'I thought you had just begun to hate me?'

'Well, I'll put it this way . . .' she began when my phone droned in an urgent tone.

'Excuse me,' I said as I picked up the phone.

'Hello, is this Mr Nakul Kapoor?' A voice asked from an unidentified Mumbai land line number.

'Yes?'

'This is Dr Neha Joshi from Mumbai Civil Hospital,' she said. I felt my pulse shoot up.

'Is all well?' I asked urgently.

'Not exactly,' she began. 'We have a patient in our emergency ward who wants to speak to you. Can you come and meet him tomorrow? Our visiting hours start at 10 a.m.'

'What patient?' I asked frantically. 'Whom are you talking about? What's his name?'

'Mr Chirayu Chaudhary,' she replied gravely.

The 'X' Element

Dear Son,

I know you are very angry with us. I did not give you the love a mother should have given when you were here. But son, we only wanted that you live here with us. That's why we didn't want you to go to that Mumbai city where you can't live a peaceful life also.

Even if you want to take some more time there, we will support you and will wait for you. But just don't be angry with us. To make your mood good, I am sending your favourite besan laddoos in this parcel.

I am also sending more tincture mixture for your oil. Apply it everyday in your head and also on whole body in the morning. Also, I hope you are doing pranayama properly with correct breathing technique.

May God bless you.
Love,
Mummyji

Kohinoor stood still like a wax statue, with the letter in one hand held upward towards me, and an open box of beckoning besan laddoos in the other. He looked at me, half-smiling, half-crying his heart out. A large familiar teardrop was threatening to make its way down his nose and right into the box of laddoos when I snatched the box away from him.

'Easy, easy, easy,' I said in panic. 'Let's eat the laddoos now. You should be happy after reading that letter.'

'Yes, brother, very much happy,' he said, smiling fully at last. 'Now I know they love me.'

'That calls for a laddoo,' I declared, picking up one and greedily stuffing it into my mouth. 'So what have you planned – are you going back home?'

'No brother, not right now,' he said. 'I have some other plans.'

'I know,' I spoke through a stuffed mouth. 'You want to go to America, don't you? That's why you are studying for GRE.'

He looked at me in surprise. 'Oh, how did you know? I was preparing so furtively. . . .'

'It's your vocabulary.' I winked. 'By the way, your words have been getting better everyday!'

'Thank you, brother,' he said proudly. 'I want to go to America, but not forever. I want to go there only to learn some useful course which helps me handle Papaji's business better when I return.'

'Do them proud,' I said. 'They deserve to see you successful.'

'Yes, I will,' he said, puffing up his chest in an exaggerated gesture of determination. 'I will do them proud.'

'Good,' I said, tying my shoelaces. 'Now it's time to go to work. Are you coming?'

'I'll come late if you don't mind,' he said coyly. 'It's Saturday anyway, and I want to complete wordlist "T" today!'

'Yeah, why not? Mark my words – your *tenacity* will bring you *triumph*!'

He blushed and dug his face deep into his books. I stepped out on the busy Linking Road in Bandra, trying to catch a cab to the Mumbai Civil Hospital. Not that I cared otherwise, but the thought of Cheapo lying in the hospital's emergency ward was surely not exciting. I had tried asking Dr Neha Joshi for details, but she could not explain much on the phone. It was I who had to find out.

I stood engulfed in a sea of thoughts right opposite Bandra's lake point, even as thousands of vehicles buzzed past me like a storm, honking deafeningly and bellowing smoke blacker than black. And then suddenly, in the midst of the mad rush, I spotted a man no more than thirty, his bony back bent almost into a semi-circular arc. He had piggy-backed on him a young boy who was even skinnier than he was. The boy's eyes were half-closed, and in the brief moments that he opened them a bit, I could see that they were bloody red in colour. The father was sweating profusely from the labour of carrying a child and walking around. But the burden on the back seemed insignificant if you compared it with the lines of worry running down his worn-out face. Undeterred by the simmering heat, he ambled from car to car at the traffic signal, rapping his knuckles on the tainted windows of each car to plead for help. But it goes without saying that he was not getting an audience. It's a painful travesty of the developed India that he failed to realise – a busy 10 a.m. city road can never be your agony aunt. Once the signal turned green, the cars again honked their way through and left him waiting patiently for the next lot of 'we-care-two-hoots' passengers to reach the junction.

I signalled to the man to cross the road and come to me, lest he get knocked over by some callous driver.

'What do you want?' I asked.

'Sahib, my son is very ill,' he replied in a shaky voice. 'I need immediate help.'

As an instant reaction, I felt tempted to rubbish that line as yet another tactic of getting some quick money. I began walking away when he stopped me. 'Sahib, I don't need any money.'

'Then what do you need?' I turned around in surprise.

'I just need to be taken to the hospital,' he said frantically. 'I have come all the way from Dhokli to get him checked. But I don't know where to go.'

I looked at the child, hesitated for a second and then touched his forehand. It was so hot that I had to immediately withdraw my hand.

'Just wait here with me,' I instructed. 'I'll get a cab that will take us to the hospital.'

I got off the pavement and began waving desperately at every passing cab, hoping to find an empty one that would take us to the hospital. Eight rejections were bad enough, and I had no capacity to walk any further. After a few dozen cabs passed by, an empty one finally pulled over to our side with a screech.

'Civil Hospital,' I said.

We jumped into the cab and ordered him to speed it up to the hospital. The man sat in the front seat, placing his son in his lap and lovingly caressing his forehead. Every few seconds, he would moan as though in pain himself.

'What's wrong with your son?' I asked after some time.

'I don't know,' he replied. 'But he has high fever since the last one week.'

'Why did you not get him checked before?' I asked. 'He could have recovered by now.'

'I come from a village that has never seen a hospital,' he said without sarcasm. 'I came here as soon as I could. But in these two days of travel itself, his fever has risen drastically.'

I examined the boy's pale skin. 'It could be jaundice.'

The man's eyes widened in horror. 'Is it something dangerous?'

I was taken aback by his reaction. 'Take it easy, jaundice is not something that cannot be cured. It happens to people all the time.'

'Yes, but in our village nobody survives these illnesses,' his voice had begun to quiver. 'When the Goddess is enraged, we have no say whatsoever.'

'Don't worry, your son will be fine,' I reassured him. 'But how come your village doesn't have a hospital?'

He laughed mockingly. 'I wish I had the answer to that question!'

'But I've read that medicine has reached even the most far-flung villages in India,' I said. 'How has Dhokli got singled out?'

'It's not just Dhokli,' he said. 'There are many villages and tribal areas like ours with no medical centre for miles around them.'

'But the government keeps claiming that medical facilities in rural areas have been improving steadily over the last decade. Is that a false claim?'

'Yes, it is false,' he explained, 'but the government can't be blamed for it. A village's prosperity depends a lot on its villagers' willingness to let it prosper. In a village like ours, blind faith and belief in ridiculous superstitions is too prominent to allow for any scientific or medical progress to happen. And frankly, beyond a point, the bigger cities do not care. I am sure most of you would not have an idea of the darkness and sickness Dhokli lives in.'

He was right. Keep its way of living aside, I did not even know where on the map was Dhokli located. I had not even heard of Dhokli before. But how could I? I myself was a victim of the ways of destiny – till recently, a self-proclaimed loser who thought life had given him a really raw deal. I had a job I could not respect, a boss I would never want to respect, and a ruthless society from whom I demanded a modicum of respect. I had a highly unsatisfying social circle – a friend who turned out to be quite a slimy fox, a roommate who was a case study of misery, a girlfriend who dumped me because I was not rich enough, and a friend who could not be my girlfriend because she preferred dating women in hot pants. Add to that my own financial stature, which I thought sucked big time.

Now that this stranger permitted me a peek into the miseries of thousands of his brethren, I did realise, though a bit late in the day, that what I called miseries were mere trifles. Even if I did not respect my job, I at least had one. I hated my boss, but I was at least grateful to my company for giving me a congenial atmosphere to work in and a brand name to boast of. And yes, I had my issues with society and with my social circle. But then, I needed to get real – I am sure they had their share of issues with me too. So it was a fair game at the end of the day.

Yet, something was amiss. And I was not the only one who complained. The whole world around me believes that we all live only in part. We may be at the bottom rung of society or we may well be some corporate czars. But the unhappiness is with all of us to stay. And it's just a small 'X' element that it will probably take to make our lives feel worthwhile, to make us feel that we are of some use to the world, to make us feel proud of our being. But for most of us, it is that very 'X' element that always plays truant with us.

'Here we are,' I said as we reached the hospital after a long drive through the crazy traffic.

The man looked at me as he got down and smiled feebly. He was about to bend down in gratitude and touch my feet when I stopped him.

'That's fine,' I said. 'Come, let's get your son in first. I know one of the doctors here.'

I took him to Dr Sudhakar Pandey, a general physician I had met about six months back when I had brought Kavya to him. She had stubbed her toe against the foot of a restaurant table and had lost half a toenail and half a square centimetre of skin around it. In order to avoid the risk of being labelled insensitive, I had rushed her to Dr Pandey, who had felt mighty amused when Kavya had made a big deal of her 'serious injury'.

'Ah, Nakul,' Dr Pandey exclaimed as I knocked on his door. 'What's the emergency this time? Did your friend get a mosquito bite?'

'No, doc,' I said, ushering the man and his son in. 'It's this boy. He needs to be examined immediately. He is burning like a furnace.'

Dr Pandey touched his forehead and let out a squeal. 'Damn! That's a furnace alright. Make him lie down.'

The man helped the boy lie on the patient's bed on the corner. The doctor fetched his toolbox, bringing out one sharp shiny object after the other. The man and the boy looked on in complete bewilderment.

'Open your mouth,' the doctor ordered the boy as he stuck a pair of forceps inside his tiny mouth, simultaneously throwing torchlight into his feeble eyes. The boy cooperated quietly throughout the remaining processes of examination.

'It could be jaundice,' the doctor spoke after some consideration. 'Look at his pigmentation – all yellow. It looks like he has been ill for long.'

The man's face contorted into a crestfallen expression. 'But can he be cured? Please, sahib, he is all I have.'

'Relax,' the doctor consoled him. 'Of course he can be cured. But he will need to stay here for some days under observation.'

The man folded his hands. 'As you say, sahib. Just please make him alright.'

I looked at Dr Pandey. 'Doc, please let me know the expenses. I'll try pitching in if it shoots up.'

'Sure, I'll keep you posted,' he replied.

I patted the man on the shoulder and walked out of the room towards the reception, when the man called out to me. 'Thank you very much, sahib!' He came and hugged me.

I was overwhelmed. 'Don't worry. I didn't do anything special.'

'You did, sahib,' he said. 'What you did was a gesture I'll always remember.'

'I'm glad I could help.'

'My neighbours in the village told me I would not get any help in the city,' he said, 'but you proved them wrong. Now I have the courage to fight my son's illness, sahib.'

'I'll come by and check on you again,' I said as I began walking away.

'Thank you, sahib.' He folded his hands and smiled at me in gratitude for a gesture I myself did not consider all that lofty.

But when I saw his expression of gratitude, there was one thing I was beginning to feel confident about: that I had finally found a way to discover the 'X' element – the pursuit of bringing a smile on someone's face. I was not sure if I was right. But it wouldn't hurt to try. In fact, my life had become quite a bore chasing a dream which I myself did not understand thoroughly. I had been running along, like Eric, and like the million others around me, in pursuit of the pinnacle. And finally, just when I had begun to feel smug after reaching the pinnacle, today's incident made me realise the bitter truth that after a temporary feeling of ecstasy, even the view from that magnificent height becomes mundane. You have a choice either to explore other pinnacles, which, by the way, will give yet another mundane view, or you can try other thrills that might bring you the contentment of being worthy to the world. I just had a feeling I had discovered that thrill.

I scampered up one floor, my heart beating fast. The corridor was completely abuzz with patients lined up outside wards, waiting impatiently for their turn with the doctor. Yet, the entire area gave me the creeps. This place bore an uncanny resemblance to the hospital in Baroda, where as a kid I was brought every month to get a monstrous injection in my bum for a reason I never found out. Today, I could sense the same pain. A part of me wanted to run away, but the other part was duty-bound and made me want to know what had happened.

I reached the emergency ward, which had its door ajar. I peeped in to have a look. He was lying on the bed, surely asleep, for his snores reverberated in the largely empty room with the potential to scare the living daylights out of Goliath. A thick wire connected to a bottle of blood was plugged into his plump wrist at the other end.

'Chirayu?' I knocked lightly on the door.

He opened his eyes and raised his head a bit. 'Who is it?'

'Nakul,' I said.

'Oh, come in, mate,' he said in the same irritating twang of an accent. He was strapped to a hospital bed, but his mannerisms wouldn't leave him. 'What's up?'

'I am OK, but you tell me,' I said. 'How are you?'

'Unfortunately, still alive,' he said, looking the other way.

I was taken aback. 'I'm sorry?'

He raised his right wrist and showed it to me, smiling sheepishly. There were three deep gashes on his wrist. The blood had clotted, but the colour was still a deep crimson. The gashes were deep enough to let a lot of blood ooze out, but evidently not deep enough to penetrate through his thick skin. Finally, his fatness had come to some use.

'You . . . you did this to yourself?' I asked disbelievingly.

'No, the witch from Kirri Kirri came home last night and did this while making love to me,' he grunted.

'I mean, why? What happened?'

'Let's say I deserve this,' he said softly. 'I've not been a nice person.'

'Yeah, but ending your life doesn't make you a nice person either, does it?' I said unwittingly.

Cheapo glared at me. 'Thanks for the compliment, Nakul. I am much moved.'

'That's not what I meant,' I said, 'I meant suicide is not cool at all.'

'Life isn't cool either,' he rued. 'I have screwed up big time.'

'Why, what did you do?'

'Tell me, Nakul,' Chirayu said. 'What do you think of me as a person?'

I shrugged uncomfortably. 'Let's not discuss all this right now, Chirayu. You need rest.'

'No tell me, please,' he insisted. 'How much would you rate me on a scale of 1 to 10?'

'Well, Chirayu . . . ' I avoided eye contact.

'Not applicable, eh?' He laughed. 'I know, I know, you think I am a complete asshole. And I can't blame you either. I have been a very self-centred man throughout my career. Today I can feel its repercussions.'

'Is there something you'd like to share? Can I help in any way?'

Now, most of us say the above words in purported sympathy, without really being sure we can help the afflicted in any way. And if the afflicted is someone like Cheapo Chaudhary, you have to be doubly sure of what you are saying.

'Yes, today I'll tell you my story,' Cheapo began.

I bit my tongue. 'Chirayu, you should rest,' I suggested. 'Let's discuss this some other. . . . '

'No, it's all pent up in here,' he said, beating at his chest dramatically. 'I want to let it erupt today.'

'OK, shoot,' I said, reclining in my seat, readying myself not to yawn.

'You know, when I joined the corporate sector fifteen years ago, I was just like you,' he began. 'Even I didn't have that drive, that zeal to work; to do something worthwhile.'

Correction one: I had all the drive and zeal when I joined the corporate sector, so that comparison stands void. Correction two: I don't see that drive and zeal in Cheapo even today. But what the hell, it was his story!

'But a time comes in our lives when a single trigger sets you raging into the competitive arena like a mad bull, when all you know is that you must win and stomp forward in life, by hook or by crook,' he continued. 'That trigger in my life came when I got married, and further again when my daughter was born. Seeing my family happy was my purpose in life. I loved them so much, I knew I could push myself to the wall at work, only to ensure that whatever they ever needed in life could come to them on a silver platter. But I learnt a tad too late that my efforts were completely askew, and I could never really figure out what is it that they really expected of me.'

'Where are they right now?' I asked hesitantly. 'Are they aware you are here or do you want me to call them?'

He smirked. 'Like hell they would be aware of what's happened to me. My wife hasn't called me once the last three years. One fine day, I got up and saw a note stuck on my laptop screen. She wrote that she was tired of playing the dutiful wife who pined endlessly for some attention from her workaholic husband. According to her, my job was the only thing I was in love with and everything else was secondary or rather non-existent. So she decided to run off with some guy in her office and then she never looked back at me.'

'Did you try talking her into staying?' I asked.

'Of course, I did,' he said. 'But once a person closes the doors of his heart on you, that heart becomes impermeable to even the loudest drum rolls of your love. I was shattered, but I still held myself together because my daughter was still with me. She was my strength, as well as my weakness. The tragedy is, that I still did not realise where I was going wrong. In order to avoid brooding over my wife, I started spending even more time at work. For three years, I stayed convinced that my daughter was treading on the path of becoming a mature, sensible daddy's darling. For three years, she behaved in my presence as though I was her hero. And I indeed thought I was so, because for three years I did not let the gloom of my wife's absence from our lives affect her. But I really wish she had been bitterly upfront to me rather than leaving behind this chit like her mother.'

He handed me a note.

Dad,

It's not like I hate you or something. But I must be frank and tell you I am not happy with the way my life has shaped up.

Mom first left us and ran away, but I said nothing. Yet, the least I expected from you after that was some attention towards your daughter. I used to come back home from school at four in the evening and you never returned before ten in the night. Did you ever wonder what those six hours of daily loneliness did to me? Those six hours broke me bit by bit every day, but I still did not complain. But over the last few months, I have been feeling shackled by your embargos that you try to put on who you feel is still your daughter who has only Barbie for a friend. I have my own life, Dad, and my own friends with whom I like to spend time. They mean something to me, and frankly, they are at least around me when I need them. I don't have to wait six hours to share my day's experiences with them.

So please, Dad, I want you to let me live my life on my own terms, just like I've let you live yours. I am sixteen now and I am mature enough to go my own way. By the time you read this, I'll probably be gone. A nice Nigerian friend of mine called Zusha, whom I met two months back at a rave party, has offered to take me along with his group of friends who are going on a long cross-country expedition. I have agreed because this is a chance I get to discover myself finally and know what I want. Zusha is a sweet thing and I know he will take good care of me. He has promised to teach me the Kalabari if we go to Nigeria. I love him, Dad and I want you to feel happy for me because this is what really was meant to be.

Take care, Dad
Yours,
Natasha

'What the hell is Kalabari?' Cheapo asked after I was done reading.

'It's some kind of African tribal dance,' I explained, 'where you sway your hips and. . . .'

'OK, leave it,' he cut short. 'I don't want details. I actually called you here to say sorry. I know what I did to you the other day was mean on my part. Personal grudges should never be settled in a professional circuit.'

'It's OK, Chirayu,' I said. 'I've moved on. Moreover, I am not a hero either. We all have grey areas in our doing.'

'You're right,' he nodded. 'And all this to achieve something you never get. Look at me – I look successful to the world outside me, but internally I am a dead soul. My niece often pokes fun at my lifestyle. She has often told me that my struggle for success is but a race whose finish line does not exist. And God, today I so feel she is right!'

I smiled. 'That sounds weirdly familiar.'

'Oh you must see this,' Chirayu said, fetching a large packet out of his airbag. 'She made me some sketches which she said give me a peek into my own life. Look at this, it can so be related to!'

He held out an A4 size sheet in front of my face. I was shell-shocked to see the sketch.

Eric is in chaos. He falls prey to the trap and reaches no-man's-land. But he must understand that this is the worst that can happen to him in

this race. He thinks he is lost. He stares listlessly at a signpost that shows four arrows in different directions, clueless as to which arrow he must follow. A tornado is blowing over his head, ready to fling him away. But he must remember that the world is round, and everything in life goes a full circle. He can choose any of the options at this chaotic crossroad, and he can be assured that he will be able to make his way back. It's a long walk, but the destination is still within bounds.

At the bottom of the sheet was the familiar signature of Payal Saxena. I looked at Cheapo in surprise.

'Is this your niece's work?'

'She is one hell of an artist, isn't she?' He was looking at the sketch in admiration.

No, I could not believe this. Payal was not that ugly. I refused to accept she belonged to Cheapo's family. Thank God I had decided not to marry her, or else I would have had to bow down and touch Cheapo Chaudhary's feet for the rest of my life!

'She sure is,' I said.

'She asked me to send her some sketches on this theme too,' he continued. 'And if you see mine, you will know that I've not been a morally clean man. And I do hate this about myself, but I didn't see another way to move ahead. People used me as a ladder to move up, so I had no option but to get back at them in the same way.'

Cheapo's mentality – reflected in the sketch – reeked of deceit. Not that I was surprised, knowing the way his wily mind had always functioned, but this sketch was nasty. I wished I could hate him for it, but the irony of the whole matter was that my sketch in response to Eric's chaos was not too different. The villain was all pervasive in me too, and it was with great difficulty I tried to get it out of me. He showed me his remaining sketches, which were very similar to mine. Very expectedly, he also sketched Eric as seated proudly on the pinnacle finally, taking in the view from what could be considered the ultimate height of success. But unlike mine, this was not his final sketch. He put up yet another sketch in front of my face.

'This was my state of mind two days back,' he explained. 'Natasha's letter entirely changed the way I looked at this goddamn pinnacle.'

Eric is on the pinnacle, but the glory is all lost. The view is beautiful, but there is nobody to share it with. It is lonely up there and the ecstasy the pinnacle offers is just not worth the cold loneliness. It's time to surrender to the will of destiny.

'Frankly, I didn't like your last sketch,' I said, still examining it closely.

'Nor did I,' Cheapo replied. 'But Eric didn't have a choice.'

'I think he did have a choice,' I said, 'or at least he could have mulled over his options. By brooding dejectedly, or worse, by jumping off the pinnacle, he would have altogether eliminated the possibility of those options coming to his mind.'

'Eric can't live alone, Nakul,' he said.

'Nobody can.' I nodded. 'But one can surely try and look for ways to minimise the loneliness. Success and happiness are better experienced when shared with someone.'

'So what do you think would have been a nicer way out?'

'I'll think about it and tell you,' I said, getting up. 'But for now, I suggest you take rest. The team misses you and we want you back on board!'

'I'll be back.' Cheapo raised his thumb in the air. 'Very soon.'

I went back to office and took out yet another sheet of paper from the stationery room.

Eric is on the pinnacle, but something is missing. The view is beautiful, but he realises it will be more beautiful if the experience can be shared with his fellowmen. It's time to help others scale up to the pinnacle.

The 6 a.m. Romance

I found Mehek early in office the next morning, reading an internet article on how yet another case of dowry harassment had got muzzled amidst the noisy claims of modernism the city made. She shook her head in disgust as she read along, swearing heavily at the wretch and his family who brought a bad name to mankind.

'It's a bad world, isn't it?' I asked from behind.

'Oh, hi Nakul,' she said, closing the browser window as she turned to me. 'I was just browsing through the news for a bit.'

'So, how do you like things here?' I asked. 'Is the company treating you well?'

'Yes, absolutely,' she replied. 'It's awesome.'

'I have an offer for you that can make your experience doubly awesome,' I said. 'I considered for long your suggestion that we can pursue our desire to do something for the underprivileged alongside our professional aspirations.'

'OK . . . and?'

'And I thought you are right,' I said. 'In fact, I can take your suggestion one step further. How about we use our professional abilities to do something for the underprivileged? It serves both purposes, doesn't it?'

'That sounds noble indeed,' she said. 'Do you have something in mind?'

'Yes, I do,' I replied. 'Look, I have something to show you.'

I bent over her tiny head to open a new browser on her machine. I entered the URL www.be-compassionate.com and waited for the homepage to download.

'It's a website begun by an old friend of mine,' I explained. 'If you click the "Facts" section here, you will get to know many an ugly detail of the squalor many of our people still live in. In fact, poverty is only a secondary culprit. Plain ignorance and lack of basic amenities are vices that are killing these people bit by bit. It's a situation so bad we can't even imagine.'

'This is what I was talking about when we met the first time.' Mehek looked at me indignantly. 'But you dismissed my suggestions then.'

'Well, I have got my eye-opener; let's make amends now,' I said. 'I met a man last week from a village called Dhokli. His story made me realise there is a lot we can do to improve their living conditions.'

'I am all ears,' she said excitedly. 'So is there a way we can channelise our IT capabilities in this direction?'

'Sure,' I said. 'Have you heard of telemedicine?'

'Yes, I have,' she said, 'but I have only just heard. I know nothing about it.'

'Put simply,' I explained, 'it's a technique of treating a patient sitting at a remote location, without the patient having to travel hundreds of miles to see a doctor. If we can put our heads together, this could be a miraculous feat.'

'Educate me!'

'Here you go,' I said, tossing a booklet on her table. 'It's a report on a telemedicine project I had done with a friend way back in engineering days. It's elementary, but I suggest you go through it to get some dope on telemedicine. Once we are clear with our basics, we have grounds on which we can go and put a request to Anand.'

'This is very thick,' she said, flipping through the pages containing an extremely small font. 'Why don't you give me a verbal synopsis?'

'You are a lazy girl!' I quipped.

'No seriously, it's logical,' she insisted. 'It will save us time.'

'OK, I'll be frank,' I said. 'I don't know anything about telemedicine myself. I am a novice too.'

'But this report . . . ?'

'I was a member of the project, yes,' I said. 'But I'm afraid I wasn't really into the mumbo-jumbo of telemedicine.'

'So how did you fare on this project?'

'We fared well, thanks to my friend.' I grinned. 'I only presented the initial part, where I spoke to the audience about the introduction and history of telemedicine. Then I went like, "I now hand over to my friend. . . .", and I watched the rest of the show.'

'Was that all of your contribution?' she asked in surprise.

'No, I also got the prints of this report once it was ready,' I attempted feebly. 'That was a big task too!'

'Whoa!' She laughed. 'And someone preaches diligence to our team!'

'We are not here to poke fun at me,' I scolded her in jest, swatting her on the head with the booklet. 'Let's focus. We must go and meet Anand at 2 p.m.'

'Don't worry,' she said reassuringly. 'I'll be done reading soon. We can even go before that.'

'No, 2 p.m. is fine,' I said. 'He is high on fish curry then and likely to be in a good mood.'

At 2 p.m. we rapped ten nervous knuckles on Anand's door. He looked up from his plate of nearly-finished food.

'Ah, come in,' he beckoned, licking fish curry off the edges of his fingers. 'Tell me, what brings you here?'

'Good afternoon, Sir,' I said. 'I hope we are not disturbing you.'

'That's alright,' he said, 'I am done eating. Go ahead.'

'Sir, this is Mehek Gupta.' I pointed at Mehek. 'She is on my project.'

'New employee?' Anand asked his favourite introductory question. Fortunately, this time he was right. Mehek nodded and smiled.

'Not me, Sir,' I was quick to add. 'I have been here for a year and a half.'

'Of course, I know that,' he said confidently. 'Your impressive performance has been in my line of sight for long now, Nikhil.'

'Sir, Nakul,' I said, this time rather indifferently.

'Yeah, what's in a name,' he admonished with a wave of his hand. 'They are all the same! Tell me the issue.'

'We have come to you with an important request, sir,' I said. 'Mehek and I were discussing the prospect of initiating a project for a social cause.'

'And what may that be?' Anand's curiosity meter rose sharply.

'Introducing telemedicine in remote villages,' I said, trying to sound as confident as possible.

'Wow, that sounds fancy!'

'Sir, we want to convert this into reality,' Mehek spoke eagerly. 'We are really determined. We just need the go-ahead from the senior management.'

'Are you trying to say you want to do this on behalf of Bytesphere?'

'Yes, sir.'

Anand burst out laughing. 'Guys, let's get real. Bytesphere doesn't do these projects.'

'Sir, but we do believe in corporate social responsibility, don't we?' I argued. 'If we treat this project as one of those exercises, I am sure. . . .'

'We have enough initiatives that come under the corporate social responsibility tag, sonny.' Anand raised his hand. 'But the project that you are talking about comes with huge complexities. And I am not talking only money here, mind you.'

'I absolutely agree, sir,' I said. 'But a project without formidable challenges is like playing Ludo at twenty-five. Moreover, doing something for a cause is only going to add to the organisation's repute in the long run.'

'But the telemedicine you are talking about here is nothing innovative,' Anand said. 'It's been on for years. And medicine has penetrated villages through the length and breadth of the country. How do you think Bytesphere can project this initiative as something unique?'

'There are still a lot of remote villages with very poor medical facilities. Every other day, we hear reports of villagers and tribesmen dying of otherwise curable diseases, simply because they did not get proper medication in time,' I said. 'If we can do something for them, it will be an immense achievement.'

'I don't know, Nakul,' Anand resisted. 'I hate to discourage you guys like this, but the idea seems a little far-fetched. Even if we get the nod from the board of directors, we cannot do this without the cooperation of the top medical institutions of the country. What I can surely promise you is that we can offer some kind of monetary aid to these villagers. That's what all companies do anyway.'

'Exactly, sir,' I explained. 'That's where we can be different. Please consider this: we will be using our pool of professional talent to do something extraordinary, and in the process we will be changing a few thousand lives forever.'

'You always have the right words, my friend,' Anand quipped. 'You always do. I am very impressed!'

'Sir, we can at least try,' Mehek pleaded. 'My mother is a doctor herself, so we know some good Mumbai doctors who are in our fraternity. I am sure I can pull some strings here.'

'And we have two big teams – the telecom vertical and the life sciences vertical – we can all put our heads together to make this work,' I said. 'Please, sir, we need a chance.'

'Do you have an approach in mind?' he asked.

'We have some steps in place, sir,' I said. 'Mehek and I have gone through certain study material. We will need to get in touch with the life sciences team and come up with an effort and time estimate. We will need some time to prepare our plan and then roll out the instrumentation.'

'OK, I can give you a deal,' he said after some thought. 'You know Bytesphere is always willing to support its employees who are trying to do something as nice as this. Your effort will be no exception. But you have to prove to the board that your idea is the best thing that could happen to society.'

'We will do our best, sir!' we screamed excitedly in unison. 'Just give us some time.'

'That's the only luxury I can't grant you,' he said. 'Early next month, everyone on the board is going to get busy because there is a major acquisition being planned.'

'Oh great!' I said. 'What's the acquisition?'

'I have my lips zipped right now,' he said. 'All I can warn you is that you have no more than twenty days to finalise your plan and keep every modality ready. If you get the permission, you will be expected to take the project to market immediately.'

'Sure, sir,' I said, though a little apprehensively. 'But we will have to begin with a pilot project.'

'That's more than obvious,' he said. 'But that itself will be a big achievement if you can pull it through. So for now, take whatever help and guidance you want from the senior technical architects in both these verticals to get the framework of your project in place. If the board approves your request, Bytesphere itself will liaise with the doctors for their help.'

'Thank you very much, sir!' I said gratefully. 'Your support means a lot to us.'

'I do hope you get the support from the rest of the board too,' he said. 'I'll speak to them about this in the next meeting.'

'Thank you sir!' Mehek said. 'We can assure you the company won't be disappointed.'

I loved her confidence. We had no basis to make that statement yet, but the confidence with which she said it made it sound like child's play.

'Now here comes my main question,' Anand said, banging his palm hard on the table. 'Setting up a project here is one thing. I trust your capabilities on that. But who goes to the village to teach the uneducated and change-resistant villagers the use and benefits of this project?'

'We will go, sir,' Mehek shouted in excitement. 'We'd love to!'

'It's easier said than done,' he said. 'Have you ever been to a village before? Life there is not just about fancy folk dances and golden paddy fields that you see in the movies. And if you go there, you can't just give a single demo to the villagers on the use of the telemedicine equipment and then walk away merrily. You will have to stay there for at least two to three weeks to oversee the project's execution. If anything goes wrong, it will be a huge embarrassment for us.'

'We understand, sir,' I assured him. 'But we are willing to take up the challenge. For once, I get the feeling I am embarking on something that can make me proud of myself. I can promise you we won't let go.'

'I thought you should also have felt proud of the offer Julian made to you last month?' he frowned. 'Do you realise that offer may not hold good for you if you are absent for so long?'

'The offers will keep coming, sir,' I smiled. 'I am sure I can wait.'

'Alright, you will also have to provide me your backups on the project,' he warned. 'Two resources staying absent from one project for so long can be a significant impact. And we can't forgo business for philanthropy, can we?'

'Surely not, sir,' I concurred. 'We will provide you with the entire team plan before we leave. And all our effort right now on the telemedicine project will only be after hours. We will keep dedicated time aside for Britcell. Moreover, Chirayu will also be rejoining the offshore team in a few days. So things should be smooth.'

'What do you mean by rejoining?' he asked. 'Was he on leave or something?'

'Yes, sir,' I said, 'he was in the . . . he was on leave for personal reasons. He has just come back to India now.'

'Cool,' he said. 'Get rolling. I will inform you soon once I speak to the board. By the way, which village are you guys thinking of targeting through the pilot?'

'Dhokli,' I said.

∞

By 7 p.m. the next evening, I felt like a zombie. I couldn't recall if it was the same afternoon or the previous one or the one before that when we discussed our telemedicine proposal with Anand.

'It was yesterday,' Mehek helped me remember. 'I think you need a break.'

'Yes, I do,' I said, rubbing my eyes. 'I can see images of ECGs and EEGs running through my head. This subject is tough!'

'Let's go home,' she suggested. 'Or maybe we can take a short walk? It would be easier to discuss things.'

'Haji Ali?' I offered.

'Sure.'

We sat at Haji Ali's juice centre, greedily scraping strawberry cream from every corner of our cups.

'I feel confident,' Mehek said after a while. 'Things are working smoother than I thought.'

'Of course,' I said. 'The life sciences guys are an amazingly intelligent lot. But this is just a framework we are preparing for the presentation. Designing the equipment and rolling it for live use is another headache that will take at least a couple of months more after the presentation.'

'But that headache is not ours,' Mehek reasoned. 'We are not equipped to design the equipment. That's the technical team's work. We only need to go to the village and help the people use it there.'

'Exciting, isn't it?' I mocked. 'That's going to be the toughest part, Mehek. We have a lot of ground to prepare for that too.'

'Like what?'

'Setting up chemist stores in the village, for starters,' I elaborated. 'What does the patient do after the doctor prescribes him his drugs? Dhokli doesn't have proper chemist stores either.'

'I know,' she nodded. 'We will need to plan everything.'

'Anyway, let's not discuss work for sometime now.' I winced. 'We are here for a break. And the sea is just too beautiful to allow any stress.'

'It's beautiful indeed,' she said, inhaling deeply to take in the breeze. 'I've come here for the first time.'

'I came here often during college days,' I said, 'with friends. Those moments were beautiful.'

'Romantic, eh?'

'Nah.' I waved my hand dismissively. 'Romance isn't my kind of thing.'

'Why not?' she asked. 'You would not know if it's your kind of thing until you've felt it.'

I had felt it. The problem is I had felt it twice, and both the times it had left a very queasy taste. I was now nauseous and I could bet one more mention of the word 'romantic' would make me throw up.

'I don't wish to feel it,' I said dryly. I turned my face the other way to indicate I was not interested in the discussion, but Motor Mouth Mehek didn't seem to get the hint.

'I do wish to feel it some day,' she said, smiling to herself. 'Because I feel love is something as limitless and beautiful as this sea right in front of us.'

I was sure that was a line from some soppy Hindi movie. But I didn't care to ask. To me, love was a sea alright – a sea which you can drown in if you jump without testing the waters. I had jumped twice, and I almost drowned to death both the times. I had barely come to the surface after a long haul to catch some breath, and now she was suggesting I taste the salt again.

'You seem to know a lot about love and romance without having experienced either of them, don't you?'

'I'm a dreamer.' She shrugged. 'I have this fancy of spending romantic 6 a.m. mornings with my guy cycling on the empty roads of the city and then stopping by at Marine Drive for a corn on the cob breakfast, where he sings for me. . . .'

'Wow!' I laughed out loud. 'That's funny, I must say – talking of romance at 6 a.m.!'

'Funny?' she asked, visibly offended.

'No, it is sweet,' I said, trying to pacify her. 'I guess sometimes you laugh at others' dreams simply because you have forgotten how to dream yourself.'

'What?'

'Nothing,' I said, changing the topic. 'Hey, I think I just might have a solution for the chemist stores to be set up in Dhokli.'

'What's that?'

'I'll just tell you.'

I took out my phone and called Shomu da. I explained to him in detail about our proposed plan, and what benefits we thought it could bring to the people there.

'Bondhu, I don't know whether this will go the full distance,' he said. 'But the fact that you have decided to try has made me very happy. I'm sure mom must be proud of you.'

'I'm glad to hear that, Shomu da,' I said. 'And I want to take this the full distance. But for that I will need your help.'

'Anything for a cause, Nakul. Tell me.'

'How is your NGO shaping up?' I asked. 'Has a good number joined in?'

'We are about two hundred strong already,' he said happily. 'The scene is very encouraging.'

'We might need some assistance in setting up chemist stores in this village called Dhokli in Maharashtra,' I said. 'And we will also require some volunteers who will be willing to run these stores, at least for about six months.'

'I will need more details from you,' he said, 'but consider it done.'

'Thanks bro,' I said. 'I knew I could count on you.'

'You sure can,' he said. 'And keep me posted on the developments.'

'Sure, bye.'

'What did he say?' Mehek asked.

'He says he can get it done,' I said. 'But of course it will take some start-up time . . . Hey, I just got a missed call from a landline number. It seems to be from office.'

'Check your voicemail,' she suggested.

I went to my voicemail. There was one unread item. I clicked it open and we listened with bated breath:

'Hi Nakul, this is Anand. The board is very impressed and moved by the cause you and Mehek have taken up. They have agreed to hear you out, and have promised they will lend you 100% support if the idea seems plausible. Now get your act together – you have to make a presentation to them next to next Monday, that is, thirteen days from now. If that goes through, you and some other senior members will coordinate with leading doctors of Mumbai. All the best, and Godspeed!'

The Redemption

More than ninety laborious days and sleepless nights later, Mehek and I finally reached Dhokli. But our challenges had not ended with the management approving our proposal. In fact, they had only just begun. The stage was set from our side – we had the telemedicine equipment ready, Shomu da had got his volunteers to set up a chemist store and a twenty-four hour assistance system for the villagers, and we had met Mansukh to explain what we were there for, so he could arrange an audience for us. The only key detail we missed anticipating was the human mind's innate tendency to resist change.

'People here are somehow very comfortable with the way their lives are moving at the moment,' Mansukh explained. 'I'm not certain how they will react to something so complicated and incomprehensible entering their culture.'

'That's where you will play a key role,' I answered. 'I want you to make them understand how medical facilities saved your son's life.'

'I am forever indebted to you for helping me then, sahib,' he said, 'and I'll do my best to repay in whatever way possible. I will ensure you get your audience.'

A half-broken platform decorated with *mogra* flowers, two cups of aromatic masala tea, and around four hundred curious eyes greeted us the next morning at the village square. Mansukh stood dutifully beside us, in case we should need any amenities before we began the session. But we had much to do in very little time and so we began our work without much ado.

'Our objective for coming here is very clear,' I began. 'And that is – to share some interesting snippets of our lives with you that can change your lives for the better. We want to introduce to you a medium that can bridge the formidable distance between the places we live in and bring us together. In the process, it brings about a revolution here as well.'

The audience listened with bated breaths. There were a few murmurs here and there, but they died down in a few seconds before I spoke again.

'This little bag on my shoulder is what I'm talking about,' I said, raising my laptop bag in the air. 'We are aware that diseases like jaundice and malaria are rampant here. Unfortunately, a number of people here have fallen prey to these otherwise curable diseases simply for want of medical facilities. But now the time has come for you to rise against these evils. And this little machine here is going to aid us. It is the harbinger of change that is waiting to brighten up the future of your children.'

'All of us have a right to live a healthy and happy life,' Mehek continued. 'We all have a right to medical facilities. And obviously, it is very inconvenient if people from here have to travel all the way to a city in order to get treated just because their village does not have a hospital. This machine will allow you to talk to a city doctor and get your treatment done right here, in your very own village. We expect your cooperation in understanding how this works and in helping us make our effort a success.'

'All this is meaningless for us,' someone suddenly shouted from the audience. 'You are wasting your time as well as ours, *memsahib*. We don't really need any of this.'

We turned to the source of the outburst. A small group of men supported the initial voice, giving us a mixed look of contempt and confusion.

'We are quite happy and satisfied with the way our lives function,' another man from the group added angrily. 'We don't need your assistance. We maybe backward as compared to what you city folk are, but we know how to live our lives.'

'So you mean to say you are comfortable seeing people from your village die everyday, succumbing to diseases that could have been easily avoided?' I asked, dabbing at sweat beads on my brow.

'Those are not diseases,' the man yelled back louder this time. 'Those are indications that the Goddess dwells in our homes. We have known of the rituals to be followed in case of such situations for ages now. We know how to please the Goddess.'

'Where does the Goddess come from?' Mehek asked in disbelief. 'Who has told you this?'

'Baba Bhordev,' one of the men shouted out with pride, followed by the others in his group chanting the name in chorus.

'I told you, sahib,' Mansukh leaned to me and whispered. 'They are rigid in their beliefs. And it's probably not a good idea to refute them right now.'

'OK, I've got your point.' I stepped forward, raising my hand in the air to calm them down. 'Now can I get five minutes of your time so that I can talk?'

'No, you can't,' yet another man snapped back from the crowd. 'I, for one, don't even have a minute to spare. I toil day and night so that I can just about make my family eat. Now if you expect I take out time for this new gimmick, then I'm sorry – I can't cooperate.'

Before we could respond or even take stock of the situation, others in the crowd followed the protesters and dispersed, leaving us clueless and dejected. We knew this was never going to be easy, but the villagers' resistance was much more than we had prepared ourselves for.

'Who is Baba Bhordev?' Mehek asked, as we sat for dinner in Mansukh's hut that night.

'The head of the village,' Mansukh replied. 'In fact, a demi-god of sorts for everyone here. If at all you want this to work, I think you will need to get him on your side.'

'And how easy is that?' Mehek questioned.

'Not easy at all,' he replied grimly. 'Baba exercises control over the village through his preaching. It's not likely that he will let your idea come in the way of the respect and awe that he enjoys.'

'Introduce us to him,' I demanded.

'Let me take you to him tomorrow morning,' Mansukh agreed promptly.

We nodded, and finished our dinner in silence. Then, we walked back to our tent and resigned ourselves to another night of unbearable anxiety.

∞

The next morning, we reached Baba Bhordev's hut. A man in his mid-sixties, dressed in tattered rags, opened the door. We saw Mansukh bow low to him like an arc and understood this had to be Baba Bhordev. We bowed dutifully too. Mansukh had told us to flatter him a bit during the discussion, so I made a mental note of bowing to him every few minutes thereon.

I examined the man more carefully now. He had curly, long tresses and an overgrown beard, and bore an uncanny resemblance to Anand. Baba Bhordev could pass off as Anand's ugly cousin who was ten times more intimidating than him. His eyes were bordered by dangerously thick kohl, black as the darkest night. Most of his teeth were broken, and of what remained, all I could see were tiny white fragments covered by something as dark as soot. I knew one more look at him would leave me an insomniac for life, so I decided to gaze downwards for the rest of my conversation with him.

As we took our seats on the mud floor of the hut, Mansukh did the introductions and briefed Baba about the purpose of our visit.

'We are here to get your blessings,' I said, bowing again.

'They are always with you, child.' Baba patted my head. 'But I have not got the slightest idea of what you are talking about. It's too complicated for my people to understand. And then, we have our own ways of dealing with these problems that you just mentioned.'

'Pardon me, Baba, but the ways that are being followed right now are doing no good to your own people,' Mehek spoke, even as I gasped at her courage. 'We have no personal gain from this work, but we have come all the way only to help everyone here. All we need is one chance to show what we have.'

'Are you trying to tell me that my preaching is all false, girl?' Baba's voice rose in anger. 'Let me tell you that these people here equate me to the Almighty himself!'

'Of course,' I quickly jumped in, bowing yet again. 'But isn't the sign of a true leader also that he shows his subjects the path to a better way of living? Let me assure you, Baba, your respect will only increase if this village can wake up to the potential that medicine has to offer. Please give us just one chance.'

'Hmm, OK.' Baba stroked his beard thoughtfully after a long, heated debate. 'One chance is something I can grant you. Talk to the villagers again the day after tomorrow. Till then, let me speak to them. I know for a fact that if I tell them, they will surely hear you out once.'

He smiled broadly, self-acknowledging his power.

'Thank you,' Mehek smiled. 'You are indeed kind and wise.'

'But let me warn you that I can't force them to implement your idea,' he interjected. 'Their acceptance or denial of the same will be their decision. And, of course, my decision will rule over theirs!'

'We promise to convince you,' I said excitedly. 'Thank you very much!'

I bowed for the last time before we left. One more time, and I would have heard my spine snap.

A notch more encouraged, Mehek and I busied ourselves with laying the groundwork for the big day. Anand had informed us that this was to be a big event and the media was to arrive at Dhokli to cover it. It made the tension all the more palpable and both of us began freaking out continually at the littlest of visible lapses.

'Let's check out the arrangements at the medical store,' I suggested in the evening. 'We need to ensure everything is in place.'

We walked down to the store, which had been set up right next to the solitary temple present in the village. A thin, twenty-something lad was perched on a stool, busy rearranging stacks of medicines across the shelves.

'Jagdish?' I called out.

He turned around. 'Nakulji? I've been waiting for you!'

He got down and we shook hands.

'This is Mehek,' I gesticulated to my right. 'We're working together on this.'

'Yes, I know.' He brought his hands together in greeting. 'Shomu da told me. He has great regard for both of you for having taken up this bold step.'

'Thank you,' I said, 'though he is our inspiration. Setting up an NGO and motivating so many of you to participate is no joke.'

He nodded again. 'He has conveyed his best wishes to you for this project. He might try and call soon.'

'Nakul, can you lend me your phone, please?' Mehek asked. 'I need to speak to my parents, and my phone's signal is down.'

'Sure.' I handed her the phone.

She dialled a number and walked a few steps away to talk to her parents, while I busied myself in the meantime chatting with Jagdish on what activities the NGO was into.

'You have a voicemail message,' Mehek held the phone upwards as she walked back to me after her conversation ended.

'Open it,' I ordered. 'It must be Shomu da. He wanted to wish us.'

She opened the message and kept the phone on the speaker mode. Unfortunately, it wasn't Shomu da. I wished I hadn't asked her to open it.

'Hi Golu, this is Kavya. I wanted to share a piece of news – I am getting married on the twelfth of next month. I'll give you details when we talk. I know this was not the dream we had seen together, but I guess fate had something else in store for us. Anyway, I have moved on, and I am sure you have done so too. I wish you all the very best in life. If you still think I am worthy of being in touch with you, do speak to me. I will wait for your call.'

Mehek froze in embarrassment and kept staring at me with a pitying look that I despised. Jagdish pretended he was not privy to my personal moment of angst, and disappeared somewhere behind his counter. As for me, well, I had nothing much left to say. I fidgeted awkwardly, looking here and there to avoid eye contact with my sympathisers.

'I'm sorry,' Mehek said. 'I shouldn't have opened that.'

'It's alright,' I said. 'I shouldn't have opened it either.'

I took my phone back and walked off to the fields, where I rested myself against a huge tree trunk. I stared languidly at the crimson horizon, watching the sunset in comfortable seclusion. I had tried hard to forget Kavya and was almost sure I was over her when the irresistible beauty of her voice came and hit me again like shrapnel. The wounds were open once again. But I had too much work, and little time available. After a few worthless minutes of brooding, I walked back to the tent.

'It's her loss,' Mehek spoke after a long spell of silence, as we lay in the tent under a starless sky. 'You are a nice guy, so you deserve better.'

'Am I, really?'

'Yes,' she replied half-dreamily. 'I only wish you were a little more chivalrous.'

'What do you mean?' I turned to her.

'It's so bloody hot in this tent,' she complained. 'Don't you think you should fan me till I fall asleep?'

'I'm sure I don't need to answer that,' I said, flopping over to the other side. 'Now if Your Majesty permits me, I'd like to sleep.'

'Bad boy,' she mumbled sleepily.

I tried flipping from one side to the other, but it was bloody hot alright, and I just couldn't sleep. I looked at Mehek. She was mildly asleep, but there were beads of perspiration on her smooth skin. And there was a frown on her forehead, which was an obvious mismatch to the usual pleasantness she carried on her petite face. I was tired and in half a mind to close my eyes. But if I recall correctly, I groggily fetched a magazine from my bag and began fanning her till the frown fell away and she gave a few short snores in gratitude.

∽

The big day arrived. Baba Bhordev lived up to the reputation of his clout and pulled the entire village to the square to attend the demo. The media was there, ready with its shutterbugs to capture the moment everyone had waited for. There were anxious ears near the telephone in the Mumbai office. There were two hearts beating so fast, they could jump out of us and wobble into the crowd. But the audience was, not surprisingly, not half as thrilled. Evidently, they were present only at Baba's behest. Baba himself was perched on a pedestal placed in the front row of the audience, giving us a reassuring smile.

We asked the first patient, a sixteen-year-old girl, to come up on the stage and face the laptop. Within a few anxious minutes, a doctor's image appeared on the screen, who joined us online from Mumbai. As he greeted the girl with a warm, affable smile, a sense of excitement ran through the crowd.

'Tell him about your problem,' Mehek prodded her.

The girl spoke to the doctor, a bit hesitantly initially, and it took the doctor a few minutes to gauge the problem. He then instructed the volunteers standing next to her to take her blood sample and send its screenshots to him. He assured the girl that she would be cured soon, and then briefly addressed the crowd, welcoming them to the new world of telemedicine. Once he went offline, we turned off the laptop and looked expectantly at the crowd. But all we got was another round of murmurs.

'I understand you cannot relate to this effort right now,' Mansukh suddenly took control of the situation. 'But ask me how it feels to see your loved one slip into the jaws of death and then miraculously leap out alive! And let me tell you that this miracle occurred only because I took the risk of believing in something. Now it's up to each one of you if you would like to follow me.'

'In any case, the adoption of this technology is not being imposed on you,' Baba Bhordev now spoke, standing up to face the audience. 'If we feel that this is of no use to us, we can boycott it. But let's give it a fair chance. I urge each one of you to make full use of this facility. There are volunteers available throughout the day to help you understand whatever you need to.'

His word was the final verdict. After a few moments of confused hush, a middle-aged man rose from the crowd and got on to the stage to face the laptop. This was followed by a mild cheer from the crowd, an applause much less in intensity than what we had hoped for, but a start nonetheless. I looked the crowd in the eye, and let the gratitude show. I flashed back on my life gone by in the last year or more, but I couldn't remember much. Or maybe I didn't care much. The flashes of the media's cameras blinded me; I looked at the sky with a lump in my throat and whispered to Shomu da's mother: 'Love you, aunty. I hope I've earned my redemption.'

The World isn't a Supermarket

I got a resounding thwack on my back. I turned around to see Cheapo Chaudhary towering over me like the shadow of the devil himself.

'I didn't know you were that good,' he grinned. 'You've proven me wrong this time.'

'That's OK, Chirayu.' I winked with due vanity. 'We all make mistakes.'

'Ha ha,' he roared, his expansive belly juggling like a mound of jelly as he laughed. 'But remember – a tough cookie I am and a tough cookie I'll be. More work to follow.'

'Sure,' I smiled cheerfully before I turned back to face the stage.

Short-Skirt Shirley got onto the stage with her usual élan, following her staunch principle of minimum clothing and maximum flaunting.

'We are proud to have with us tonight Nakul Kapoor and Mehek Gupta who together share the award for the Young Achiever of the Year,' Shirley spoke into the mike. 'Can we please have them on stage to share their experiences with us?'

If the deafening sound of claps filling the air was music to my ears, the icing on the cake followed soon too. As I reached the podium, Shirley strode up to me, leaned forward and planted a kiss on my cheek – in front of some few thousand people! I felt faint. I somehow held my own, and walked up to the mike.

'Thanks folks,' I began. 'I'm going to take a couple of minutes to share with you how this project changed me as a person. Thus far, I had remained stuck in a swamp of my own worries and had only been trying to take futile steps to walk out of it. But each step that I took pulled me deeper into the swamp till one day I found myself neck-deep in it. Today, I want to take a moment out of my life and recall when was the last time I was free of all hassles. When I was in school, I was under pressure to score well so I could make it to a big engineering college. When I was closing graduation, I was in the competitive race to get into a B-school. Then I went bonkers worrying about the company I would join during placements, and once I joined one of the best companies in the world, well, I still remained a worried man, now going crazy about what roles and levels of importance I deserved and yet was not getting in the company.

And not too surprisingly, most people around me admit that they go through the same restiveness in their lives. I ask myself if this cycle ends somewhere in life and I get an answer in the negative. The reason for this permanent unrest is that I have been trying too hard to put various parameters together to derive the equation for contentment and happiness. Unfortunately, there is no fixed formula and no fixed parameters for happiness. This world is not a supermarket where I'll get signboards at every corner showing me directions to those parameters. Nor is my life a grocery basket into which I can stuff a certain number of parameters and feel satisfied. It's an elastic bag where the more I fill, the more vacant space I find. And a time comes when the bag gets so heavy that you begin crumbling under its own weight.'

I looked at all the faces staring back at me and continued, 'To be frank, it's not like this project was always at the back of my mind like a passionate dream. In fact, it will be fair to say I just stumbled upon the idea, moved by a one-off incident I witnessed on the roads of the city. But once I went the full distance, I felt a change. I felt that I had finally done something I could feel proud of. When I saw the excitement and gratitude in the eyes of those villagers, it gave me a satisfaction undoubtedly beyond any recognition or reward I ever received in my life. And these are not the words of an altruist, but simply those of an ordinary human – for the human mind is conditioned to desire the love, respect and goodwill of fellow humans in equal, if not more, measure than his other material interests.'

I paused again, hoping I wasn't rambling. 'If asked would I like to dedicate the rest of my life purely to social service, my answer would probably be no, because I know I need to eat before I can feed. But I will certainly look forward to more opportunities where I can give back to society in some measure what it has always so lovingly given me.'

The audience broke into loud cheer and applause at this point. Some of them stood up and acknowledged me. I was finally living my dream and I had to pinch myself to ensure I was awake.

'So what is the point I'm trying to drive home?' I asked more confidently. 'Is it the importance of social service? Well, no. What I'm trying to convey is the importance of stepping back a bit from our usual humdrum lives and doing something different that brings us the contentment that always seems to elude us. We slog every hour of our lives to poke our heads up through the world and say, 'hey, I'm here too!' We lust after the sound of our cash registers ringing. But in the scheme of events, we often end up forgetting the end objective of all this maddening effort.

'The end objective is to be happy, which rarely ever gets fulfilled. The entry-level executive is as unhappy about being unrecognised as the CEO of a company is about being laden with endless responsibilities. And funnily, when situations like the recession arise, everyone is screwed alike. The only people who can survive the onslaught, then, are the ones who can find the "x" element that can make them happy. In my case, I found social service to be the "x" element. In your case, it could well be the ability to reach home early from work once a week and take your kid to an amusement park. Or it could be the will to take out your rusting guitar from the attic and strum a few chords. Or it could well be a decision to accompany your retired parents on a weekend trip to Khandala rather than affording them a foreign holiday without being able to meet them for years together. Whatever is your "x" element, find it soon, and you will see the difference it makes to your lives.'

'Coming back to the project,' I went on, 'I need not mention that the entire management, especially Anand, has been very supportive towards our cause, and we could not have budged an inch without their encouragement and guidance. So I am grateful to them. But most importantly, I am grateful to my colleague Mehek. Her boundless energy and zeal for things has left me awestruck time and again. She pulled me up when I fell lax and she drove me to work harder each day on this. But besides her team abilities, I dare say that it's impossible not to adore her. I truly, really love her!'

Oops. I didn't say that. I swear I didn't. Even if I did, I'm sure I didn't mean that. But something funny had surely happened, for I could see that the audience was in splits, and was whistling over and over again. Mehek was standing next to me on the stage, her face tomato-red with anger as she stared at me. I was petrified and just about managed to mumble a quick 'thank you' and scampered off the stage.

'Nakul, that was fantastic!' Lekha came and congratulated me. 'I am proud of you!'

I hugged her. 'Thanks, Lekha, I missed you while I was gone, by the way.'

'Liar.' She punched me. 'By the way, there's someone else you're going to miss soon. Kohinoor is leaving the company.'

'Why?' I asked. 'Has he got a call from some US university?'

'No,' answered Lekha. 'He is going back to Pali to set up an English training school there. He said that was something badly needed in his town and he needed to take up the cudgels. He said you were his inspiration.'

'I'm glad to hear that,' I laughed. 'But I wish I could meet him once.'

'Your wish will be granted,' she said. 'Tomorrow is his last day at work, so you can meet him in office. But for now, you have a more important mission to accomplish.'

Lekha pointed towards Mehek, who had just finished her speech and had gotten off the stage in a fit of embarrassment. Her face was still red and I very cautiously approached her.

'I'm sorry,' I said meekly. 'I shouldn't have . . .'

'Nakul, that was not a place to propose,' Mehek said angrily. 'Not like this. . . .'

'Propose?' I got defensive. 'You must be crazy. That was not a proposal.'

'Oh, yeah? Then what exactly did you mean, o wise one?'

'Get off it, *yaar*,' I protested. 'Is this what I get for praising you on stage?'

'It was more than just praising.'

'It was an offhand remark,' I said. 'Don't read anything else into it. I didn't mean it literally.'

'Are you sure?' she demanded.

'Of course,' I replied.

'Swear on me.'

'You must be crazy,' I said. 'I got to go home now – early office tomorrow. Catch you later!'

'Catch you later.' She waved back at me and smiled.